Muffled voices reach me, but I can't tell what they're saying.

Another moan comes from Cam.

Should I do something? How can I keep her silent?

More sounds come from the front, a little louder, until I hear, "... in the back," as if someone has just spoken right through the trolley.

"Empty space for supplies for the commerce center," June says, his earlier country twang gone from his voice.

A few clangs follow along with a few gurgles from Cam, her stomach, I guess.

Please don't throw up. What if she throws up on me? My stomach mimics hers. I don't do well with vomit.

The back doors jiggle.

They won't open.

"Get the driver," someone says from outside.

DELTA STREET

EMI GAYLE

MM&I

DELTA STREET

Published by MM&I
www.emigayle.com

This book is a work of fiction. Names, characters, places, and incidents are either the products of the author's imagination or are used fictitiously. Any resemblance to actual persons, living or dead, businesses, events, locations, or any other element is entirely coincidental.

ISBN 978-1-937744-60-1

First Printing: May 2017

To my daughters,

who just couldn't wait for me to get this one finished.

1

"Sixty miles from the District center," Zane says, after a big stretch of nothing but the transpo's own noise rumbling along the pathway. Only the dark outside has connected us—our own silence a growing oppression.

"Three hours to spare, too." June's voice is somber, a hint of *please take me with you* still lingering though he wouldn't directly beg. "Plenty of time to get *you* back, so you *and Anna* can go to the—"

The brakes of the transpo screech, and my head slams back against a solid surface, hard enough to send flashing lights through my brain.

Screams fill the cabin—mine, Zane's, June's. I think. I don't know. Reaching for something to grab, I try to lift my head, but I'm tossed right, my hair swinging out and whipping my cheek as I flip around once.

Twice.

Three times.

Landing hard. With a jolt. A crash.

A creaking song plays through my mind.

The night's silence breaks through once again.

2

"Anna."

My name sounds in my head but disappears into emptiness and silence just as fast. Shifting to the right, my cheek brushes up against the softest fabric ever, and I curl into it, but can't bring my body up. It's as if I'm bound. Held in. Strapped. By something.

My heartbeat speeds up as panic takes over.

"Anna."

Again, my name comes through, more a whisper, a hint that I should wake up, or look up, or do something. I twist to the left, but held in my spot, I don't really move, just sink into softness. I think. Maybe. The contrast doesn't make sense, and neither does the fact I can't get up.

"Anna, wake up." The voice has an insistent tone this time. A shove to my shoulder makes me blink, and Zane's face looms right in front of me. "Finally. Wow. You're a heavy sleeper."

My lids open and close a few more times as I take in the fact I'm in the front seat of Lucie's and Marlena's stolen—no, *borrowed*—transpo, strapped in with the safety harness.

Lucie and Marlena's? I thought I was in June's transpo.

Zane's brow scrunches. A snap of his fingers in front of me jolts me upright. "There you go. You're like a morning zombie."

Running a hand through my hair, I expect it's going every which way, but unless someone shares a mirror with me, there's no point trying to fix it. "Sorry," I mumble, covering my mouth. Without a dental tablet, I'm going to have some nasty breath. Sitting up and trying to re-orient my mind, I remind myself that I'm not at home, not at registration, haven't slept in a real bed in three days, and apparently, I'm no longer in June's transpo on the way to the District center in the middle of the night.

Was that a dream? I must be exhausted. "Where are we?"

"In a holding lot." Zane finger-combs his dark hair. Unlike me, his blue eyes seem wide awake whereas I've probably got crust and gunk to clean out from mine.

"Are we ... here?"

"You mean, are we at the fire? Yes. Actually, it's across the street."

The fire. We were on our way to see it. I spin in my seat toward the window, but all that greets me is another private transpo, and beyond that are dozens more. All stopped, not moving. No fire. No obvious signs of one. What am I missing?

"We're on the fifth level of the holding lot," Zane says, "so we should be able to see it all over the barrier."

Oh. Okay. Weird how he seems to read my mind but even weirder that I can't get a grip on what I'm seeing.

He opens the transpo door and slides a leg out while I stare and wonder why on Oz's-green-earth I'm in a holding lot, somewhere in the A.U., with a guy I barely know, to see the remains of a fire.

"C'mon, Anna. You've told me you want to understand, so I'm going to show you." He disappears through the open door, leaving me alone. When it closes, I jump, but on a deep breath, I exit, too.

The stench of burning something-or-other assaults my nose.

I pin my nose shut with my fingers. "What is that?"

"The rubber, plastic, or burning flesh smell?"

Yes. That. I wave to Zane, hoping he understands I mean all of it. It's overpowering, and a bubble of acid burns as it rises up my throat.

"This way." He holds out his hand. I take it with my free one—no way I'm letting those smells in again—though breathing through my mouth isn't helping much. Whatever is in the air has a taste, too.

Another bubble comes up. *Don't think about it, Anna. Don't, or you'll vomit.*

Staying in the shadows, we walk to the edge of the holding lot, right to where the sun reflects off the still-smoldering rubble of a building. Smoke billows up from it in small wavy lines. Twisted metal stands tall, but other parts have caved in.

People meander on the street, some crying, others holding each other. A dozen long black lines are neatly ordered on the ground. "What are those?" I ask.

Zane eyes me for a second before his face goes blank. "Body bags."

"Dead people?"

He nods.

"Why haven't they been taken to the death repository?" My voice is nasally as each time I release my hold, the smell makes my stomach curdle.

"If they can't ID them, they can't take them in."

Shock has me stepping back and opening my mouth, gasping in a brutal wave of disgusting, acrid air and doubling over involuntarily. Luckily, I have nothing in me to throw up.

Zane's hand on my back makes me jerk upright again. "Sorry," he says. "But you have to see this."

I wave him away, sucking in air through my mouth, through

the shirt I've had on for a day, ensuring my nose stays pinched. "Where is the security? The fire brigade?" I still want to vomit. Why doesn't he?

Zane's head cocks to the left. "You didn't see them?"

I shake my head.

"Guess they weren't here, then."

What? A raging fire that could take down an entire building and with the the destruction and debris that litters the ground should have brought dozens of support personnel. It should have started the auto-fire-prevention mechanisms, too.

Why didn't the fire get shut down right at its start?

I force myself to lean over and stare at the missing building, which had to be at least fifteen stories tall if it matched the ones on either side of it. "How did the other two buildings not even get damaged?"

Zane shakes his head and tucks a strand of my hair behind my ear. "This was an incineration, Anna."

"A what?"

"A planned demolition ..."

Okay, that happens.

"... with people still in there."

My heart thumps in my chest, the tips of every nerve ending in my body sizzling. He's got to be kidding—making fun of me, maybe, of my normal naïveté.

All my thoughts swirl, sounds of chaos breaking through as if the fire has started up again. People scream words I can't understand. I must be hearing them from within the building—a building that doesn't exist anymore.

How can that possibly be?

Forcing myself to look, to see, to understand doesn't help. I can no longer open my eyes. No longer think.

The world bursts into a cacophony of noise so loud my ears ache.

Spinning. I remember spinning. Stopping. Hard. My mind struggles with the vague recollections. Blinking brings brightness, illuminating the space above me. Bright, but small. Orange light. Pinpoints of it. Trying to reach out with my left arm sends shooting pain radiating through me. My breath comes out in a puff, and my right shoulder is squished against something pinning me in place.

I tell myself to move. Will myself to, but I can't. Nothing hurts if I don't move, but nothing works, either. Shouts and calls fill my head, growing farther away, like echoes, with each repetition.

Something obnoxious burns the inside of my nose when I inhale, and coughing doesn't help, but instead mixes cold and heat at the same time.

"Anna!" The word clears my ears, just as it had before, but I can't figure out who's saying it, where they are, or how they know me, because it's not Zane, and I'm only with Zane.

Aren't I?

"In here!" someone else yells, but I don't recognize their voice either.

Holding my breath against the fumes, I force my eyes to focus, to take in what has happened.

What *has* happened?

I stare into darkness alight with various blotches of color—swirling, bleeding reds.

June's transpo. Not the little personal transpo.

An accident. Not the fire.

This has to be a film. I'm sleeping and dreaming and none of this is real.

That has to be it.

Like back in my dad's living quarters.

My head throbs, piercing my skull until nothing seems real at all.

c——✦——o

"This isn't a film, Anna." Zane's voice is crisp and clear, coupled with fear and uncertainty. *Danger* might be a better description as he glares at me. There's no other way to define the flatness of his eyes—the seriousness in them.

I spin to the ginormous screen on the middle wall of my dad's living quarters, on which people run everywhere, pushing each other out of the way, switching directions, going left, right, forward and back in the dark, in the red, in blobs of moving, blazing orange. It looks like people are actually on fire.

Whirling to Zane again, I say, "This *is*, too, a film."

The headshake he gives is small, but I catch it. His hands slide up my arms and hold on. "It's *not* a film."

A blast of noise fills my ears, and I turn again, covering both ears, wishing I knew how to shut it off. Bodies litter the ground. Dozens of them as if they've fallen from the sky and landed like meteorites.

What if it is real?

Being there would be horrendously hot, searing to the eyes, to the skin, lung-constricting with all the dust and debris in the air. The display switches to ten mini-screens, all showing the same thing from a different angle. There can't be hope for anyone inside that fifteen-story building, engulfed in burning red on every floor. I imagine it'll fall at any moment.

Because it did.

I saw it.

I was there.

A rapid series of pops jerk the screen, and a teddy bear lands in the lower left frame, its head on fire.

⚬══╋══⚬

The scene playing out in my head blends again with that fiery redness and the dark of night as I force my eyes open. Pain, once again, sears through my shoulder.

Real pain. Not dreamed pain. In June's wrecked trolley, not the little transpo with Zane.

I don't know why I can't stay awake. Can't call out for help except when I pass out, except in a dream state.

This ... the wreck ... did happen. I'm in it. Right now. Right here.

In front of me is a crumpled metal pole. I reach for it, but a burning pain stops me, and I visually trace a line of fabric up and around, to the seat where I sat, orienting myself—or trying to.

Stay awake, Anna.

As the scene before me comes into even better focus, I realize I'm completely, absolutely stuck with no way of getting out.

Even a slight turn of my body brings a misery beyond the extraordinary to my shoulder. "Zane! June!" My yell comes out hoarse. Light crosses over and back. What sounds like a screech behind me makes me want to look, but I can't figure out how, not without hurting so much that nausea curls my stomach. "Help!"

"Anna!" There's that urgency to the call of my name again, though I still can't figure out who it is.

Where are Zane and June? Are they okay? Are they even alive? Fear grips me, sending my limbs shaking.

Metal against metal, scratching and ripping, tears through

my ears. Bright lights shine down on me, giving me a view of my mangled position on the floor, squished between the front and the back—or what once had been separate areas of the trolley.

"Fire!" someone yells.

"No! There's another occupant!" *Zane's voice.*

He's alive!

A deep breath torments the inside of my nose.

Is there a fire in the trolley? Did they get everyone out?

Oh, my Oz! Cam! She's with us.

I pull harder, but my efforts are pointless. My feet bend and flex, but I can't bring them forward. My right shoulder screams at me with each movement, and my left is as useless as a wet noodle, though I can flex my muscles and my hand a little. I just have no strength.

Behind and around me, people call out to one another, their words punctuating the air, but I ignore them. Hands reach toward me, and as one slides under my shoulders, I'm the one who yells.

"I'm so sorry." Zane again. "You're stuck between two seats, and the seatbelt is wrapped around you. I gotta detach it first to get you out."

"Cut it," someone says.

"I need a knife!" Zane yells back.

"Hurry!" comes from yet another unknown, panicking voice. "We can't move it out of the path, and it's heading right for you!"

Move what out of what path? What's heading for us?

Shivers and tremors wrack my body. "Help me!" I don't want to die. I just want to be with my family. Tears start to fall. "Zane?"

He spins back and leans over me with some device in his

hands. Something snaps above me.

"Can you move your legs?"

"Yes. Where's Cam? June?" My legs, which had begun to tingle, are free.

"Push on anything, so I can slide you out." His hands go under my shoulder like before.

"No!" Throbbing torture radiates across me. "My arm. I can't." Hitches take over my breath.

He releases and takes my right hand. "It's going to hurt."

Staring at him, his face shadowed by the dark, I know it is, and as much as I trust him to get me out, I expect I'll vomit if he tries again.

"Now!"

No!

He pulls, and my body inches forward as agony pierces my everything.

"Again!"

No! Biting my lip to prevent the scream doesn't do any good. My mouth opens involuntarily and lets free a guttural sob. *Please stop! It hurts so bad.*

"Again!" He pulls, and my shoulders are free of whatever trapped them—and me—leaving me laying on something soft. "Relax, Anna."

I do, or try, as my limp, right arm falls to the side, scorching every fiber of my body and sending me into the blackness again.

⚬══╪══⚬

Zane steps in front of me, the screen in my dad's living space unblinking. The grip he has on my arms is going to cramp up my muscles. "You'll never understand. Not in time. You're too blind to it all, Anna."

Thanks for the pep talk. "So just go, then. Wherever is going to make it better for you. You should go." My heart lurches. "I'll just go back to my mom's." Not really, but if it would help him, I'd concede to leaving Dad's living space again, on purpose, even when we're not supposed to.

"You can't stay here," he says.

I jerk back a little. "I just said I'd go to my mom's."

"Only the U.S. can make this better." He lets go of me and spins in a circle I know is made from frustration.

So, we're back to that. My heart seems to be pumping in my arm again as the Zane-tourniquet releases. Everything is about going to the U.S., where the grass is apparently greener, as the saying goes. "Of course *I* can stay here, Zane. This is my home." Okay, so it's my dad's, who I barely know, but he did tell me to stay here.

Zane's chin drops a little. "I don't mean that. I mean … this country … it's … it isn't … isn't good for you. It's not. For any of us."

"I know it's not *for you*, Zane, but—"

"Don't, Anna." He turns away again and smacks his fist into his open palm before turning back. Staring right at me, he says, "I'm going to convince you."

"Convince me? Of what? To what?"

"To—"

3

"Anna, come back to me." Zane's tone is insistent, his palm gentle on my cheek.

Reality sets in yet again. I'm outside. At the wrecked trolley. Not even ten feet from it. Around us, sirens blare, red and white lights drown the area in blinking shadows, and people move about in what anyone would call mass chaos. Someone, I don't know who, runs a hand over my shoulder.

"Where's Cam?" I twist toward what I think must be the back of the trolley, where she was asleep, but I can't tell. "Zane! Where's Cam?" My body shivers, as if it understands that no one's answering me because they know and don't want to tell me. She was in the trolley with us—in the back—in the part that doesn't seem to exist anymore. "Zane!"

"Shh," a man above me says. "You've dislocated your shoulder. I'm going to reseat it, and you'll feel a hundred times better."

I don't care about me. I want to see Cam. *And June. June?* "June! Zane, where's June?"

"He's fine," the man above me says. "Saved your life, is what he did. Now, on three." He slowly rotates my shoulder back, bent at the elbow.

A thousand-degree fire rages all through me for what has to be the four-hundredth time. My scream must fill the entire world.

Stretching it out above my head, he pulls, not stopping, harder and harder, my voice never ceasing.

Until it does.

Completely.

"There you go. It's going to be sore, but you should have full use of it in a few days, and strength in a week." He guides my hand back down to my side and across my chest, laying my other hand on top so I can hold it in place.

"Thank ... you." That comes out an embarrassing hitched sob.

"No problem. Just remember, there are good people in this world." He pats my head and rises, disappearing into the night.

Zane leans over me. I must be on the ground.

"What happened?" Using my nearly useless abs, I try to rise, but Zane pushes me back. "Where's Cam?"

He hangs his head and shakes it a little.

"Is she dead?"

His head pops up. "No. Why would you think that?"

Why wouldn't I? is a better question, given all the unsaid words. "Well ..."

"She's with the street team medics. They think she's unconscious because of the accident, so June and I decided to let them keep thinking that. Maybe they can wake her up."

That actually sounds like a good idea. "And June? He's ... is he okay?"

Zane lays next to me in the dirt, face up toward the sky. "Yeah. We're all okay. You, too. Now, at least. Anything else hurt?" He doesn't turn to me as he asks.

A check of my fingers and toes, a bent knee, or two, and a big deep breath reveals nothing else serious, though the stench implies something still burns. *The fire.* "Fire ..."

"Not here." Zane squeezes my hand. "One of the other three transpos."

"What ... what happened?"

The sigh Zane releases says it all.

"You promised you'd tell me everything. Remember? You said you'd convince me by telling me everything."

His chest heaves, a blown out breath following as he nods. "Remember how June and I told you that if things went bad, everyone would try to converge on District Eleven? Well ... we're in District Nine. One border away from Eleven. Actually, we're twenty yards away from Eleven's border, and ... it's happening."

"What is?" My question is tentative as if I don't really want the answer. Maybe I don't, but I do. I think.

"The center of District Nine has been overtaken. So, the border around Eleven was activated. Of course, no notice was given, and the border wall went up *as* we crossed it. Four of us did."

"I don't understand." I stare off toward the right, where lights blaze, big, giant streams of brightness facing us like small suns, cloaking whatever is behind them in darkness. People stand in the light, outside the light, and meander between the beams. Their words are both muffled and clear, all filled with anger.

Zane flips toward me. "This pathway is the main way through Nine into Eleven, and ultimately into One. It's the fastest route. They closed it with a push of a button in District One. That's the only place that can activate all the barriers at the same time."

"You're saying that someone pushed a button, like with their finger, to close up all pathways to the Capitol. Really? All of them? Or just this one?"

"All of them," he says.

"Why?"

"Because they've been expecting this. I told you they knew what was coming, and I told you they knew how to protect themselves. Since One is at the center and has the people with the most to lose, they've activated their protection protocols. That means no one leaves their district, and no one gets into a district until our leaders shut off the emergency protocols."

Before Zane can stop me, I sit up, my arm aching with the movement, though not as painfully as before. "So, we're really locked in here? Even if this isn't our living District?"

"Exactly."

"But—" I don't know what to say, but my heart hurts as badly as my arm does. If we can't get out of here, that also means Zane can't get to the border of the U.S., and I can't get to my family.

Zane goes back to facing the sky.

June rolls toward us in his medical cart, a tablet-like device in his hands. "All grids are up."

"Where'd your screen come from?" Zane asks. "I thought it was crushed in the wreck."

"One of the guys who helped me out of the trolley extracted it. As great as new. Good people."

Good people. That's the second time I've heard that in the last few minutes. Or hours. I can't tell time right now.

June holds the device on his lap and faces me. "How are you, Anna?"

Alive. "Sore."

"I'm sorry I couldn't get past the wall before it went up." He heaves a sigh he's probably been holding in since it happened. "Didn't even know it was coming ..." His head shakes slowly. "... and we were right on top of it when it activated. Threw us over and around a few times." He turns toward the wreckage of the trolley, which is mangled and nothing like the one I rode in for so many hours. Like me, I expect his heart is hurting, too, since that trolley was everything he had.

"And you guys are okay?" I ask after a long quiet.

Zane gives me a nod. June says, "Enough," and releases another deep breath. "All the breakaway material broke away, just like it was designed, and all the safety puffs worked. I just wish I'd had Cam strapped in better."

"Well, at least you secured her at the last stop," I say. He had, too. I thought it weird at the time, but both Zane and June said, as we got closer to District One, we shouldn't take any chances. "It's not like we could have put her in a seat."

"That's true." June nods. "She'll be okay, since the whole back stayed intact. You actually took the hardest hit. Right in the middle seats. Honestly, I'm surprised you're not dead."

"Tactful," Zane says.

June chuckles. "The truth isn't always *tactful*. But I am glad you're okay, Anna." That sounds more like June than the con-templative version from moments before.

"Thanks for making a trolley that's so tough it can stand up to ..." I face the burning lights, trying to see what we'd almost made it past, but can't get a visual.

"It's a twenty-foot tall, solid steel wall. Goes plum around the entire district. All of them, actually. Well, no, not all, but One, Nine, Eleven and a few others. Then ..." He turns the tablet toward me, showing green circles, red circles and yellow circles in the order our districts are organized. Like a spiral-based dartboard, the districts are numbered around it with One in the center. "... everything in red has this wall." He points toward the giant one that we basically fell off. "Green is more like a gate. Yellow is armed by guards who'll be on alert non-stop until someone deactivates the protection."

"Won't people use air transpos to get across?"

"Electronic and magnetic barriers above will effectively make the wall reach to the hundred-thousand-foot level and stop anything that's airborne."

"What about air shuttles? They go—"

"Grounded. All of them. Anyone in the air at the time of the barrier raise would have been forced to land in the District they were over."

Which means we're stuck here, just like I thought. In the biggest cage I could ever imagine, and completely impenetrable. The night's chill tears a shiver through me, as my earlier adrenaline, or whatever, wears off, and fatigue makes me want to close my eyes and sleep, despite what's happening all around me.

"Cold?" Zane asks.

I only give him a nod, and he scoots closer, putting his arm around me, as June rolls away, talking to someone else.

"I'd offer you a coat, but, well, we didn't bring them," Zane says.

"Yeah, I remember." I remember it all.

If I hadn't gone with Zane to see that fire, would I even be here now?

4

EIGHTEEN HOURS EARLIER
A sub-zero holding lot where a dozen or more personal transpos wait—that's where Zane leads me after dragging me out of my dad's living quarters. It's barely five in the morning, and leaving my dad's place for the second time really isn't smart, but what do I have to lose?

The lights brighten on a two-door model that looks about twenty or thirty years old—at least—from what I know of transpos.

"This is us," he says and moves around to the left side, leaving me standing on the non-driver's side.

I stare at the gleaming, metallic-purple, miniature contraption. "What are we doing? Where are we going, Zane?"

"Get in, Anna." Zane disappears, and the door closest to me opens.

I don't move. This thing is a death trap in the making, especially when running by other personal transpos and trams, and whatever else is legal to take from one place to the next. It's bad enough he won't tell me where he's taking me, or why, but putting my life in danger in the process of something I don't understand seems wrong.

Zane pops back out. "If you don't get in, I'll never be able to show you." He says it like a regular person—one who isn't on some unsaid mission.

I still don't move.

His chin drops to his chest, exasperation or exhaustion—I don't know which—surrounding him. He never seems sleepy, though, like he runs on some alternative fuel. Adrenaline, my mom would say. Mia, my sister, was—*is*—the same way.

As he lifts up and meets my gaze, he says, "Please," in the softest voice ever.

Mia's words roll through my mind: '*Trust Zane, Eri. Trust him*'. With a ping, I open the door farther and slide onto the smooth seat. A yawn tugs at my lips as I strap myself in.

Zane zooms forward, we exit the underground, and moments later, he merges in with a bunch of other transpos in the middle of a sleepy city. Pinpoints of light flicker in the distance, crisscrossing each other with every blink I take.

My lids fall a few times as I try to concentrate, to follow where Zane's taking me, to pay attention to everything around me in case I have to find my way back. Alone.

"Lucie designed this transpo, you know."

"Lucie? As in—"

"Yeah. This is hers."

I jolt upright. "You *stole* her transpo?" We stole a transpo? Heart beating way too fast, I stare at Zane, blinking in time with the rhythm of my heartbeat.

He turns a corner, and a blaring noise involuntarily forces my hands to my ears.

"Not stolen. Borrowed." A quick zig-zag gets us out of the way of oncoming vehicles.

"Did you ... did you at least get permission?"

His single eyebrow raise suggests I should have known better than to ask that question.

"Oh, Oz, Zane!" Now, not only am I kicked out of registration, my mom hates me, my sister is missing, my dead dad is alive, but I'm also going to get caught in a stolen transpo with a guy I thought I could trust and go to a rehabilitation facility for thieves, where stress alone will make me insane.

"Relax, Anna." Zane's palm lands on my arm, soft and warm. "I have a starter. She gave it to me for just these purposes."

So, he didn't steal it. Why didn't he just say that? Why doesn't he just tell me stuff without leaving the details for my mind to come up with some crazy scheme?

Because that's how Zane is. Need to know basis.

"I only take this when I absolutely have to, and I gave Lucie and Marlena the signal, so they'll know it was me," he says.

"What signal?" Spinning around as if I might see something seems pointless, since we're already pretty far away from the Delta Street building. Maybe we'll get back fast enough that Lucie won't even notice it's gone. Maybe I can reimburse them for the energy to run it.

With what? You have no credits. You have no job. You have no future unless you go back to registration.

Why does my mind have to bring that up now?

Zane presses a few buttons and leans back in his seat. "We both might as well try to get some rest. We've got at least a six-hour trip."

Six hours. Six hours. *Six hours?* "Wait ... what? Six *hours*. *Where* are you taking me, exactly?"

"You need proof stuff is happening in the A.U., and I'm going to show you."

"We're supposed to stay at my dad's place, you know."

"So, going to your mom's was ... *staying* ... at your dad's?"

The heat rising into my cheeks will definitely show. That he'd use my trip against me is a cheap and dirty trick. My step was necessary. I needed to understand what happened before.

His lips curve into a smirk. "*Stay here* is a lot different than *don't leave this place*. Anyway ... to answer your question, I'm going to prove to you, going to show you, going to convince you to go with me to the U.S. I'm going to make you want to get to the other side of the wall with me."

It doesn't matter how many times he says it, this is home. This is my life, where I live, where everyone I love lives. Things may not be perfect, but no one, no place, ever is. "I'm not—"

His finger to my lips stops me. "Say nothing. Just watch. Listen. If what I show you doesn't prove the A.U. is bad, you can go back to your old-life-that'll-never-happen, and I'll walk away. Forever."

⊂══◊══⊃

NOW

June rolls back up to us, pulling me from my memory. "I have a way out." He stops just at our feet, a thick blanket covering his shoulders and another folded up on his lap.

"See?" Zane smiles wide at me.

"How?" I ask. "Where?"

June hands us the extra blanket, which Zane throws around our shoulders. "The one place you're never going to believe it."

"Where?" I ask again with more insistence.

"Underground," June says.

"Underground?" Surprise coats my tone.

A flash of light crosses June's face, a spot of blue decorating his cheek. His right eye is swollen and partially shut. He must not have been as unharmed in the wreck as I thought. "It's the one place someone our age can go right now without a huge security check."

Zane palms his forehead. "Of course!"

I want to know what they know, but I feel like I should

already know.

"I can't believe I didn't think of that right off," Zane says.

I hate being the one who doesn't *get* stuff. It's always me in that role, so I should be used to it. I'm not, though.

"Of course, *I* can't go," June says.

"No, that's true. Me, neither. At least not seen," Zane says. "But maybe we can make that work in our favor." He turns my way.

I don't know whether to look at him or keep staring off into space, because, somehow, I gather I'm going to be doing something I don't want to do.

"Anna ..." His tone is soft, comforting, and definitely deceptive. He's probably about to ask me to crawl through some muck, or through a hole, or something. "The only way through the walls is *through* the walls."

And probably through something where only a tiny body can wiggle her way from one side to the other.

Zane squeezes in closer. "I mean to get to the other side, we gotta let the powers-that-be take us. But they won't take *us*. They'll only take *you*."

"I have no idea what you're talking about." Heat seeps into my cheeks.

"Registration, Anna."

Oh, no. I'm not going back to registration. No way. No how.

"And ..." he continues as if he doesn't know I'm starting to freak out in my head. "... if you can get back home, to your dad's place ... you can contact him securely and tell him where we are. He can send some of the Delta Street ops here to get us out and at least get us back to headquarters. We can strategize there on next steps." Zane takes the blanket off himself and wraps me in it.

The chill that runs through me, though, doesn't come from

the temperature.

"All you have to do is go back in, claim you were forced out against your will, and they'll take you back."

"I'm a spy, Zane. Remember?" How can he have forgotten *that*? All that running to get away from people in registration just a few days ago.

He shakes his head. "You aren't."

"Huh?" My eyebrows come together as I stare up at him, while he paces back and forth between me and the beat up trolley. "I'm not *what*?"

"A spy. You're not a spy." He says it as if I already know this.

My mind whirls with the contradictory information. I know I'm not a spy, but Zane said I was. Didn't he? "You said we had to leave registration because they found a spy. You said it was because of me. You—"

He cringes, complete with one closed eye, the other directed away from me as he paces away.

"Zane?" Anger heats my tone and my core. He *did* say that. *That* reason made me run with him, go up the garbage riser and smell disgusting for hours after we got out. "*Zane?*" I ask with a little more insistence. "Did you lie to me?" I thought I could trust him.

Ripping off the blanket, the night's cold only prickles my skin. The fire burning through me will keep me warm. "You did! You lied to me!" Mia. Mom. Dad. Cam. All my friends from school. Now, Zane.

Everyone I've ever loved, ever cared about has lied to me.

I've spent the last few days running, and I didn't even need to.

"Why do people *do* this to me?" My voice comes out a squeak as I rise, intending to walk toward the wreckage of the trolley. None of this makes sense. I stare down at the ground below as I stand, but being on my feet is just not a good idea with the spinning going on in my head. I steel myself anyway and make myself stay upright, in place.

Every time I put my trust in someone, I get screwed over. "Why?" I ask no one but myself.

"Can I answer?" Zane asks somewhere close behind me, wrapping the cover over my shoulders again.

Does it matter if he answers? Should I even believe him? Every time I start down what I think is the path of enlightenment, I find out I'm just a fool. This is no different.

The blow-out of breath behind me sends cold air against my hair. Zane's air. Because it's him, I want to turn, to listen. Like I always do. Same old Erianna—the girl who's not just *normally* naive, but *ridiculously* naive.

"Does it help if I say I'm sorry?" he asks.

"No." It doesn't, either.

Zane promised to show me what's going on in the A.U.. He did. Or I thought he did. The problem comes in how he's done it.

Maybe the problem is how everyone has done everything. All the way back to the fire.

5

TWELVE HOURS EARLIER

They burned the building, on purpose, with people inside it.

I pull away and take in the seriousness in Zane's expression, the downturned lips and stern gaze. "There were people in that building." I saw them on screen back at my dad's place, falling out and down, on fire, scrambling to get up and failing and now laying in body bags on the ground. Zane knows that, too, but that's no real consolation.

"It was meant to happen today, not last night."

"You *knew* this was going to happen?" I scamper back from him, the flip-flopping of my stomach sending another wave of bile up. "You knew someone was going to—and you didn't hel—"

"No, no." He moves closer to me. "The people weren't supposed to be in there."

A huge breath escapes me, like relief blowing away from me, except for the fact people *were* in there.

On a deep sigh, Zane says, "An incineration is meant to level a building and everything in it. To destroy everything in a controlled way, but to not affect the buildings around it. Fifteen stories, and you saw nothing else was damaged, right? Not on the screen and not here."

"Yeah. But why would they do that if they knew people

were in there?"

"The smoke will kill them in their sleep—the humanitarian way. Then the fire will incinerate them so they don't go to the human repository. It's a cost savings."

I jerk away. "That's not even a bad joke, Zane. Only people living in uncivilized countries ... no one would purposefully—" Facing away, staring back down at the mess, at the people, at the lack of support personnel, I can't believe it, yet somewhere inside me, I do. "No one would just kill people like that. This'll make world news."

"It would in a free country like the U.S., but the only people who'll hear about this are the ones who live in this district, probably just this sector of the district. Maybe even only those on this street. And me and you, since we walked in last night and saw it happening live."

"Murder is against our laws. All laws. It's inhumane. You must be wrong."

Zane straightens and steps back. "Yes, Anna." His voice is clipped. "I'm wrong. *Again.* What do I have to do to prove to you this is happening? Right under your stupid nose!"

Everything inside me disagrees with him, and the pressure in my chest builds until I want to sob, curl up in a corner, and wake up from the bad dream I must be having. There's nowhere for me to go as I drop to the concrete floor, caged between Zane and the wall. Knees up to my chest, I breathe into my jeans. This can't be something the A.U. does. It can't be.

He lowers to me. "Look, Anna. You don't believe me when I tell you what's happening, so I'm proving it to you by showing you. I wouldn't believe me, either, if it was just on a screen, but you're here witnessing it. How can you come to any other conclusion?"

"Why didn't they leave, Zane?" I still can't believe an entire building would be incinerated with people inside. Someone had to have tried harder.

"They didn't have new places to go."

I lift up and stare hard at him, searching his face for the lie. "Our leaders would have found new places for them to live." Arms crossed, I'm sure of this statement. No way would they leave the people inside on purpose. Dying of smoke inhalation or being crushed in their sleep is *not* humanitarian. It's murder.

"Where would they put them? Construction has stopped everywhere in the country. I already told you the A.U. doesn't have any credits. They can't even take care of the places they have, let alone build new ones. People are told to leave, but where will they go? Where would *you* go? Would you believe the government if, all your life, they gave you everything, and the one time they say *leave, but sorry we can't help you*, they actually don't? What would you have done?"

I'd have left. Yes, I would have. Wouldn't I?

"We've been waiting weeks for this. Weeks!" Zane stands and spins away, pacing to the holding lot's stair door and back. "We sent in rogue teams to try and convince people the building would be leveled, and if they were inside still, they'd go with it." Facing me again, he asks, "Do you know that not a single one believed us? None, Anna! None!" His hands slam the frame of the door, sending a metallic clang through the air. "No one would go with us." He pleads with his arms extended my way. "None of them."

"But if the district leaders knew—"

"Locals don't know what goes on. Or if they do, they're bought off with enough mystery credits to keep silent." His sour expression makes me think I should have known that. "A directive comes from Osso, or more likely Osso Junior, that gets filtered to the right place, and the job is done. Period.

The building was condemned. It was rotting out from under its own shell because of shoddy construction fifty years ago—when they were throwing up buildings like they printed that paper money before we went to electronic credits. Had to have places for people to go, so up they went. Half those buildings are falling apart. This isn't even the first ... or the last."

"Why didn't they just let it be, if they have no place to go, though? Why didn't they—" *take care of them like they always do?* "They'll get caught—"

Zane shakes his head. "They'll say—*prove*—that all protocols were put into place. They'll have paperwork documenting that the building was condemned. That all the people inside were supposed to have moved. That they did move. That they somehow returned with all their furniture after the last check. They'll say the triggers accidentally went off early—before the marshals could go through and ensure no one snuck back in, and it'll all be lies."

I drop my head back to my knees. I don't want to know my own country did this. On purpose.

Once again, life as I know it, *knew it*, has changed. It makes no sense why no one came to help, at least. Keeping my gaze on the rise and fall of Zane's chest, and the blue of his jacket, I tell myself not to look again. *You're too sensitive*, my mother's voice speaks in my mind. I don't want to even consider that someone planned this—that someone could keep safety and security away.

Someone, please tell me this is a dream! Yet, I'm right here. Just outside of it. Smelling it. In my own country.

We burned down a building rather than find people other places to live.

What more can we do to ourselves?

Oh yeah, we can sterilize the next wave of adults permanently.

I can't control or help the tremors.

"Are you okay?" Zane asks in a flat monotone.

I nod, though I'm not. Not in the least. I try to wave off the emotions running through me, but even I know the action is pointless. Air breaks through my lips in spurts as I hold back tears. "Are you sure, Zane? A hundred percent sure that's what happened? It wasn't an accident?"

⚬═══╤═══⚬

NOW

The wall going up didn't "just happen", either.

Though, how do I know?

I have to force myself to stop taking everyone at their word. Make them prove their claims. Stop letting people push me around. Like with the necklace Cam gave me. Never should have accepted it because it felt wrong at the time. I should have known.

How can I trust anything Zane has to say, when he lied about *why* he took me away from my dad's? Does that mean we didn't have to run at all just two days ago? Could I have just finished registration, the way it was all planned for me, and not be stuck here, outside in the cold, with a busted up shoulder, away from home, away from everyone who's important to me?

I need to be more like Mom, but I walked out on her, too.

What am I going to do?

"Anna?"

I know. I know exactly what I'm going to do.

I'm going home.

Just like Zane suggested, I'll use registration to get over, through, or whatever it takes to get past the wall, somehow get to the surface and find my way home. To Mom. To the one person who knows how to deal with the circumstances of life, and she can teach me how to be more like her. I'm getting out of this new life Mia forced me into. Out of this mess Zane put me in.

"Anna?" Zane takes my hands and holds them as he stares down into my eyes. "Before you go ... um, I have to tell you one more thing."

Uh oh.

"I might have hinted that you were a spy ... you know, before, but ..."

So we're back to this topic.

He shakes his head.

"Why are you shaking your head?"

"Because you weren't. Aren't."

"Weren't, aren't, what?"

"A spy." He says it so matter of factly, like I should just take it as truth. "I promise the spy thing was the only lie I told, and it wasn't totally untrue." His voice is calm. Genuine. At least, I think it is.

There's a deep pull inside me that wants to listen to him, but I can channel my stubborn-as-all-get-out-mom when I want to, and right now, I want to.

"I'm really sorry, Anna. I know what I said, but I did it because it was the push you needed."

The push I needed? As if I wouldn't have gone with him otherwise?

Tearing myself from him, I whirl away, but just as quickly storm back toward him, anger heating my cold body. "You said Mia told us to run, that she had to, too. I'm standing ... *here* ... *in the cold,* with a busted-up shoulder ... with *you* because *you* said—"

"I know. I should have told you, but we were so caught up in everything, and you looked so happy when I mentioned going to the coast that I ..."

"Don't. Just don't." That's the problem with people. *That's the problem with you.* Emotion tightens my chest, and tears threaten to fall. Next to the word *naive* the name Erianna Price Keating should be emblazoned in some precious metal. I'm just a pawn in everyone's game.

"Anna." His voice is soft and closer, pushing the dam of water building at my eyes toward the outside.

I don't want to be mad at him. Right now, he and June are the only two people I can count on. *What good does that do if he's a liar?*

"Anna?"

"What?" I finally manage after a few cleansing breaths.

"First ... I'm truly sorry. Second ... Mia suggested I tell you that it was you so you'd to agree to go with me, since we'd thrown so much at you all at once. I—I didn't know how much more you could take before you'd think we were lying about everything."

Because I don't believe that now?

"So, I twisted the story a little. You aren't the spy. I am. And you know that."

Do I? Do I? What else has he lied about? "What about the people chasing us down the hall at Registration," I ask. "Was that true, or did you make that up, too?

"Um ..."

"There were people coming down the hall, Zane! You said *now or never* because *you* heard them!"

"Well ... yeah ... I don't know if those people were coming after me, or just bringing their trash to the bins. We had a very limited amount of time to get out, and I didn't want to be left with no time—"

"The garbage riser? Did we have to?"

"Um ..."

Idiot comes to mind. "Um ... what?"

Zane glances back for a second before returning to me. "I didn't want to tell you, but you ... kinda ... delayed the opportunity, so I had to improvise."

I step back. "Delayed? *I* delayed us? What do you mean?"

He closes his eyes and pinches the bridge of his nose before coming back to me again. "We ... were late. You sleep really soundly, and I didn't want to wake you, and then my time ran out, and so we had to go an alternate route or risk getting caught."

My breath catches in my throat. If it weren't for me, he'd have been just fine doing whatever *he* needed to do.

Does it change anything that I know this?

No, it doesn't.

It's just reinforcement that I've gotta get away. Away from Zane. Away from June before I mess him up.

I have to get back to my life.

Right now.

6

"Be truthful with me, Zane. I really, *really* need this. And don't sugarcoat it this time. Don't hide the truth, and don't baby me. I can take it." My voice hitches on my last sentence. "Is this wall *really* because of economics?"

"Yes."

"Is it *really* true that District One made it happen?"

He nods.

"Is our country *really* falling apart, or are you making it up?"

"It's real. It's *all* real." He hesitates for a second, and that hitch in his stride piques my curiosity.

"What?"

"There's one thing that isn't totally real."

"What's that?" I ask.

"Me. The A.U. has no record of *me*. Of Zane Warren."

I can't believe him, and I'm sure my body is giving me away somehow. "You were there in registration. I—You got a tablet with a job assignment. How can you not be ... you?"

His chest expands and deflates. "Remember how you thought Mia was a fluke?"

"Yes." Of course. I remember that like I learned it yesterday. "What does that have to do with anything?"

"Because she was one. *Is* one. Your mom made that happen by going off the grid. Mia, though, she wanted in with the resistance, and a true test was to come through registration as someone else. With an assumed name. So ... to them she's ... well ... someone else."

My brain is starting to hurt with all the information I didn't ask about. "The A.U. doesn't know my sister, but they *do* know my sister?"

Zane nods. "As someone else."

"Not as Mia?" I don't know why I need to ask again, but I do.

He gives me another head bob.

"Okay, but what about you?"

"They know me as Warren Zane. Because I'm young, my uncle wasn't sure I'd be able to handle a completely different name, so they played name swap and reduce when they got me in. Not even a very clever trick, but in a world that exists by numbers, that little switch is all it took. It confuses everyone. And better yet, people mix it up all the time, reading the first and last name at random and calling me by either one as if they don't know for sure. Kinda funny, if you think about it."

Funny? Not what I'd call it. I saw his name on the tablet, including the Warren and Zane. I thought it meant they'd reversed his name. "What ... about me? They know me, right?"

"Yes, because your dad put you in. But the A.U. thinks you're a normal person. They don't know that you're connected to Eric. To Mia. Or that you have anything to do with me."

"How did they find out about Mia?" She'd gone into the wind, as my dad said, but both Dad and Zane had told me not to worry, that Mia knows how to take care of herself.

"Not sure. Haven't heard from her since all that went down."

All the information Zane has shared swirls in my head. He lied to me so I'd believe him. He's telling me the truth so I will believe him. I really don't know what to believe anymore.

This is exactly why this life is not for me, and why I have to get out of here.

Now.

"How would it even work ... I mean, me going back in?"

A small smirk graces Zane's face like he's happy I'm following his plan—though it's not *his* plan. This one is mine.

"One story, multiple ... let's call them embellishments," he says. "For your return to registration, that is. Stick with the facts, don't share anything that isn't absolutely necessary, and you'll be fine. It's how Delta Street stays undercover."

"So, if I go back in, they won't come after you, or Mia, or Dad, if they figure out all the connections?"

He shakes his head. "No. *You* can go back to registration. You've only missed a couple days. You're officially on the roster, and the A.U. is expecting you. And *wants* you."

I huff a laugh. Right. They aren't going to let a girl who broke the rules just return with a smile and a nod. No way. Who would do that? "They're not going to let me back in without some proof."

After a big sigh, he says, "Yes, Anna. They will. And you have proof." He points to my arms, tucked against my chest. "That injury is enough. They'll let you in, just like they let everyone in. Like I said, it's part of our problem. Come here, get free stuff. Screw us over. Get more free stuff. Leave and come back ... get more free stuff. That's why we're out of credits, and China's set to take over. You see?"

"Right. The whole *our country is bankrupt* thing."

"If you want freedom, you have to be prepared to take the road *less* traveled. Like Martin Luther King Jr. said back in the mid nineteen-hundreds, 'The road to freedom is a difficult, hard road. It always makes for temporary setbacks'." He seriously knows his history. "It wasn't all for nothing." He rubs at the side of his nose, which has healed—mostly—since I kicked him.

"You're crazy, you know." I mean it, too.

His head bobs in what I take as agreement. "Since we're on this truth kick, I have one more thing."

Didn't he say he'd already covered all his lies?

"Remember on the bus, when you thought you first met me, and I was kinda all geeky and weird?"

I do remember.

"Well, I'm not. Weird. Or geeky."

Could have fooled me.

"That was all a setup so I could get you to stick by me. Which you didn't, by the way, and made my life seriously hard for a few hours. You're a tough one. Tougher than your sister, actually."

I face Zane straight on. "Me? Tougher than Mia? Now you're lying, and I know it, but at least it's straight to my face."

"I'm not." He adds to the statement with a slight headshake. "That's why you're the right one for this mission." He reaches out and tucks my hair behind my ear, sending a chill through me. "In a good way, too. I kinda wish we didn't have to meet like that. Like I could have just asked you on a date at the commerce center or something." He gives a small shrug of his right shoulder.

Really? *Really?* A date? We're in the middle of a warzone, or a small one at least, surrounded by cold weather, don't have a trolley to get anywhere, and he says he would have asked me on a date? Now? Heat flushes into my cheeks. If only we could have had a date. He might— *No!* my subconscious yells at me. *You want a life. A real one. One with less possibility of death and dismemberment.*

My inner head is truly loud, and it's right. I never wanted to leave registration. I just wanted simplicity in my life. A decent job. A warm house. Not this mess Zane has gotten us into. If I get back in, I can go find Mom and beg her forgiveness and team up with her. Zane, June, Cam and everyone else can figure out how to live their own lives. Delta Street can disappear into the recesses of my memory. I'll miss Mia and Dad, but I haven't had them in my life long so I shouldn't worry about that much.

I stare up at Zane. It seems I'm on a never-ending cycle of choosing this or that. That or this.

You have to do what's right for you. Get a move on with it.

"So, what do I have to do ..." ... *to get you to just leave me alone for the rest of my life.* I can't bring myself to say that, so instead out comes, "Just tell me what to do."

⁓

Zane claps his hands as if my agreement to go back to registration is the best thing that could ever have happened. To anyone. The light that flashes over June's face from the giant spotlights over the wall reflects a more somber attitude—I assume toward my departure. Does he know I have ulterior motives?

"How do we get her to the red house in *this* district?" Zane asks June.

Tapping on his tablet, June focuses on that for a minute. Maybe two. "It's about two hours south from here. Ish. Maybe three, depending on how this is calculating distance and what transpo she takes. It's a little foggy because of the accident. But ..." He holds up one finger. "... it's not too far. We just need to get you a ride." June rolls back and disappears behind the trolly.

"You're sure about this, Anna?" Zane asks me.

I give him my best, most realistically-fake smile. "You think

I can do it, so yes, I can."

"Awesome. Once we get you in, just tell them I took you out without consent—"

Which you did. Sort of. "Wait, tell them *you* took me? But won't that—"

"Yes, tell them Zane Warren took you. Zane. With a Z. First name Zane." He taps me on the nose. "Then tell them you never wanted to leave, and tell them you just want to get through registration like everyone else."

Which won't be hard, at all, because all of it's true. Except for the last day, which is only one or two days away, if I've counted right.

"And then, tell them to expedite the last forty-eight hours of training so you can catch up. That will force them to send you back to *your* district—to Eleven, because they can't expedite training an Eleven anywhere except *in* District Eleven. It's the rule. So, they'll send you, and once you have your schedule, you'll be able to go off grid quickly because they won't track you the way they track everyone else, what with the *expedited* schedule." On a small laugh, he adds, "This will be the easiest inside job ever, since they want you back. I know it. You know how to get to the surface from Eleven?"

I nod. I really don't, not that it matters since I'm staying this time.

"Perfect." Zane seems exceptionally happy about this. "Think you can do it?"

Can I go back to registration, claim I was stolen, get back in and finish, and disappear from Zane's life forever? I worry a little about Cam, but now isn't the time for me to think about her. I can't help a lifeless girl, whether she was once my friend, or not. Other people will do that. The 'good people'. I just have to focus on me. The way Mom wanted me to. To just be me and do the best I can.

Which means going back to the place I left.

"Yes, absolutely."

⁂

The old man who reset my shoulder shows up with June about ten minutes after Zane thinks he won his argument with me about going back to registration.

"I'll be happy to transport you," the man says.

My heart softens as he offers a ride in his transpo. He's another person who I'll have to make amends with in the future, and pay for the energy for his transpo at some point.

"And how is your arm?" he asks.

"Better. Thank you so much." I have my right arm still tucked against me and hold it with my left because it hurts to stretch it out, but it is better. "How did you know what to do?"

The old man smiles. "I was a medic in the war, almost eighty years ago. In my late teens. Fought to bring this country into its glory days. Haven't forgotten a lick of what I learned."

"Well, thank you, then, for lending me that treatment."

"You are most welcome. Shall we be going, then?" He holds out a hand like an old gentleman would a lady in one of those big old dresses, where the skirt flares out three feet on all sides. He takes my elbow and guides me around the trolley.

For the last half hour, or more, my view has been the black trolly. I knew people milled about everywhere, but I never saw anything beyond Zane, June, the old man, the broken transpo, and the lights glaring from the new barrier.

Beyond the trolley, and with the lights a little lower, my view is of four small transpos toppled upon each other, one with flames coming out of the front and people spraying it down, while others tend to two of those body bags, like at the scene of the fire.

Someone died in this accident. No, not accident. Homicide. There's no other way to consider it.

The worst part about it is that there are no security forces here either. Everyone that's helping is just another, average, everyday human. Or that's how it looks, anyway.

Why couldn't they have given a warning to the other transpos? Why did the wall have to go up with such force that it would leave at least two people dead? By the looks of the mess, there could be another in the burning transpo, from the way people cut at the metal, or whatever had once formed the transpo's frame.

Pain rips at my heart.

My escort tugs on my elbow. "Come with me, young lady. You don't want to watch this."

He's right. I don't, but at the same time, something inside me compels me to stare as we pass. Right until Zane pops up in front of me and blocks my view.

"You have everything you need? Know what to do?" he asks.

"Sure," I say and keep walking.

"One second, Mr. Perez. I just need Anna for one moment."

My guide nods and steps away.

"I have one more thing." He holds out his hand, and something shimmers on his palm.

"What's that?"

"This is a listening device."

"A what?" I've never seen anything like it.

"It's so you can hear us. I lost the communicator in the wreck, but I do have this part. So, at the very least, you can hear others. Not June or me, but others in Delta Street. They know the code to reach me, which will mean they'll share information with you, but they won't be able to hear you, or anything."

"Why are you showing me this?"

"Because I want you to take it. This is how we communicate, and I want you to, at least, know what's going on in case there are problems."

"But they'll catch—"

Zane shakes his head. "No, they won't. It's undetectable."

"Is this how you've communicated with ... my dad ... and Mia and ..."

"Yes. But I'm not supposed to let anyone know. I just want you to be safer inside. Just in case."

"Just in case what?"

"Anything, Anna. I can't do anything from here, but knowledge is power, and if you're going in alone, you ought to have something to help."

"Where ... does it go?"

Zane's lips curve up. "In your ear."

"And this has been in yours for ... how long?"

"Since the start of registration. So, see? Undetectable. If anyone does an ear check, they'll see what looks like a freckle. That's how well it sticks to your skin and blends in"

"This is weird, Zane."

"I know, but I just don't feel right leaving you without anything, since I can't go with you."

Maybe I don't want to know. "I—"

"Please, Anna. It's better for you than me stuck here." The light that pans across his face shows me how sincere he is, and once again, that stomach-sinking feeling hits me.

"How do I attach it?"

"Hold out your hand."

I lower my right arm so my left hangs at my side without too much pain and stretch out my uninjured one. Zane places the little device on the tip of my index finger.

"Now, just act like you're going to dig wax out of your ear, and put your finger in, pressing to the inside. This'll just wrap to your skin like a contact."

"A contact?"

Zane laughs. "Sorry. It's an old medical device for correcting vision." He waves me forward.

Awkward doesn't comes close to describing my feelings at sticking this thing to the inside of my ear, especially when it's been in Zane's. On a blown out breath, I do as requested.

Sound fills my head.

Hand out, I cringe.

"Give it a second. It auto adjusts," Zane says.

The noises continue, scrambled and messy, fading until they are soft and clear. Voices speak over one another. "How do you turn it off?"

"Tap your ear once. Here." Zane reaches out and touches the spot just at my cheek, on the outside of where the device is.

It goes silent.

"It has a sensor. One tap is off. If it's off, one tap is on. The volume will auto adjust continuously. It's on based on surrounding noise, decibel levels, and how sound is passing through your ear canal, so on and off is really it."

I tap like he did, and the sound returns.

"You get used to it," he says.

"Okay." Another touch and it's off. "Thanks."

Zane takes my hand, my good one, and holds it, staring down toward it as if he's thinking about saying something. When his gaze meets mine, he says, "Good luck," and lets go.

"Ready?" the old man asks.

"Uh ... yeah." I follow him toward an old beat-up transpo, something that has to be as old as him—an antique, if I recall the word people use. The transpo is one of those ancient ones with a long empty space behind two seats. I don't think I've ever seen anything like it.

He opens the door and helps me climb in, before making his way around to the steering side.

As he closes the door, I ask, "I don't mean to sound rude, but what is this exactly?"

"My truck?"

"This ... transpo. Yes."

"It's a *truck*. Had the engine converted to the new energy, but used to be that this ran on gasoline."

"But that's dangerous!"

He chuckles as he presses a button, and the truck, as he calls it, rumbles beneath me. "Back in my day, before everything went generic and gender neutral and bland as can be, we had cars and trucks and all sorts of makes and models. Should have known what was coming, what with the colors going to muted, boring colors, that the transportation units would, too. But I saved ole Bettie here. She's nigh on eighty years old herself."

"Is she pathway safe?"

He regards me as if I've gone crazy, complete with raised up eyebrow. "Of course. Did all the upgrades myself."

"Aren't you supposed to go to a center for that?"

That same look graces me again as he turns onto the pathway. "Darlin', I may be a hundred and three, but I don't need someone else messin' with my stuff, and ain't nobody gonna tell me what to do with my truck."

I don't know what to say to that. For as old as he is, I kinda can't believe he still has a pathway controller certificate. I'm guessing he doesn't and him transporting us is another illegal activity. I swear I can't get away from people who don't follow the rules.

"Now, you ready to go?"

On a deep sigh, and with a quick glance back, revealing Zane standing just where I left him, I say, "Yes, please."

The truck lurches forward. "Perry Road it is, then."

As long as I make it to registration, I'll be happy.

Or content, at least.

Maybe.

Probably not.

7

"You know, back in my day, we didn't have this . . . registration," the old man says, driving us away from the crash scene. "If you wanted a job, you either got a degree, or interned, or did whatever you could to learn how to do it. If you didn't like that one, two, or twenty years later, so be it. Just go back to square one and learn how to do the new thing."

"How did people know what they wanted to do, then, if no one told them their skills?"

He narrows his eyes, glancing toward me before facing the pathway again. "You didn't always. We just did what we were best at. But *we* picked it. All this selection and testing . . .. My great-great granddaughter just went through it, and I tell ya, she came out wrong when it was done. All she's doing now is waiting for that check. Gave up on everything I thought her mom and dad instilled in her."

"I'm sorry." I don't know what else to say, but he sounds sad, it seems appropriate.

"If you ask me, which, of course, nobody does because I'm old school, the moment we gave one red cent without requiring work in return was the moment this country started down its path to failure."

So, he's one of Zane's people. An A.U. hater.

"I've worked every day of my life—well, up until my own

boy put me out to pasture on his own dime. But what's going on now ..." He gives a slow headshake. "... it's a damn shame." For an old guy, he's a chatterbox.

"If you don't like what you're living ... with ... why do you live here?"

He shakes a gnarled finger my way. "Now, that's a very good question. My boy, number two, now, he wanted me to go to the U.S. with him and his wife and my grandkids. Could have. Probably should have. But I don't believe in giving up. Like I told him, this is my house, my land, my country. It ain't over until the fat lady sings, and she ain't sung yet."

Why does someone with a physical ailment have to sing for the situation to be over? This man confuses me more than anything.

"So, here I am, just biding my time until my ticker stops ticking."

We continue our drive in amicable quiet, all except for the whoosh or swish as the air wheels pass over different types of ground cover, and Mr. Perez humming to himself every once in a while. "You can sleep if you want. We have a little while to drive."

I don't think I can sleep. Or should.

"Or you could talk. Don't girls your age still like to talk about everything?"

"About what?" I ask.

Mr. Perez shrugs his boney shoulders. "Tell me how you got here today."

Surely, he doesn't want to hear about that. Then again, if I tell him, maybe he'll see just how wrong Zane has been and prove me right. Prove that going back and staying here is the right decision.

"You sure you want to hear my story?"

"What else we got to talk about?"

⊂━━┼━━⊃

12 HOURS EARLIER

Never in a million years did I expect my 'What do we do about it?' question to Zane to lead us to a goat farm in the middle of nowhere. I am glad, however, not to be smelling or breathing in the air around the burning building anymore.

Goats are everywhere, though. In all honesty, I can't remember seeing so many animals in one place. The apple trees are bare, branches empty of all fruit, though in the middle of winter, I would expect that. It's the sheer number of goats and the bleating that's making my eyes twitch.

"Why are we here?" I ask.

"I wanted to show you one of the places affected by the A.U.'s policies over the years."

Brow furrowed, I ask, "Okay, so why are you showing me—this?"

"Because this is what happens to small farmers when they don't follow the rules. Non-negotiated rules, I should add. Rules imposed at random, by select E.P. officials whenever they want."

"E.P.?"

"Oh ... environmental protection. They get to control what everyone can do with A.U. resources. Like land. Water. Stuff like that."

"If no one controlled it, wouldn't things be in ... chaos?" Like back at the burned-out building where no one came to help, I want to add.

"Sure it would."

"So, how's this bad?" The sound alone, the incessant bleating, would bug the living daylights out of me, and that's coming through closed windows.

"Okay, so ... we make a rule, right? Something that's good for most. Like, for ninety-nine percent. Then there's this one percent who fight it. And oddly enough, they'll have the credits to do that, and they get all these people to agree with them, whether they do or not. Then, for that one percent, they end up imposing a law that doesn't work for the ninety-nine, and the ninety-nine suffer."

I have to bob my head and let his explanation filter through. "So, it's not majority rule? And they get goats?"

He chuckles and shakes his head in one, hard, determined move. "Whoever has the most credits wins. So, let's say your apple orchard, a farm that's been in your family for six or seven, maybe eight generations, has produced apples that you've shared with hundreds, if not thousands, of families at a local market, but it sits on land that the goat farmer next door thinks he should have for his goats because goats produce meat and milk and fertilizer—which are three things instead of one. All he has to do is prove that his need is greater than yours, and the E.P. will side with him."

"But that's not right."

Zane says nothing.

"When you own something, when you've worked so hard for it, how can they just take it away? Aren't there ... records, or something, that say the first person owned it? How can this E.P. group just take it over?"

"Oh, they don't *just* take it away. They'll compensate you— by paying you a pittance of what it's worth, and telling you that apples can be imported, and that goats need land. Of course, then, they import from Brazil, who gets paid by Russia, who's really backed by China, and once again, China has a stronger hold on us than we do on ourselves."

He makes my head spin when he talks like that, but I get the point. I think. "Why didn't the apple farmer fight back?"

Zane's head tilts just a little. "If they ... do ..."

Waiting for him to finish and fill in the blank he's probably expecting me to complete, I turn and face the outside again. Snow covers much of the landscape, and under the sunlight, it glistens a beautiful white.

"Those trees are all dead," Zane says without a hint of joking. "That orchard doesn't operate anymore because the goats ate every bud for so many seasons that the trees stopped producing. But the original owner of the orchard still has to pay his property tax, his self-employment tax because he owns the orchard, and it's registered as a business that no one can change because of zoning laws, and he has to now pay a limited use tax."

"A what?" I stare at the decimated rows of brown, barren trees.

"Well, he can't produce, but the land is his, so he has to pay to own it and not use it. And he's even fined for not using it because he could have been."

"But the goats ate everything. How—*that's not fair!*"

"Exactly."

"Why doesn't he sell out. Can he? To—I mean, if the A.U. had credits, could he?"

"Could have, yes. But not everyone will. No matter what, some are determined to bring the A.U. back to what it once was ... a thriving economic power house, merged with the U.S.. For prosperity and individuality and laws, but less control. Think about this ... would you give up your most prized possession just because someone said you couldn't, or shouldn't, have it?"

I have nothing to claim as 'prized', except maybe the three

books in my room back home with my mom. I wouldn't give
them up, but I have thought about selling them many times
when we needed food. "But this is different, right? This is land.
It could be re-cultivated and—"

"Eaten up by more goats. *Baaa*."

My laugh comes out, but I force it to stop. "That's really
sad."

"Yup."

"This is depressing." I slump back in my seat.

"There's so much more out there that I could show you,
but I if we go back to your dad's, I can explain and show you
exactly what we plan to do about it. Or hope to."

As Zane operates the transpo, he talks. Incessantly. The
goats' stop leads to decimated butterfly fields, ruined because
the person who lived next to the butterfly field became aller-
gic to flowers and forced the flower shop that owned the field
to shut down. Compensation from the government is never
enough, Zane reminds me.

Beyond that is an apparent catastrophe, or so Zane tells
me, about another implosion site—like the fire—where every
building along an entire block disappeared. He says over one
thousand people died. I didn't believe him, until he pulled up
a recording dated ten years ago. Nothing has been rebuilt because, also according to Zane, no one in the town could get a
construction permit, and the closest families with construction
job titles didn't feel like working on them, because after their
business closed, they found out they could get assistance and
earn more on assistance than working, so they didn't. Worse,
they file, every year, to register the ground they own as dangerous, claiming, repeatedly, that there are sink holes. Since no

one can prove otherwise, everything stopped, they earn money for nothing, and the entire sector is empty.

According to Zane, it's all a big fat lie. It makes my head spin, is what it does. There's nothing logical about it. We work to earn credits to live. Simple as that. How it can be justified seems silly, but surely there's a legitimate reason. Zane must just not know it.

After an hour, and a stop for some much-needed breakfast, Zane says, "The Department of Agriculture would be great, if Osso hadn't mucked it up."

"What do you mean?" I ask, biting into an omelet sandwich complete with a cheese I've never had before that's sharp-tasting and orange and really delicious. The lady who sold it to us called it cheddar and she apparently makes it herself.

Back in the transpo, Zane says nothing, and I turn to him, realizing he's just done the same as me, his mouth full. Who knew cheese would be good on eggs? Who knew real eggs could actually be sold in small road-side restaurants? It almost seems like the country areas don't follow all the rules, because unlike Milton's, which has a list a mile long of things they have to do to meet health codes and the types of food they can serve by their permit, the little three-seater restaurant where we stopped had no lists, no details, and no menu. Just 'breakfast'.

"No one wants to be a farmer," Zane says after swallowing. "Did you know eggs can't be eaten by the owners of chickens because that would prevent someone else who might need them from eating them, so they must be provided to the farmer's market by courier each day. Since that's too expensive, they're all disappearing."

"Say what?" I spin to him. "If I have a chicken that produces food for my family, I can't even eat it?"

His head goes back and forth. "Same for gardens. Well water.

Any animal that could be consumed—"

"But not goats?"

"Goats, too," he says with a grin. "Unless you let the E.P. Officials stick their hand in your pocket."

Corruption. The more he talks, the more irritation builds up in me. How did I not know all this before? How did Mom keep it from me? Did our educenter people know? They never said anything that I remember. Did our cafetorium people do the same thing they did at registration to our food so we'd all comply?

We pass through a small, deserted district town. There's not a soul anywhere, and I expect tumbleweeds to roll by, like in the old screen films.

"Why is no one here?" I ask.

"The department of transportation re-routed traffic. This is the I-corridor. Jokingly named because capital I is the roman numeral one, and only one person ever uses the road anymore."

"Who?"

He keeps moving, slowly. "Same guy who decided the area needed a jobs boost and petitioned to have the new freeway built that bypassed this area, then shut everything down because no one went through."

"Why does he still use it?"

Zane chuckles. "He doesn't. But they say his ghost does."

I laugh. Sort of. Ghosts don't exist. Right? "What about the people who live close by? Why don't they use it?"

"Sink holes. Or so they said. A dozen houses collapsed about thirty years ago, but we think it was shoddy construction again. Only problem is, they literally slipped right into the ground, people, contents, transpos, everything. Major Stein was one."

I face Zane. "You've got to be joking. And who's Major Stein?"

His head moves back and forth. "The ghost of the I-freeway."

Raising an eyebrow, I say, "C'mon, Zane. Sink holes aren't real. Ghosts aren't, either."

Tapping on the transpo's P-Comm, he brings up a screen, and I lean forward to read.

"Sink holes are everywhere!" I can't believe it, but it seems they exist, and not just in the A.U.. A follow-on story tells the tale of one Major General Gerald Stein, who did in fact disappear in one of the sink holes—the same man who had initiated and procured the approval for the bypass. "This is nuts," I say.

"Exactly, and the department of construction doesn't check for them. Even today, they don't. They authorized construction all over the place, no matter what or where, and there you go. Disappearing stuff. Disappearing people."

Falling back against the transpo's seat, I just don't know how to take it all in. "Did they ever find the people?"

"They didn't even look."

"No way." Disbelief coats my tone.

"How are they going to? In a sink hole, everything just gets sucked in. No idea how far it goes, where it goes, anything. Probably whole cities are formed underground, and we don't even know it."

"That sounds like the making of a sci-fi film, not reality." I wish Zane would move faster because if sink holes really do exist, that means we could fall into one at any time.

At a bump in the road, I cry out.

"You okay?" Zane asks.

I nod, heat rushing to my cheeks while an underlying panic consumes me. I don't want to be sucked into the ground with no way out. Being underground during registration only freaked me out a little, but at least there I could return to the surface if I wanted to.

NOW

"You don't want to hear all this, do you, Mr. Perez?"

"This truck doesn't have the speed of today's transpo's, so we have a ways to go to get to Perry Road. If I gotta stay awake, might as well hear something interesting."

"It doesn't get better, though," I say.

"Nothing ever does, unless you talk about it."

8

The screen in the transpo blinks once, twice, and in the center appears Marlena, the stylist from registration who gave me my new look and my tattoo, and next to her, Lucie, Marlena's absolute clone. Both stare at us, knowing for sure that we're in their transpo, eating their food, using their energy, and are certainly going to turn us in, since Zane *borrowed* their tranpo.

I'll be living in a rotting security encampment for the rest of my life. I know it.

Marlena waves. "Hey!" Lucie mimics the action, adding, "What're ya'll up to?" Or the other way around—I can't tell who is whom, exactly.

Zane's lips curve up. "Hi! I'm just showing Anna some of the A.U.'s beautiful landscape."

Both sisters snort a laugh. "As if there's any left," Lucie says. At least, I think it's Lucie. The screen isn't very big, and their faces are zoomed in so I can't see their hair very well, and both have dark hair.

"When're ya'll returning?"

Zane shrugs, though I doubt either sister can see it. "Tonight, probably."

Heads bob on the screen. "You better. We got some good news, and some bad news. Which do you want first?"

They haven't mentioned anything about us being in their transpo. It makes me wonder if they even know. Can they tell?

"Good news first, as always," Zane says.

"No, wait." I hold up my hands, as if that will stop them from talking. I have no idea how much they can see of us, so I drop them again. "I'm sorry about the transpo. About taking it. You know, about borrowing it. We'll bring it back. I promise. And I'll find a way to give you the energy credits back."

Their eyebrows quirk up, just like Zane's do, and their lips twitch. He's sitting in the seat with his arms crossed over his chest, a giant smirk on his face.

"What?" I ask.

He presses a button and a big, bold 'mute' shows up on the screen. "I told you they wouldn't mind, and I gave them the signal. They know we're in here and that we're out. Why are you apologizing?"

If I could slink any lower in my seat, I probably would.

Zane presses the button again, and chatter comes up through the screen as Lucie and Marlena talk to each other. "Good news first," he says again.

"We're going with you!" they say in tandem, their voices a stereo of sound.

"Going where?" I ask.

"To the U.S.. We're on the next transition team with you! We got in officially!" They both do a little jig, faces bouncing at the same rate, smiles blooming just as wide as the other's.

I thought they were already going to the U.S., so why is this news? Beyond that, it reminds me that Zane is going to leave me soon, since he, too, told me he'd be on with the next team.

"You're coming, too, right, Anna?" one of the twins asks.

My head pops up as if I've been smacked. "What?"

"The next trip. Zane's got you on the list."

Guy-in-question stares at me as if I should say something. As if I should comment, even though a question hasn't been asked. He presses the mute button again and runs a hand through his hair.

"What just happened?" I ask.

"Uh ... well ... so, I was going to tell you—"

"*I'm* on a list to go to the U.S.? Since when? How? Why?" I can't go to the U.S. It's dangerous over there.

Zane waves my thoughts silent, presses the button again, and the chatter starts up. "So, what's the bad news, then?"

"Trip's been moved up. We leave tomorrow, at oh-three-hundred," one of the two says.

"What?" It's an exclamation of worry from Zane. "Tomorrow?" He leans back into the seat and pushes on his eyelids with his fingertips.

"No, it's not tomorrow, it's in the night of tomorrow, but it's actually the morning," the other says.

"Sisters, will you please calculate how many hours we have to get back before we have to leave?"

They stare at each other for a second. "Fourteen hours," they say together.

Zane's shoulders go rigid.

"Will you make it back in time?" Marlena, I think, asks. "Where are you, anyway?"

Zane's head does a half-turn-twist-thing. "We're in District Fifteen, I think."

"Oh, well, you got plenty of time, then. Hel*lo*, you can get all the way across the country in twelve in my little transpo." Lucie turns to Marlena, or vice versa. "I'll pack your bags. If you're not at the location by ten"til departure, I'll give it to the closest homeless guy. The whole thing, and no one will know you were there, or not."

With a quick head bob, Zane says, "We'll be there. Thanks, ladies." He clicks off and turns to me. "Ready?"

Ready for what? I drop my chin down, closing my eyes. What is he asking of me?

As he's done before, his finger ends up pushing under my chin, lifting my face up. "Will you go to the U.S. with me?"

◦══╪══◦

NOW

"So, that young man asked you to go on the trip of a lifetime, and you're choosing to go back to Registration?" Mr. Perez asks.

"I can't go there. He knows that."

"Why? Why not?"

◦══╪══◦

NINE HOURS EARLIER

"Please, Anna. I would really like it if you came with me. I can show you more about the other side. The world outside the walls of the A.U.. I just showed you how things are bad here. Let me show you how things are good over there." His gaze bores into me harder. More determined.

"I don't ... *know* if I want to go." It comes out a whisper, but I know he hears me when his finger drops away. It's the truth, too.

"Why not? What do you have to lose?"

My head pops up. How can he even ask that? "My mom? My dad? My sister? Zane ... I just—I just got my dad back. He's here. My mom may not be right, but I don't want to make what I have with her worse. And my sister—"

"Is M.I.A., literally and figuratively."

My lips crack into a smile. "That was kinda funny. She

would have liked that as a joke." *What if she comes back, though? I need to spend time with her. I've missed the last four years with my sister.*

"Mia would want you to go. Your dad would want you to go. I can't answer for your mom, but you told her why you weren't staying with her, so if you're going to do what you said, this is part of what you need to do. And it's not forever. It's a one-week trip. Like Lucie said, it's a transition trip."

"But—"

"Think about it, Anna." He drops his hands. "I'm not going to make you." Hands raised into the air, he leans back. "I don't want to put any pressure on you. I want you to go, but you have to know it's right for you."

I don't have any credits for a trip like that. I can't ask my mom. I won't ask my dad. Zane doesn't seem to understand that I can't just pay for stuff, like he seems to be able to. Besides that, what's the purpose of going to the U.S.? What exactly is a transition trip? Marlena and Lucie had a plan to get over there and start their own business, or something, but I don't have any reason to go. Zane probably just wants me to tag along because he's supposed to be watching over me, or something. At some point, that's going to get old. Using the trip as a reason is probably best for breaking the ties.

After what seems like a zillion years of silence, I say, "I just can't, Zane."

On a deep sigh, he asks, "How are you ever going to learn, if you don't experience it yourself?"

"Why are you using *them* as your measure of success? I mean, the A.U. split from the U.S. on purpose. And what transition? We're not going to reintegrate. We're two different countries. And if you're going there temporarily, that means you'll be back." *Though, you probably won't want anything to do with me, given how whiney I sound.*

Zane huffs, and an odd anger takes over me.

"I know I don't know a lot of stuff, Zane, but it doesn't make sense to go over there just to look around, or to sightsee—" Unless it's not for a vacation but forever, and he lied about the duration.

His head cocks to the right.

Arms over my chest, I face the outside again. I don't have credits to go. *Don't ask, Anna. Just leave it. You'll find a way to be happy here.* "Now isn't the right time for me."

"You might never get another chance."

I probably won't. Ever. He'll go over there and find his place in life, and I'll never see him again. That's got to be okay. Facing him again, I say, "It's okay, Zane. I get it. I'm sure this is right *for you.*"

His chuckle strikes a nerve that builds up a mix of hostility and sadness in me. "You *don't* get it. It's now or never. This trip was planned for a few weeks from now. To have pulled it up to tomorrow is both crazy and insane and totally out of the ordinary. Delta Street doesn't do anything quickly. We're slow and measured on purpose, so we don't make mistakes. We go, or something seriously bad is going to happen here."

I say nothing because he's just proved he's going to stay. That, I definitely don't want.

His smile breaks my inner, building irritation. "I want you to go with me," he says. "I *want* you to, Anna."

"I don't have a country-to-country permission book." That's as good a reason as any. A legitimate one, too. One that doesn't prey on the 'poor Anna can't do anything because she has no credits' saga that has been the staple of my life.

"Doesn't matter. I want you to come. With me."

"Because you're supposed to watch over me?" Why did I ask

that out loud? Biting my lips shut may be the only way I can prevent more stupid questions from escaping.

"No." His voice is soft. "Because I like you."

"I know you do, but—"

His head swishes back and forth. "I'm not sure you get what I mean."

My eyebrows do something funky, moving in and out above my eyes.

"Anna?" There's a huskiness to his voice. "I want you to go with me because . . ." He moves in closer. ". . . I like how willing you are to learn. That you don't take things at face value. That you process, even if it takes me ten times to convince you to try. That you're a little naïve, but you're also smart and strong. His finger touches the bottom of my jaw, lifting my head up a degree. His eyes dip down, gaze meeting mine again a second later. "Anna?"

"Huh?" It comes out breathy and unsure. "Yeah?" I manage as my breathing slows.

"I *want* you to go with me."

A chill races through me. Staring into Zane's eyes, I want to agree, to just go with him, but I can't. I just can't.

"Give me one good reason, and I mean a *good* one, why you should say no," he says.

I've told him before I'm on the lowest financial rung of society's ladder. "Zane—"

"I promise you answers. If you want them." He's promised me that already, and two promises of the same thing don't make the promise any bigger. "The U.S. has the most thriving economy of the entire world. People there are empowered. They have to work hard, but they keep what they earn, and they have opportunity like we don't. I've already told you that, though."

He has. That's how and why I know it's the right trip for Marlena and Lucie. Zane, too.

"It's not that. I just ..."

A pop and a hiss make the transpo jerk to the right. Zane grabs the steering column as I jolt in the opposite direction, hitting my head on the window. We slow, coming to a stop as a variety of contraptions whiz by us, their speed making them a blur against our immobility.

◦═╪═◦

NOW

"Blew a tire did he?" Mr. Perez asks. "On purpose?"

"What? No, why would you ask that?"

There's a mischievous grin on his face. "Carry on with the story."

◦═╪═◦

THEN

"What happened?" I ask as I rub my head, my heartbeat making its way to the spot.

"I don't know." Zane glances toward his door but turns back to me. "If I open the door over here, I'll be hit by the next thing that passes, and we'll have way more than air wheel issues. So, either I have to crawl over you to get out, or you have to get out, too."

Pushing open my door, I step out into blazing sunlight and freezing cold. Without tree cover, there's nothing keeping the sun from us, but there's also nothing to stop the wind from digging its cold into our skin. Rubbing my arms, I lean against the frame, hoping to gather some warmth from it.

Zane crawls over the console and slides out the passenger door like he's ridden in the transpo a thousand times. He moves to the front, the back, close to the other side, and says, "Sheez."

"What?" My breath comes out in a haze of white.

"I think the air wheel's broken."

"What?" I race to him, shivering the whole way. "How does an air wheel break?" They look normal to me. Round. Black. Bumpy.

He kicks the one at the back closest to us and pulls. "This one's sensor went off right before it jerked. Something could have gotten caught in it, but without a sensor, it won't let us roll because it can't guarantee it will provide the air it needs, and because it's probably the air gauge, I can't hover, either. That's the extent of this transpo's upgrades since Marlena and Lucie bought if off someone."

"What's that mean, exactly? How are we gonna get home?"

Spinning, I take in our surroundings. There is nothing anywhere, except other transpos zooming by.

Zane stands there, arms crossed over his chest.

I move to him. "What do we do?"

"Actually, Anna ... I don't know." As he answers, fat flakes begin their fall from the skies.

Oh, Oz. If he doesn't get back, he'll miss his trip.

9

EIGHT HOURS BEFORE THE WALL WENT UP

Zane faces the flying traffic, his hair blowing all around by the wind. I've hugged myself in an attempt to warm up, though really, the effort doesn't do squat.

"Can we get pathway security to help?" I ask.

He shakes his head. "Not if we want them to know we're not at registration. Or who we are."

Oh, yeah. That. "What about Marlena and Lucie? Maybe they know how to fix it." They already know we took their transpo, so maybe they'd be willing to help?

Zane chuckles as snow covers his hair. "Let's just get back inside where I can think."

I rush to the seat and jump in, all too happy to be out of the cold. Zane leans down toward me, holding the door open. "You want me to climb over you?"

Oops. I force myself out and brush off the flakes, while he slides into his spot, before I return and close the door. Warmth seeps into my every pore. The transpo shakes as others pass us. Blue. Orange. Yellow. White. They zoom by, one after the other, not stopping. Should they? Would I? Isn't it the right thing to do? Then again, Zane hasn't pressed the emergency signal. So, who would know we're even having a problem?

Quiet fills the space. He plays with the screen unit, changing information on it a bunch of times.

I slide my hands between my knees to warm them more, as Zane tilts his head toward the steering column, but screen imagery just doesn't have the same feel as being someplace. Now, I get why Zane had to show me the imploded building.

Anxiety churns in my stomach as I sit there, waiting.

"I wish we weren't in the dead zone," he says into the quiet.

"The dead zone?"

"Yeah." He points toward my side of the transpo. "That area out there, where there's nothing?" He glances back toward me, and I nod. "Used to be a housing project."

There's absolutely nothing in the space he pointed to. "Another one of those that went poof in the night?"

"Yup. They're everywhere. In every district."

There really isn't anything there. Nothing. Snow just falls straight to the ground, untouched by anything around it.

He taps the glass. "A few decades ago, this District bought that land from a chemical company for a credit."

"A credit?"

"Yes. One. Just one."

"Seriously, just *one*?" I can't help the surprise in my tone.

He nods. "And, of course, it sold for only a credit because it was really a thick clay cap overtop industrial waste, and the city, by requirements from the department of construction, went ahead and built on it." Zane continues to play with the screen as he talks. "No sooner did the first ten units go up than the basements started flooding with blue goo, and rocks shot off in every direction randomly, and eventually, whole houses exploded."

"No."

He gives me another nod. "And that was before the U.S. and A.U. split."

"Well, then, it's not the A.U.'s fault, right?"

Zane huffs a laugh as he touches the screen, pulling up information and closing it. "We're one-hundred percent in A.U. territory, Anna. The U.S. border is hundreds of miles from here. But yes, then we were all one country, so yes, blame gets handed to them all. Anyway, stuff started to go south even before the split. No more than a hundred and fifty years after the original U.S.A. was founded, this kind of stuff started happening."

"Why, then? I thought all this was because of the boom in two thousand fifty, like the film they showed us at registration."

He shakes his head, still facing the screen. "All this government control stuff started in the nineteen thirties, right after the stock market crashed and President Roosevelt took over."

"Stock market?" At least I recognize the president's name. We had to memorize all of them in level one educenter.

"Oh ... the stock market is like this invisible place where they used to trade pieces of businesses to earn credits and save for retirement. Or really just to earn credits without doing work. Anyway, the A.U. did away with it and took over all investments back in twenty-seventy-six so they could ensure the fair share of earnings."

"Traded businesses?" That doesn't make any sense. A business isn't a credit or something that can be shared or traded.

"Sorta. When you invest in a business, it's like saying, 'I want you to do better and make money for me'. You buy stocks to get that investment. To earn more. But we eliminated the need for it when our leaders thought it would be better to take away private ownership. Then nobody needed stocks to earn money because everything would be equal. Theoretically. Anyway, that's not what you initially asked. See ... way, way, way back when ... Roosevelt tried to get the stock market to grow after the great depression, because it had collapsed, and that's when things that seemed to be good went all backwards."

Zane's history lessons confound me. Half of them, I understand. The other two-thirds, I don't. Apparently, math isn't my strong point, either. Rather than let him know my head is spinning, I just stare at him and nod. His passion, though, is seriously strong.

"People figured out they could get and keep, and not give back as much. Not everyone, but it's like an itch you can't scratch. It's there. You know it, but you can't make it go away. So, yeah, all the downhill started just a century and a half after the entire country became a country. Sad, isn't it?"

I guess. Even though I don't get it all, I do understand that something awesome going bad so soon isn't good.

"Two miles," Zane says as he taps on the screen.

"What is?" I ask.

"The next pathway exit. Civilization. We actually made it farther than I thought. Still in the dead zone, but pretty far inside."

"Okay. So ... what do we do?"

"Find someone to run a diagnostic over the control pad. Make sure the air itself isn't a problem, and if it's just the gauge, override it so we can keep going."

Say what? One of those silent whooshes goes over my head. I've ridden in only a few transpos, and they've never had a problem, so this is like nothing I've ever dealt with. "So ... how do we get to these people who might help us?"

Zane smiles at me. "We walk."

"*Walk?*" I spin toward the window and stare out at the growing white. "It's like zero degrees and cold, and we don't even have our coats." This is what happens when I don't plan ahead.

"Do you have a better idea?"

He's got me there. I wouldn't know what to do if the answer hit me in the head like a snowball. "No."

"Well, then, we walk. Or run. If we go fast, we can be there in less than thirty minutes, and the run will keep us warm. And if we find civilization, as I expect we will, we can hitch a ride back here, hopefully with a diagnostic tool."

"You're serious." I can't believe it.

"I am." His eyes dart left, toward the clock. He has to be worried about time.

I would be, too, if I only had hours left before I had to be somewhere important, to go on a trip that's probably the one thing I've always wanted to do my entire life. Not that I do, I'm just guessing. Actually, I can't think of one thing I've wanted 'all my life', not the way Zane does. Nothing has ever been in front of me in a way that made me truly passionate about it. Does that mean I'm boring?

"Anna? You in there?"

Shaking my head, I say, "Yeah, sorry." I've been lost in my other thoughts a lot more since I met Zane. "All right, then. I'm ready." If he can run two miles, so can I. Actually, running and walking are my specialties, since Mom had no transpo of her own, and the trams in our area go quick.

Opening the door sends a chill through me, but I push through and, cupping my hands together, breathe into them to keep them somewhat warm.

Zane follows and shuts the door. "Ready, set, go!"

We take off, our shoes kicking up little bits of snow, but at least it stopped falling. My cheeks burn with the cold; my eyes, too. The brightness doesn't help one bit as I have to squint, but in doing that, I end up closing my eyes. Alternating right and left eye open, I keep pace with Zane, who has a nice rhythm to his run.

We stay together for the first mile, or what seems like one, but a stitch hits my side, and I have to slow.

Zane does the same. His cheeks are as bright pink, as is his nose, and he swipes a hand beneath it at the same time as I do, probably getting rid of the snot he can't suck up—also just like me. I'd call him cute, but I'm pretty sure my lips are frozen shut.

I point to my side where I press, and Zane nods, but we keep going, walking instead.

A gigantic, white, double-level transpo passes, sending a flurry of air at us and making what I thought to be cold frigid. Red lights illuminate on the back of it, and it slows, pulling over to the side.

Great, a ginormous transpo is broken, too. Must be the weather.

A guy in a white coat steps out and waves us forward.

Oh! Salvation. "Race you to the warmth," I say and lift my hand.

Zane grabs it and presses it against my side.

"Hey—Wha—"

He spins to face me, eyes filled with determination. "We can't."

"What? But—" I try to point, but he holds me still. "They can help! It would be *warm*."

"No, Anna." His breath is cold by the time it reaches me. "You don't understand."

Of course I don't. I take one step backward, out of his hold. "That's someone willing to help us, Zane. Someone with probably a seat and heat and—"

"Are they still there?"

Why is he asking me that? "Yes. Of course."

He shakes his head. "You don't understand."

"Of course I don't!"

Zane's eyelids lower, and when he meets my gaze again, he says, "That's a cleaner."

"A what? Like people who clean buildings?" Or people who clean up messes like the building that burned?

Zane moves in close again. "We probably look like runaways, Anna."

"But our car just—"

"A mile away. In the dead zone. They have every possible reason to pick us up."

I peek around Zane's arm. The guy in the white coat stands there as if waiting. "Should I wave him away or something?"

"No. Just wait here. Act like you're talking to me."

"But I *am* talking to you. Why do I have to act?"

Zane chuckles. "I mean, act like you're mad at me."

"Mad at you? I'm freezing, Zane, not mad."

He rolls his eyes. "Just do it." He pushes at my shoulder. "Think about everything I've done that could possibly make you mad." He nudges me again.

"What was that—"

Again.

"Hey!" My voice is a little louder.

Zane throws his hands up and glares at me. "What're you gonna do about it? Not have me tell you why this country sucks? Why you're not good enough for it?"

I cock my head at him, my hands slowly raising. "Wha—" A glance around him shows the white transpo lights blinking and the whole contraption starting onto the road again. "They're leaving."

At a quick glance, he says, "Keep going."

"But—"

Another poke does make me mad, and I return the jab into his shoulder.

"You can do better than that," he says.

I knuckle the spot.

"Oh, come on, Anna. Put a little muscle into it."

With a right hook, I give him all I have, right in the shoulder.

Zane steps back, a giant smile on his face. "Not bad. For a girl."

"That didn't even hurt, did it?" Shaking my hand to get the tingles out, it doesn't seem like Zane is even affected by my little punch. My knuckles and hand, though, are another story altogether. Clenching and unclenching to get the blood flowing again, I say, "It's gone."

Another glance and he says, "Okay, let's go."

"Where?"

"Same place as before." Lifting my hand, he brings it to his lips and kisses the back.

The tremor that runs through me is not from the cold.

"I'm sorry, Anna. For this morning. And just now. Forgive me?" He stares at me like some lost puppy dog having just found its owner.

I nod, and we start our walk again, building up to a jog, and a full-out run a few steps later. With limited breath, I ask, "Why did we just do that?"

"Because cleaners don't mess with people in conflict. They go for the eager meagers."

I run out of air and heave to catch it again. Slowing to a walk, I ask, "Eager meagers?"

Zane nods, blowing into his cupped hands as he slows to my pace. "People who *want* help will go with them, no questions asked. People who're pissed at each other won't. They'll be fighting the whole time. They want the people who'll be docile."

"Why?"

"So they can get rid of them."

"No."

"Yes."

"What do you mean *get rid?*" I have to know if I interpreted that right.

"Ship them to another country, if they test well, eliminate if they test poorly, convince them they're nuts if they are and get them to ask for elimination ... whatever they want. It's another method of getting rid of people. It's why they call them the cleaners."

"That's just wrong." It's also yet another piece of my country I don't get. "How do you know this?" Even as I ask, I figure I know the answer. Zane knows all sorts of stuff, about all sorts of things, thanks to my own dad and Delta Street.

He raises an eyebrow.

Yup, he knows because he knows.

Every part of me is frozen, my feet ache, and the wind going up my jeans has probably caused ice to form on my skin. With this new knowledge about the cleaners, all my hope in my country disappears. I'm definitely one of the oblivious, and if I didn't have Zane at my side, I still would be.

The other half of our run is slower and less steady, but as we reach the exit to the stop sign, living spaces and a small, one-story commerce center that appears to have been a relic from the nineteen hundreds, stand there like a beacon to salvation. The outer facade is nothing but planks of what looks like wood, faded, dusty and crumbling. If there's life inside, I'll be surprised.

Next to the building is a rundown something, or other, covered in vines that have worked their way up to the top of the building's roof.

Zane's unit must have had some old directions. "Wow," he says.

"Wow, what?"

He points toward the building. "That's a nineteen-fifties soda shop, though the chrome is pretty rusty and the windows are pretty grimy. Next to it, there, on the left, is the carcass of a train."

"A train? *That's* a train? Like in the old films where the thing is on those rails, and it always falls off, like over a cliff?"

He smirks at me. "Yes. Like that. It's kinda sad they got rid of the wheels. That's what made the sound, that chuga-chuga—" He stops as I giggle and takes my completely frozen hand. "Let's go get warm."

My adrenaline pumps at the thought, and I start forward with him, but halt when that gigantic, white transpo rolls up the hill and stops in the holding lot.

A second joins it.

I can't really see through the tinted glass, but it seems like eyes stare back out. Averting my gaze seems the right thing to do, but an insane curiosity has me staring, trying to see who would pick that kind of life, whether they know it, or not.

"C'mon. We'll sneak in the side entrance, away from where the cleaners have stopped." Zane takes my hand, and we prepare to finish our polar-bear-like run toward the far edge of the building, near the train. On the other side of the building, the cleaners sit in the holding lot, engines running.

A person dressed in all white and another in all black exit the transpos and saunter over to the commerce center.

Zane holds us back, stopping us outside by the train. It really is a carcass, empty except for the outer shell—just like he said.

Through the poorly washed windows, we watch as the two cleaners go to the counter. The person behind hands them something, and they walk toward the front doors, heading back toward the giant mechanical beasts, I assume.

"Let's go," Zane says.

He and I nearly jump through the commerce center's double doors, the sting of warm air actually hurting worse than the cold that has long since taken over.

An old woman with gray hair pulled tightly back against her forehead sits on the other side of a long wooden counter, surrounded by mostly empty, dusty shelves. It's as dirty inside as it is outside. Zane called it a diner, but there are no tables, no chairs, nothing really that suggests it's even a commerce center—like stuff to buy.

She rises and tilts her head as if perusing us both. "My, my. If it isn't the princess herself."

Blinking doesn't bring to mind anything about the woman, so why has she called me princess? She doesn't look like anyone I know, with her grey hair wrapped up on the top of her head and a pink shawl around her shoulders. "I-I'm sorry?" I manage through chattering teeth.

The woman squints through a set of bottle-like spectacles. "I'd never forget a face like that." I haven't seen corrective lenses on a person in forever, but hers look ancient, and I've never seen her before, so she can't have seen me. "What can I do ya for, missy-miss princess?"

I rub my hands together, basking in the awesome warmth which has started to defrost the rest of me, but I really don't like that she's called me princess twice.

Zane takes my hand. "Our transpo says there's an error. I don't see one, but it won't let us go without running a diagnostic, and I forgot my sensor. So, we'd like to borrow one, please."

The woman cocks her head to the side. "You mean to tell me you ridin' with this'un and you ain't got a diagnostic sensor? Who do you think she is?" One wrinkly, crooked finger shakes in my direction. "You need some better sense." That same finger shifts toward the brown, wood wall.

Following it, a sign listing the options we have, including sensor rental for a hundred and fifty credits, is tacked over a giant crack. Given how old this place must be, it doesn't surprise me that it's falling down around itself.

Though, at a hundred and fifty credits for a rental, how can it not be totally kept up? That's what my mom makes in a week, when she's fully allocated. Staring at the woman again, I can't help but wonder why she'd price something so high, and why she suggested Zane's done something wrong.

"I'd like to rent it, please." He lets go of my hand and steps forward, withdrawing a pouch from his pocket.

She thumbs over her shoulder. "Junebug'll take ya. June Bugger!" The call of the person's name comes out a yell.

A boy, no older than Zane and I, shows up, sitting in a moving seat. His legs lay at an odd angle, resting on platforms at the bottom front, and he pushes giant wheels on either side of him. "You need a sensor?" He doesn't have quite the drawl the old lady has, but it's there.

"Yes, please," Zane says.

"What make and model?" The kid taps on a screen, his rolling cart thing inching backwards every couple seconds.

Zane says something I don't even recognize. I'm guessing it's whatever kind of transpo Lucie and Marlena have.

I, on the other hand, can't stop staring at the kid's legs and the contraption he's sitting in. Instead of walking, all he has to do is roll and can be anywhere he wants just by pushing the wheels.

"Anna."

I jerk up to Zane's call of my name as the kid rolls away.

"Yeah?"

"Why are you staring?"

"Because that's a really neat personal transpo. I've never seen one like that with no roof, or anything."

Zane tilts his head. "You've never seen a medical cart?"

"Medical cart?"

Getting close to my ear, Zane says, "His legs don't work. By the looks of it, he had Polio, or something like it. A disease that probably paralyzed him as a little kid."

"No." I shake my head. "That can't be right."

"Why not?" Zane's question comes with a serious frown.

"Because we fix all those things."

June returns, rolling in with a package and a starter fob. "If you'll come with me, I'll give you a ride out and test it." He backs up, spins, and goes forward toward the inner part of the building, past the counter.

The old lady says, "See you later, princess," and I'd swear she says, "that's your ticket out of here, June-boy," as we pass, but that doesn't make sense. The growl rising up my throat at my continued reference as 'princess' has probably tainted my perspective.

Once June's grabbed a coat and hat for himself, he leads us back out into the frigid air through a door in the rear of the building. The bite to the cold is worse than when Zane and I walked miles through it. Making our way from the back to a trolley, with three doors on one side and a long back for storage, I glance over toward the cleaners that still sit in the holding lot.

"Za—" I gasp but stop myself.

My heart beats hard in my chest. It had to be. It can't have been. No way. Yes, must have.

I grab Zane's arm and pull him toward me.

"What's wrong?"

"I think I just saw my best friend Cam on the second level of the white one."

⚬━✦━⚬

NOW

"That person on the transpo your friend who was asleep in the back of the trolley?" Mr. Perez asks after the longest story-telling run I've had thus far.

"Yeah."

"Cleaners got her, didn't they?" His head shakes as if he knows exactly what I'm about to share.

"Yeah."

"Now this, I gotta hear. No one, and I mean no one, gets a body off a cleaner transpo. How on God's green earth did you manage that?"

10

SEVEN HOURS BEFORE DISTRICT ONE CHANGES MY LIFE FOR-
EVER

Zane's head turns, as if he's looking for Cam up on the giant transpo. "On the cleaner?"

I nod.

"Your friend from home? The one you told me about?"

"Yes! Why is she on there, if they are the cleanup people? She went to the white house, not the red. Why is she on there, Zane? We have to get her off."

"Oh, you don't wanna do that," June says from the other side of me. "It's easy to get on those cleaners, but you pretty much gotta be dead to get out." He rolls himself away from us.

"He's right." Zane tugs me toward our intended destination.

"But—" I can't leave her in there. Not if what Zane described to me is true.

"I'll tell my uncle, and he can look into it, if that helps."

Heart speeding up, I want to run to the vehicle and pull her out. "But—"

"Anna." Zane turns me to him. "Your teeth are chattering. The cold is making you crazy."

I hadn't even noticed, but as he mentions the cold, it all comes crashing down, and my entire body goes into one massive, uncontrollable tremble.

How can I just leave her in there?

"Of course, as the princess, you could probably get her out if you wanted," June says in a tone that seems like it's sarcastic, but I'm not sure it is.

Whirling to him, I ask, "What do you mean? And why do you and that lady inside keep calling me a princess?"

"'Cause you are." He nods like that's the final answer, and I should know it. "And that lady in there is my granny. She's been taking care of me since my mama left when I was born."

My heart falls for him. "I'm so sorry."

He shakes his head. "Nothing to be sorry for. She didn't get a perfect kid. I didn't get a perfect mom. We're even. But I did get granny, and she's the best. Old. But best."

"What about this princess thing?" Zane asks.

"Like I said. Granny never misses a face. She can trace bloodlines and heritage back ten generations just by looking at someone."

"That's not possible," I say. *Is it?*

Zane spins to me. "There are documented studies of people with imagegraphic memories who have other sixth senses."

I don't know even know how to respond to that.

Turning back to June, Zane asks, "So, she sees Anna in ... *who* exactly?"

"Osso, of course. She doesn't call anybody a princess, 'cept when they are. You related to him?"

Fear more than the cold keeps me silent.

"What if she is?" Zane asks. "How would she get her friend off the cleaner?"

"Tell 'em you're here to take her. Show some I.D. Or let them do a scan."

A scan? I'm sure I don't want to know what that is. Worse, if I do tell them who I am, even though *I* barely know who

I am, will that get back to Osso? Could that hurt my mom? What about my dad? I only just learned, in the last two days, that I'm the great-granddaughter of the A.U.'s sitting CEO, but that doesn't mean others need to know about it.

A blurt from the transpo has us all turning. The lights on the back blink bright for a second as the engine revs.

Cam's on there. I know she is.

I plead with my eyes for Zane to tell me what to do.

His blank expression doesn't help.

June chews on a fingernail as if nothing else matters in the world.

"I can't leave her on there."

Cleaner number one starts moving, pulling out onto the pathway in a slow, laborious struggle to get up the small hill we ran down only minutes before. If I'm right, Cam's on the other, but if they leave, how will I catch them?

"You have to leave it be, Anna. My uncle can—"

"I can't, Zane. She might have screwed up our friendship one time, but true friends don't leave each other at desperate times. If she's on that cleaner, this is desperate." I can't help the worry and fear in my voice. It, topped with the frozen white breath I'm creating, must make me seem terrified.

"You can't risk it, Anna. Think about your mom and dad."

I already have.

"And Mia. If they find out, we could be going in deep. Fast."

I get that, too.

The second transpo starts forward, jerks back, and starts again. It stops at the edge as if waiting, I presume for the personal transpos coming up the road to pass.

Shaking my head, I meet Zane's gaze. "I have to." Racing to the back, as it starts forward again, I pound on the panel, sending a wimpy thump through the back. Holding my hand to the side, I run up, banging as hard as I can with my fist, all energy sapped from being so cold and from the long run we had. Knowing this is my only hope, if Zane told me the truth, I can't let them go without getting Cam out. No matter what happens to me.

"Stop! Stop!" I hit it harder, though the sound is faint against the rumble of the engine. "Please!"

The ginormous machine jerks again, and the wheels freeze. The lights on the side brighten. Jogging in place to keep up some semblance of warmth, I wait at the doors until they open, and the person in the white suit steps from within.

"Are you in need of an escort, young lady?"

Bobbing up and down on my heels, I say, "I need to have a passenger removed from your ... from there." Pointing up to the windows is all I can do, since I don't really know where she is. I haven't seen her a second time, but I know. It's that gut feel that eats away at my insides when I know something is wrong.

"Name, please?" He withdraws a comms unit and taps on it.

"Um ..."

"You don't know your name?"

What do I tell him? I didn't think that far ahead, except to know I'm going to screw over a lot of people. I glance back and find Zane walking toward me while June sits with what looks like shock and some other expression plastered on his face.

You're in this now, Anna. Get it over with.

Facing the guy, I wipe my nose, building up the courage and fortitude it takes to out anyone, let alone myself. "My name's Eri—"

"She's no one, but I'm Zanethew Kenten Warren the third." Zane's full name has me stepping back. Not only did I not know the whole thing because he never told me—now I see why, because that's seriously long—but why has he used it and not had me use mine? How is his name going to help Cam?

Or is he trying to avoid getting her off?

"A Kenten?"

Once again, a mix of fear and outright anger at him interrupting me boils within.

"Now, what would a member of the resistance party be doing out here in the middle of nowhere?" The man tuts as if we've just told him the biggest lie in the whole world.

I withhold a gasp. Did Zane just tell a government official he's part of the group that wants to overthrow the current regime? He wouldn't even let me tell my mom, and she'd have been on our side. At least my name would have just brought family ties down on me without giving up the entire operation. Isn't that a huge risk to his life? Will he be tried for treason?

"*Former* resistance party," Zane says, as I think through my thoughts which always go faster than saying anything. "Fully integrated into Osso's organization since twenty-one-oh-two. And I'm searching for a traitor."

A traitor? Is he calling Cam a traitor?

From his pocket, Zane takes out an ID-card and hands it to the man. "You can scan that, and me, if you'd like."

"Very well."

"We need to confirm one of your passengers first." Zane rubs his hands together as I stare at the faces peering out through the window.

In the third from the back, on the second level, I meet Cam's gaze. The windows are dark, so it's hard to tell what she's thinking, or feeling, or even guess any emotion from her, but I won't ever forget her eyes. Not Cam's. She's been my best friend for too long to not know deep inside after just a few days.

The man shifts back to the door and waves, motioning Zane in.

Grabbing Zane's hands, I stop him, and leaning up to his ear, I give him the direction for where she is. For some reason, I don't want him to get on the transpo to tell the guy.

"Level two. Fourth row from the back. Blonde girl, eighteen. Goes by the name Camilla J. Hopper the third. We need to see her out here."

White-suit man disappears inside and returns a minute later with Cam—the girl I've known forever, who threw me out as a friend in our last hours, but who's shaking like a tree in the bad part of a hurricane. She's dressed in a solid grey jumpsuit that covers her entire body up to her neck; grey gloves and grey shoes add to the overall doldrum. In her eyes, I read fear and hope and something else, all at the same time.

I start forward, but Zane stops me with a hand out. "She'll be leaving in our custody," he says.

"Under what terms?" Man-in-white asks.

"Court order. She's due in for her role as an accomplice to theft."

"And you have documentation?"

"Of course." Zane digs in his pocket and retrieves a mini chip. I'd swear it looks like the one on the bench in the bus from days ago—one Cam had said wasn't hers, and I'd meant to find the owner of it but didn't. Then again, they all look alike, and there's no telling where the one I found is now. "You're welcome to scan this."

Suit-man plugs in the chip.

"The code is oh-one-two, A-B-six-seven-fourteen. Date of December twenty-eighth. District Eleven commerce center. Rise twenty-one," Zane says.

My jaw drops open. How did he know about that? *Does* he know about it? Does he know something else I don't?

He always does, Anna. Why question it?

Was he there? Did he see me go to the security office? Did he see Mia?

Mia. I remember her being in the bakery, but I only *thought* she'd been. The chip, though, I found that before all it happened. Before Cam got me in trouble. How can he know?

The man taps on his comm and lifts up. "Confirmed. Retina's please."

Zane leans forward, and the man holds up what looks like a pen. A bright red beam shines from it, moving left to right across Zane's face. When it shuts off, Zane steps back, pinching the bridge of his nose, his eyes closed.

"Identity confirmed." The man turns to Cam. "You're remanded into their custody." He pushes her forward, gets on the transpo, and the doors shut tight.

Still unsure if I should go to Cam, and seeing as Zane's hurting since his eyes are closed, I take him and draw him in close, turning him back toward the building.

"Whatever you do," he says in a whisper, opening his eyes and meeting my gaze, "don't look back. Don't look at Cam. Don't look at June. Just walk to the building like we own it."

He's going to have to explain why he just outed himself, why he lied to me about his name, and why he used himself over me, *and* how he knows about what happened between Cam and me, but I'll do what he said because, like Mia told me, I'm supposed to trust Zane.

June rolls up as we walk toward the door. "I have hot tea and soup in the kitchen. I'm sure Granny'd like to talk to *royalty*, and *you* ... and you're all probably frozen solid by now."

I'm numb. Outside. Inside. All around numb. Standing by June as he holds open the back door of the commerce center, I can't believe all that's happened in the last few days.

"Course you can't stay long, since the authorities will definitely be heading this way in, well, in these parts of the A.U., I'd say you have a couple hours, at least. Fifteen minutes flat, if this were District One."

Great. Just enough time to warm up, get answers and freeze again as we try to leave.

As Cam walks in, June rolls in behind her, and the door blankets us in darkness.

Eyes adjusting from the blinding white, I spin from Zane and wrap my arms around Cam. "Oh, my god! What happened to you?" I run my hands along her cheeks, down her arms, and hug her again. "Why were you on a cleaner? Why are you here?" Palms to her cheeks, I force her face in my direction, meeting her gaze. "Cam? Answer me. What's going on? Why aren't you at registration?"

Cam doesn't hug me back.

"Answer me!" The longer she doesn't answer, the more worry builds inside me. I hug her tight again as if that will snap her out of whatever trance she's in.

"Anna." Zane taps my shoulder.

"Come on, Cam. It's me. Eri."

"Anna, stop." He pulls me away from her. As he does, her hands hang limp at her sides again, and June rolls up with something in his hand.

One touch to her skin and he says, "She's been drugged. A lot, too." He holds Cam's hand, the device still against her palm. "Got a point-oh-nine level of Methylenedioxypyrovalerone."

"Of what?" I ask.

"It's a drug they used to sniff back in the nineteen hundreds," June says. "Docs figured out, if they force it into ya, in enough of a quantity, you'll be mostly zombie for long stretches of time. Well, that, or you'll eat people's faces off. One of the two. With the level in her, I think she'll be like this for another couple days, at least."

A moment of panic consumes me. Couple days? Cam would be mortified if I returned her to her family in this condition, and my mom would never take her in like it; she doesn't even want me around. If Cam's stuck like this, there's an even bigger reason why I can't go with Zane. *And it's a legitimate reason.* Not just one that sounds whiny.

"Of course ... I could probably help speed up the healing process, if you wanted," June says.

"How?" I ask.

June lifts his chin and says, "Credits. Bribes. If we come up with a good enough deal, I might be inclined to let you use my trolley, and I could administer some redaction solutions to your friend to make all her problems go away. Or, instead, I could let the authorities know the great-granddaughter of Mr. Osso himself is here with the great-grandson of the very late Roger Kenten."

Using our family names against us shouldn't even be allowed.

"And," June continues. "Unlike what you told the cleaners, Kentens are *current* resistance party members, not former, as you've ... suggested. So I'm sure they'd like to talk ..." He air-quotes the word 'talk'. "... to both of you, and might pay me really well for that chance." June sits with a giant smirk on his face.

"Or not," Zane says. "They could come here, I could tell them you did this to the girl, and they'd go after you first."

June's eyes light up as if he's just been handed a challenge, not shocked by a counter bribe. "Well played. Let's call it a stalemate. Do I give her the solution or not?"

"What could happen, if you do?" I ask.

"She'll wake up."

"Or?" Zane asks.

"Die," June says. "Or not." He shrugs.

"No," I say, as Zane orders, "Do it."

11

Once June disappears into the middle of the building, Zane turns to me. "We have to get out of here, Anna," he says in a whisper.

I know we do. For him mostly. "I can't leave Cam like this, though. I can't leave her at all."

Zane paces away, running a hand through his hair. He comes back and stands at my toes. "I can't get a read on June. Can you?"

"What do you mean?"

Palming his forehead, Zane says, "June. He knows the scientific name for bath salts, has a redaction for them, supposedly, and yet lives in hickville, in the backwoods of this district, where no one goes, except people traveling past. I think he's a fluke and might even be a Delta Street supporter, but I can't tell, because he's also willing to give us up to Osso, which is really bad for me, given who I am, and all."

I want to ask him about his name, but now's not the time for that. Frustration and irritation ebb from him in waves. "Is there a way you can find out?"

"That's the thing, Anna. I can't just come out and ask him. It's a huge risk even to imply it." He steps away, each pace measured. "And he already knows my side. Or enough of it."

"But you did with me ..." Even as I say it, I know I'm different. Mia's my sister, and Mia told him to tell me what I needed to know, when I needed to know it. "So, what do we do? You have to get back, I can't leave Cam—what do we do?"

Zane whirls to me. "You're seriously not going to go?"

Dropping my gaze to the floor, I say nothing.

"Great." His one word is flat. "I spend years getting ready for my first trip to the U.S., and now the one person I want to go with me won't because of some girl who nearly got her registration cancelled in the first place."

My head snaps up. "How do you know about that?" I told him some but not everything about what Cam did to me.

"Because, Anna. I had to clean up the record. You were supposed to come into registration clean. Mia saw you, stuck around to find out what happened, and made me clean it. I'm good with comms, but not great, so it took all night for me to make sure there wasn't anything on your record."

"Oh." Being thankful and irritated at the same time is a hard set of emotions to reconcile. "She's my friend, Zane. It's what friends do for each other." *And I already told you I couldn't go.*

"You call her a friend after she nearly got you arrested? What am I, when I've saved you from yourself too many times to count?" He raises both hands into the air and closes his eyes. "I'm sorry. I shouldn't have said that."

I hold in the air filling my chest for a moment before I let it out on a trickle, hoping he can't tell how those words hurt. "She must have had a reason." At least, that's what I thought when it all happened.

"A reason?" His hands jerk, still out in front of him. "Why don't you ask her? Get her to tell you why. See what she has to say about sending her *best* friend up the crooked creek."

"I would if I could, Zane, but you know, without June's help,

I can't right now." Helplessness. That's what runs through me, just like it did when Cam pulled her stunt.

"Did someone say my name?" June rolls back in. "Ready for some help?"

The way he and Zane stare at each other is like a showdown, but one of wills, not violence, or even mercy. Neither moves. Their breaths are slow and calm. Eyes sharp.

"Swear your allegiance," Zane says after a long silence.

June nods. "You swear it."

"I already did, and you know it." Zane nods toward June.

"Yeah, but this is my place, and castle doctrine applies."

There's a slight twitch to Zane's lips before he stretches out his hand as if to shake with June.

June takes it, and the connection is as if the two were brothers; their smiles are just that big. "My name is Juniper Augustus Arthur. June for short. No one calls me Junebug, except Granny. Got that?"

Zane nods. "Everyone calls me Zane. Warren. But I am a Kenten. And fourth generation Delta Street."

"What about her?" June thumbs over at me. "She's the princess."

Those lips curve up more, if that's possible. "Let's call her Switzerland. She might be of one blood, but she's not of one mind."

June's face does this up-down-up thing before meeting my gaze. "No Kool-Aid for you?"

What does that mean? "I'm sorry?"

"Never mind." June waves me forward. "Let me show you something. We don't have much time." He wheels himself into a dark doorway. "Bring the girl." His voice echoes back as he disappears.

Zane and I move to Cam's sides and, holding on to her arms,

force her to start walking.

"Come on, princess. I've got something to show you."

We follow the sounds of June's wheeled chair until we stand in front of a door, in the middle of a hallway.

At the entrance, June turns to me. "Everything you do in here is recorded." He faces Zane. "Everything you see comes around the filters the A.U. has in place." A glance toward Cam, and he shakes his head before facing Zane again. "If you go in here, you can't tell *anyone* ... *anything* about what you learn."

"Of course not," Zane says. "On my honor."

To me, he stares as if I'm supposed to say the same. "Okay, yes. I agree. What about Cam, though?"

"She won't remember anything until the salts wear off." June presses a series of buttons, and a panel slides to the right, revealing a room filled with screens.

Dozens of them. Three full walls of them, actually. Where there might have been windows, more black, rectangular boxes await, their screens blank. In the middle, a desk with yet another unit sits by its lonesome.

"Come in. Come in." He rolls in, and we, with Cam, follow.

As June presses a few keys, each of the panels fills with color. One by one, displays of various informational programs appear.

"What is all this?" Zane moves in closer, the door behind us latching three times.

June sits at the center panel and points.

Placing his hands on my shoulders, Zane turns me all the way around so I face the door we just entered, which also includes another set of screens.

"Top left is a feed from District One. Top right is a feed from District Ninety-nine," June says.

Did June see the fire, too?

"Top middle is a feed from District Twenty-three, the worst

area in the entire A.U.."

"You got that right," Zane says.

"Why are they the worst? And how do you both know that?" Is this something I should have known?

June taps some keys and says, "In Twenty-three, they've been cycling pay there already for a year. So there are riots in the streets almost every day."

Wow. I never knew.

The panel in front of me shows what looks to be a news team at an anchor desk, chatting away about something I can only assume is important, since I can't hear it.

"Why haven't we heard about all this stuff?" I ask.

"Same reason you won't hear about the fire," Zane says. "Every district's news is filtered so nothing is publicized that isn't authorized to be shared."

"What he said." June's confirmation comes with the lighting up of a dozen more screens.

I step back from the wall. "That's—that's just—that's just wrong." They can't keep this information from the people.

Zane's curving lips suggest I've caught on to something. "Of the original constitution," he starts, "there *might* be one percent of the previous laws and amendments still used in the A.U.." He pinches his fingers together in front of my face. "One percent, Anna. That means things like freedom of speech, even the old freedom of information act—all of them—gone. What Osso wants you to know, he will tell you."

"Or not tell you," June says.

Maybe that's why mom never replaced our screen. If the only stuff shown is filtered, what would be the point of watching? Holding out my hands, I turn in a circle. "So, what is all this?"

June points to the wall we face. "This is the A.U.," He turns to the right. "Those are from the E.U.."

"Europe?" Zane asks. "You have a feed into *Europe?*"

"Yeah." June's smile is wide and serious.

"Why would you monitor what's going on over there?" I ask.

"Knowledge is power, Anna," Zane answers before June says, "If you don't know what's going on around you—for real— how can you fight it?"

Listening to June is like hearing Zane in an echo. I'd swear the two are twins separated at birth with the stuff they're saying.

Zane moves to the wall opposite us and points toward it. "These?"

"From the U.S.," June says.

The grin on Zane's face is creepily big. "*You* have a feed from the U.S.? Do you know how hard it is to tap into that stuff?" He chuckles, obviously to himself, since he drops his head at the same time. "Of course you do."

"You monitor the United States?" I can't believe he'd even want to.

"Yeah. And those—" June points to the last wall—the place really needs windows. "—are Asia and the middle east."

None of the screens show anything negative. At least not to me. They're all just people talking, or those crazy pre-recorded shows that are so boring. "Do you watch them all day long?" I ask.

June shakes his head. "I have comm programs that pull up major events automatically when detected, so I can review them in my spare time."

"Wow," Zane says with reverence in his voice. "This is … man, some of our guys in Delta Street, they've been, just wow."

June rolls up to Zane, right to his toes. "I want in."

Zane glances my way before going back to June.

Shaking his head, and mumbling, June rolls back. "I've been trying to find a way in to Delta Street for forever. I can get all this replicated for you."

"If you have plans, others—"

June taps his head. "My plans are all in here. Every step. Every action. I didn't write any of it down, but I know it."

Zane beams like he's about to burst from an inner sun explosion.

"Entry to Delta Street still alludes me, though."

A small breath passes Zane's lips—one of those, he's thinking, moments. "What would it be worth to you to learn more?"

"Anything. Th—"

"Give her the solution. Now," I say before Zane can butt in with something Delta Street related. All this news scouring is wasting time. I want Cam back to normal.

As if he's been pushed away, June wheels himself right to and out through the door. A few scrambling sounds commence. They stop. They restart. As Zane and I both start tiptoeing our way toward the opening, which June left wide, he reappears with something pointy in his hand.

"What's that?" I ask.

"A syringe." He lifts it from his palm and points it at me. "A real one. Use this, and they won't know who injected ya. No tracer in this. Old school."

Memories of registration, the procedure, the pills and needles flood my mind, and cold shimmies up and through me. They used those on me. Several of them. In the dark. Alone.

"You okay?" June asks.

Zane zips to my side and holds me at my waist. "Anna, you're freezing." He guides me around and to the only seat in the room—an orange, plastic chair that wobbles on the uneven floor. Zane kneels down with me and takes me hands, rubbing them between this warm palms. "Anna?"

Worry, concern and care ebb from his eyes. "I'm okay," I say on a whisper. *I think.*

"Ouch!" Cam's exclamation comes as June slides back from her. Her body goes limp, falling toward the ground like a slow-motion ragdoll, but Zane catches her, keeping her head from knocking against the solid floor.

My gasp echoes in the silent-again room, my mind processing. "What just happened?"

June's eyes are wide. "I don't know. That's never happened before. Be right back."

Zane lays Cam down on the floor, her chest rising and falling, but otherwise, no sign of consciousness.

"What's wrong with her?" I ask as I slip from the seat and go to her side.

Rolling back in, June tosses something silver and shiny toward Zane. "Check her vitals." His fingers go to his own neck. "Put it right there on her artery."

With the cylindrical thing against her skin, Zane presses the button on top.

"Now pass it back to me," June says, sitting at the main screen in the center of the room.

As instructed, the device flies across the small space to June. Two quick clips, and data appears in the black of the screen.

"I'll be damned," he says after no more than ten seconds.

"What?" Zane and I ask.

"She's asleep. Plum on asleep. Never did figure that would happen."

"How long will she be out?" I ask.

His head goes back and forth. Does that mean he has no clue?

Now what do we do?

NOW

"That's some kind of strength of character," Mr. Perez says.

"What do you mean?" I ask through a yawn.

"Darlin', you trust intuitively." He taps his forehead. "Don't ever stop doing that. It'll save you one day, I guarantee it."

I think it may already have.

The loudest bang I've ever heard rocks the room.

"What the—" Zane says, as June snaps all the screens off, and I jerk to the left.

"We gotta go. *Now*," June says.

"What? No! She's not awake." With Cam's hand against mine, her warmth telling me she's alive, I'm not about to leave her.

"Look, Anna banana ... when Granny signals with a shot of her air rifle, it's time to go." He rolls to the door, waiting at the frame.

"Go where? Why?" I ask. "And, air rifle? Guns are illegal! They kill people." *Oh, my Oz, I'm with a fugitive.*

"First off, guns don't kill people. People kill people. Just like pencils don't misspell words, people do. Second ... air rifles are just made for sound. But we like the old-school name. Now, those people I told you would be coming are here and in the holding lot, and we got all of thirty seconds to get to my trolley, or they'll be swarming this place like ants to watermelon in the summer."

Shaking my head, I say, "I can't leave her."

"Sheez, Anna." Zane stomps to me, slides his arms under Cam, and lifts her. "Go!"

Scrambling up, I still hesitate.

"Now!" Zane says, adjusting Cam's lifeless body in his arms.

June waits in the doorway, blocking our exit. "You'll take me with you?"

Silence fills the room.

"Tick tock," he says.

"You get us out of here without being seen, I'll figure something out," Zane says.

The two guys nod at each other, and June says, "This way."

Through the back, out the door, and into the frigid cold we go, which numbs me once again. June leads. Zane follows behind me with Cam in his arms. At the back of a trolley, June presses a button, and the entire rear opens up, lowering a ramp that lets him roll up inside.

He motions for us to join him and shuts the doors once we have.

"What about the ramp?" I ask.

June drops a metal rod over the back door's interior handles. "It's folding up now underneath. Cover up in those." He points toward black tarps that are folded in a pile at the side of the trolley. "We generally use them to cover the fruits and vegetables we get from the market, but in this case, they're going to be needed to keep you hidden. And her." Moving forward through the two rows of seats, he leaves us alone in the back cargo area.

Zane lays Cam down, as I grab one of the covers and wrap it around my shoulders. "Lay flat up against her side," he says. "To keep her from shifting."

"And be quiet," June says from farther up front.

Sliding over, I position myself against Cam as Zane lowers at her other side, and we sandwich her between us. He flings another cover over the three of us as the trolley jerks forward.

In less than a week, I've run from authority, from the very people who I thought were supposed to care for me, more times than I can count. It doesn't seem real, or right, but it doesn't seem wrong, either. Why? Why not?

Something pokes me in the back, digging in where my kidneys are and taking me away from my conflicting thoughts. "Just stop thinking about it all." Closing my eyes, I pretend I'm lying in the sand at the beach; a shell is jabbing into me, but I don't care because it's warm and soon the ocean will reach my toes.

The trolley grinds to a halt, our bodies sliding against the metal floor, and that imaginary shell disappears along with my ocean scene.

Squeals follow, and next to me, Cam groans.

Oh, Oz, what if she wakes up in the middle of all this?

Muffled voices reach me, but I can't tell what they're saying. Another moan comes from Cam.

Should I do something? How can I keep her silent?

More sounds come from the front, a little louder, until I hear, "... in the back," as if someone has just spoken right through the trolley.

"Empty space for supplies for the commerce center," June says, his earlier country twang gone from his voice.

A few clangs follow along with a few gurgles from Cam, her stomach, I guess.

Please don't throw up. What if she throws up on me? My stomach mimics hers. I don't do well with vomit.

The back doors jiggle.

"They won't open. Get the driver," someone says from outside.

Silence greets us again, until June says, "You want me to detach from this seat, roll all the way back there, and open the door for you, when you could just shine your light right in here and see, plain as day, there's nothing there?"

"Detach?" Someone asks.

A scrape and creak follow as if the controller's door is being opened.

More quiet descends.

"Thank you," June says after a few seconds.

The trolley engine revs and grinds, and on a heave, we jerk forward, right as Cam sits bolt upright. "Mother of Oz, what did you give m—"

Throwing back the covers, I find Zane's already done the same thing and has his hand over Cam's mouth. Her eyes glaze over for a minute, and she slumps back down like the snoozing corpse from before.

"June!" Zane says. "What the hell did you give her?"

This chuckle follows from the front. "One ginormous shot of caffeine. Like I said, it'll take a while. Her system is pretty shot." The lights flick on. "You can leave her there and come up front, if you want. We're already on the pathway."

Zane meets my gaze with a smile and rises, and despite not wanting to leave Cam—after all, she's not going anywhere—I go with him.

⚬═╾╼═⚬

Unlike a tram, June's trolley, as he calls it, can hold only about eight people. It has a center aisle, wide enough for him to get through, and the back area truly is made for storage—wide and empty. It rumbles along just like any rickety, old transpo would, I presume.

"Do we need to go back and get your Grandma?"

June shakes his head.

"Won't they go back and interrogate her, or something?"

He spits out a laugh. "Interrogate Granny? Is she for real?" That question is clearly directed to Zane, not me.

Zane doesn't even crack a smile.

I can't understand his calmness. "You left all that equipment—"

"It's secured."

"But, what if it's not? How can you know she won't get caught up in all that? And ... how were you even sure it was safe to share all? How do you know that someone else doesn't already know about this?"

"All good questions." June holds up a finger. "And since you seem so concerned ... I will tell you that my machines, like my brain, runs on its own energy, its own circuitry, and with my own algorithm for connection to the satellites."

"Which ones?" Zane asks, turning toward June.

"U.S., of course."

U.S.? I'm sure my eyes are as wide as possible and I close them a little so it won't seem like I'm so surprised. "So, the people in the U.S. know the A.U. is falling apart?"

"Yes, Anna, they know." Zane shifts, facing away from me again.

June glances my way. "See, Anna, without information, the population is in the dark. With it, we the people can stand up to the government. The U.S. already understands that—or must, since it's so explicitly stated in their Constitution."

"They're sympathizers," Zane says.

"So, why don't they do something about all ... this ... us?"

Junes says, "Not their job," as Zane says, "They aren't going to do anything about the A.U., unless *we* ask to be reintegrated."

A thought kinda hits me like a proverbial brick. "Is that why you're going to the U.S., Zane?"

"You're going to the U.S.?" June asks, excitement filling his tone. "Man, I did not see that coming. I just thought we'd be going somewhere Delta Street related."

"He's going," I say, staring at my feet. I can't, I won't.

"Take me with you, man. You *have* to take me. Granny knew this was my shot, and like always, she was right."

Zane doesn't respond, and June lapses into quiet. We seem to be repeating this pattern: Good conversation, tense conversation, some half-yelling fit, ending with silence, so after a bit of going on down the pathway aimlessly, I ask, "Where are we going exactly?"

June's hands are on the big, giant wheel in the front of the trolley. There is no system for self-navigation, for me to figure out that answer on my own.

"Where do you need to go?" June asks.

After a moment I say, "Home," as Zane says, "To the U.S.." *Oops.*

"Awe, man. Come on! You *gotta* take me with ya." June bangs on the steering wheel with his fist.

Zane coughs into his own. "I don't think the trip to the U.S. is going to work for you."

"Why not?" he asks with defiance in this tone.

"Because it's going to be hard enough for people who can walk. Your cart—"

"You think that, just because I don't have working legs, I'm less than you are?" June's tone is serious, even threatening. The trolley comes to a complete and utter stop, tossing me forward.

"Don't do this, June," Zane says. "Look, if there was any way, I'd get you into the group, but I don't have that authority, and there's only one spot left . . ." His gaze falls to me. ". . . and right now, this trip is . . . . It's kinda unplanned."

"I thought Delta Street members were better than that. That

you didn't discriminate based on what you *think* someone can and can't do." June taps his head with his finger. "That's what the A.U. does. Can't buy food, we'll get it for you. Can't get out to get clothes because your screen doesn't work well, and you're addicted to talk shows? We'll send someone for you. Can't walk? We'll fix your legs." He huffs air. "Well, guess what? They don't always do what they say, and sometimes you gotta just learn to help yourself. I know how to get around. I may be hick, but I'm not stupid." June's chest heaves as he starts up the trolley again, jostling us all around as he returns to the pathway. "You're no different than ... *them*."

Zane's chin falls, disappointment written all over his features.

"You can have my spot," I say.

Zane whips around to face me, shock etched into his features as if I've just stabbed him straight through the heart.

"Thanks, princess," June says.

The trolley moves slower than the hills, but doesn't falter. Not for the first hour. Or the second. Or the third. I'm both grateful for the continuous movement and totally bored at the same time.

Especially since Zane hasn't said a word—to me, at least—in all that time.

Cam hasn't moved, either, except for the rise and fall of her chest.

"There's a cooler up against the left panel, if anyone's hungry," June says. "And if ya'll don't mind, I'd like to stop at the next commerce center for a few minutes."

"Is it safe?" Zane asks.

"I don't know, but I don't have much of a choice." June

fiddles with a screen at the front of the trolley that popped up out of nowhere, the only electronic gadget in the space, aside from the trolley itself.

Zane presses buttons on the screen, making it change the image two, three and four times, until he stops and says, "Here. This one. It's a Delta Street hotspot."

June grins and moves into the right lane. "Two miles to go, then."

Until they'd said we'd be stopping, I didn't have to pee, but knowing we will has my bladder on high alert. Those two miles stretch on for what seems like forever, until we slow, moving farther to the right and toward an exit with at least a dozen transpos parked on the side.

"Must be an event going on," June says, bringing the trolley to a crawl as people swarm on all side.

Some carry baseball bats. Some have metal poles without flags. The few we pass, whose faces I catch glimpses of through the tinted windows, have their lips downturned, eyes narrowed, brows creased. Angry.

I cross, uncross and re-cross my legs as the need to evacuate my bladder consumes me.

More people swarm in front of the trolley, blocking our way, as well as that of three more transpos ahead of us.

"Get us out of here," Zane says.

Fear has me recoiling, but curiosity has me peeking through the window.

The walking people tear open the doors of a transpo two ahead of us and yank the people out, tossing them to the ground. Lights on a second transpo, just in front of us, flare a bright red before switching to green, indicating they're going to move in reverse. The all-to-familiar beep signals that's just what they're doing as they slam into transpo number three, and it hits into us.

I jolt backward as people start toward transpo two and three. Toward us, too.

"Get us out of here, June!" Zane's insistent.

I don't understand why people are grabbing passengers from personal transpos. Everyone can have their own.

Our trolley jerks to the left and punches forward, sending Cam sliding, and me into the seat in front of me.

"Go right!" Zane says as chanting fills the air around me.

Bangs come from outside, and I jump to the aisle, crouching low and holding on to both sides.

"Left!" Zane calls out.

June moves so fast I don't have time to grip before being slammed into the legs of another chair.

"Punch it!"

The trolley roars ahead, bouncing over something, and continuing on until the terrain underneath smooths out. My heartbeat doesn't, though. My heartbeat is wild.

⚬━✦━⚬

NOW

Mr. Perez coughs and chuckles at the same time. "So, in one day, you experienced a massive fire, got away from the cleaners, outed yourself and your beau, went through riots in one District and got caught up in the rising of a border wall, and now I'm taking you back to registration so you can ... go home?"

I nod.

Mr. Perez whistles. "Either you're really lucky, or really unlucky. I can't figure out which."

1 3

ONE HOUR BEFORE TURMOIL HIT

"Anna!" The unbuckling of a clasp and quick-stomping feet puts Zane just at my head a moment later. He pries each of my fingers off the seat's leg and helps me up. "You okay?"

Obviously, I'm not. I have no idea what just happened, but since my hands wouldn't relax, I couldn't let go of the seat legs to sit up on my own. Glancing back at Cam, I find she's just fine, sleeping away all the excitement. Or terror. Whichever I call it, fun doesn't fit.

I manage to shake my head. "What happened back there? And where are we going now?"

Up front, June fiddles with the screen again.

"Riot. Looked just like the ones in district Thirty-Two from last week," Zane says.

"Why?"

June huffs a laugh. "Credits. It's *always* about credits."

"But that's no reason to hurt other people. People don't have anything to do with credits."

"No credits means no food, screens, you know, *stuff*, and that means very unhappy people," Zane says.

"We have rules for peaceable protest in each district. And, if there's a problem, aren't they supposed to get help from their representatives?"

"Is she for really for real?" June asks.

My eyes narrow.

Zane stares right at me and says, "She's for real. A hundred percent. Just like the other ninety-nine percent."

What's that supposed to mean?

"People out here, closer to suburbia than out in the sticks, they don't get it," June says, explaining my unasked question. "If their credits don't post to their account, they go berserk."

Going without food for a day is hard, but that doesn't mean people have to get all angry and spiteful, and hurt other, innocent people. "Why don't they just go to their capital then? Why don't they—"

"Here it is!" June waves for us to come forward.

"You have a feed in here, too?" Zane asks.

"Of course. I'm always prepared. *Always.*"

On screen, and around us, night has begun to fall. In another thirty minutes, I expect daylight will be gone. Back on screen, though, people walk in masses down a street, or a simple road, or maybe it's a pathway. I can't tell because there are so many of them. Together. Walking.

"Why aren't they in their transpos?"

"No credits means no fuel energy," June says. "And these people, these are the ones who don't save. They just know the credits are coming, so they spend every last one of them."

"But credits are restricted. You can't just spend them all—"

Zane's eyebrow arching up stops me. "People know how to get around the system, Anna."

"Well, if they're going around it, they shouldn't be given credits."

"Maybe she does get it," June says.

Zane actually chuckles a little.

"And when the credits go away," June says, "they have nothing better to do than riot and pillage."

Scowling at the ground, my bladder signaling for release again, I say, "Two wrongs don't make a right. If people expect—"

"Expectation. That's a big word." Zane adjusts in his seat, facing me more directly. "Our government decided, long ago, that people shouldn't be responsible for themselves. That the government knew best how to provide. Like the max size of food portions. How did we work around no sixty-four ounce drinks? By drinking two thirty-two ounce drinks. Healthcare. Don't want it mandated by the government? Well, then, pay the fine. It is always cheaper. Procreation. No need to even tell us that. Slip some extra chemicals in the food source, or sterilize at registration."

My mom said she'd had Mia during a time no one was supposed to have kids. Did selective sterilization happen way back when, or had it been everyone? Or had something happened to her? Now, I wish I could ask her more about it.

"People fought it. All of it. Even the kids thing ... people said it was their right to have kids, but then mental illness and other psychological issues grew worse, until eventually, they conceded that the government must have been right. They decided someone *else* should decide for them. That's when the U.S. split off, and in the end, the A.U. become a nation of takers. So, now, it's all or nothing. And when nothing becomes the norm, people get angry, and anger leads to what you saw on screen and what happened back there."

"That was a long time ago." Even though it's not a question, it comes out sounding like one. "People don't really still feel that way."

Closing his eyes, Zane pinches the bridge of his nose. "No. Now, Anna, what they didn't want but was forced upon them, they now don't want anyone to take away. It's like handing a chocolate chip cookie to a child and, as they reach for it, slide it between their grubby little fingers and take one bite, snatching it back and holding it up so they can see it, taste it, feel it, but not have it. Happens everywhere in the A.U.."

"I thought you said the credits thing only happened in one district." Hadn't he said that?

"I said it *happened* in one. I didn't say it didn't happen in the rest. Or hasn't since happened in others."

"Not in mine," I say.

"Not yet," Zane says. "Our district is too close to District One for them to make obvious changes. If they stop payments in Two, Six and Eleven, where are all the people going to go?"

"To their district cent—"

"District One!" June's exclamation is poignantly frustrated.

"Oh." Staring out into the darkness, my kidneys start up that frustrated dance that had begun before the riot.

"I need to stop." June slows the trolley and stops on the side of the pathway. "Next exit is fifty miles from here. No way I can wait." He unbuckles and rolls down through the back of the trolley where Cam lays.

"Are you … going out in the brush?" I ask, knowing that, if we have fifty miles to go, I, too, will never make it.

"Just to the other side of the trolley." He leans over and slides Cam to the side. "When nature calls, nature doesn't usually hang up." Out the back door he goes, lights from passing transpos brightening the interior for a second before they are beyond us.

"I think I might go with him," Zane says. "Do you …" His finger does a whirl as if he's asking if I need to pee.

I nod, though I have no idea how he expects me to go on the road, without any cover.

"Stay here. Two minutes." Zane zips out of the trolley, the doors closing behind him.

Time passes with the counting of transpos. After seventy-one, and at least as many leg crossing switches, Zane pops back in. "Your turn."

Standing is possible, but not without keeping my legs closed tight. For a girl with next to no credits, and very little need for important, fancy or expensive things, a bathroom with a door and a toilet is probably my only vice.

Zane faces the cars, a flashlight aimed somewhere behind him. "Best place is just up there in the trees."

In the dark.

By myself. If only Cam were awake. She'd go with me.

With June and Zane, though, this is not a time to ask for company.

⊙══╪══⊙

"Where to, now?" June asks Zane as we return to the trolley.

My adventure in the woods was the least eventful time in the last few days of my life. I expect Zane will focus on getting back home so he can go to the U.S., and I really hope he agrees to take June instead of me.

"How far will this keep going without running out of fuel?" I ask.

"This baby's built with a special fusion that'll last for twenty-four hours of straight operation. So, just tell me where to."

Zane glances in my direction before rattling off a series of roads and names and turns, the last of which I recognize as my dad's place on Delta street.

He's taking us home. *Me* home. Oddly enough, disappointment fills me. I shouldn't be sad, since that is exactly what I asked for.

"And that's how I ended up with you," I say. "All we were doing was taking me home." I've blathered on to Mr. Perez for what seems like hours. I don't know why he wanted to know all that, but he never asked me to stop talking. Quite the opposite—he prompted me with questions.

Leaning back against the seat in Mr. Perez's truck, I close my eyes, reflecting on all the details I've just shared with him. Zane's going to hate me when I don't really do what he expects me to, but he's already mad that I'm not going to the U.S. with him, so why does it even bother me? I'll just finish registration, Delta Street will eventually find Zane, and then the last week of my life will disappear from my memory banks.

Right, like that'll happen.

Maybe I can find a way to become Cam's medical supervisor and get her to wake up, and manage her until she's ready to be released back into the population. Maybe Mom won't hate me—too much—for leaving in the first place.

Maybe everything will just go back to the way it was.

Mr. Perez slows and turns onto District Nine's version of Perry Road. Unlike Eleven, my district, this road is clear and pothole-less, and given registration is going on right now, it's empty. He continues on down the path, all the way to the end, where the three houses back up to the giant wall.

In the dark, the wall—the border between the U.S. and the A.U.—looms as high as ever.

"May I ask you something, sir?"

"Oh, darlin', you can ask me anything." He stops in front of the red house. "But only if you call me George."

Okay. Weird. "Mister—George ... have you ever just gone over there to see if it's better? I mean, even if you thought you could fix here, why not go and see?"

"Well, now, that's a tough question." He scratches at his chin a moment. "Here's how I'd like to answer that. You see ... there's an old saying that the grass is always greener on the other side. There was also another saying to never drive your dream car, for fear that it will never live up to your expectations ... I combined the two."

I'm pretty sure the man is senile.

"If the U.S. is the greener grass, *and* it's the dream location, what happens when it's not? If that happens, the experience of just going there will ruin all the hope I have about what *could* be here. So, rather than sneak a peek and dash all my hopes and dreams, I'd rather just believe that the right way exists over there, and someday, instead of being separated by this giant monstrosity, we'll tear it down and reconnect."

"Oh, okay." I turn to the truck door and search for a lever to open it.

"Hang on. This one I made myself." He presses a button in the front, and a click noise sounds through the cabin. "All free now."

Yet, it seems I'm more closed in than I was just a day ago. An hour ago. A breath ago.

Mr. Perez leans toward the passenger seat as I push the door open. "One last thing, Miss Keating, if you don't mind."

I turn back to my kind driver.

"Don't forget what you just went through. You may want to, but sometimes, the tough road is what makes us who we are, or who we are meant to be."

"Okay."

"You take care now, young lady. Make the most of your future."

I give him a nod of thanks as I slip out and shut the door. Turning, I face the red house. It's an exact replica of the one in Eleven. So is the black and the white, from what I can see in the dark. They always are, supposedly, and seeing them, even in the dark, brings back all the memories of a week ago, when I started this nightmare.

The lights are off everywhere, leaving only the moon to provide any contrast to the shadows.

Just knock on the red house door, and someone will arrive.

That's what Zane told me, at least.

I step forward, the frozen ground under my feet crunching in my wake. At the door, I want to knock, but I don't want to, at the same time.

What if Zane is right? What if the A.U. is out of money, and they're selectively targeting people for sterilization? What if Cam left her spot because even she learned something dangerous? What if June not being invited in really is because the country wants him gone, and most flukes don't know how to take care of themselves, so even their families kick them out?

What if—

The red house front door opens, and the interior lights flash. A man in a white suit, just like before at registration, walks out, holding something long and black over his shoulder. "State your name and purpose."

"Uh ... ah ... Erianna Price Keating, sir." At least, I think it's a guy—his voice is low. "Um ..." I rub my earsm and the ear piece screeches inside the canal. I grab my head instead and shake it, as if that will stop the noise, until I remember to tap it silent. At a click and stomp, I peek up and find that black thing pointing straight at me.

"State your name and purpose."

"Eri-Eri-anna P-price Keating. And I was stolen from registration! Please help me!"

14

"Stolen from registration, were you?" the man across the desk asks. For the tenth time.

My response, for the tenth time, is, "Yes, sir."

We've been sitting in his office, inside District Nine's registration unit for at least an hour. Has to be. If not more. I wouldn't know, though, because there isn't a single clock anywhere in the sparse, empty white room. Just a desk. A tablet. Two chairs. This official. And me.

"Explain that to me one more time?"

I bank the sigh and say, "There was this boy—"

"Zane Warren, you say."

I nod, holding back the cringe that I've just given the guy Zane's real name and not his mixed up one. "And he tricked me into going outside." True. "And then he wouldn't let me back in." Sorta true. "And then after he wrecked the trolley we rode in, I got away." True. Mostly. "And a nice man brought me here so I could get back into registration." Totally true. That is, of course, the super summary version of the events.

"I have no Zane Warren in this list."

"Maybe he lied about his name." Fact. He did. "All I know is I didn't want to go, he made me go, and now I'm back. I just want to get through registration, and get my job, and my living quarters, and work for the A.U.."

"Well, we have had people run kidnapping operations before, so your story is plausible."

It is? They have?

"And your identification does prove who you are."

Thank goodness.

"And without a coat, or any other type of covering, only a crazy person would go out in this cold."

Or someone who forgets their only coat.

"Here's what I'm going to do. The next transport vehicle is set to leave in two hours. Until then, you're remanded to this space. You are not to leave this space and will have no contact with anyone else in District Nine. You will be placed into that transpo at oh-two-hundred hours and will be taken directly to District Eleven, where you'll be sent down for remediation."

Remediation?

"At that time, they can deal with the indiscretions."

Indiscretions?

"Am I clear?"

I nod, not knowing a better answer to give him. I have no idea what he means, except that I'm going to Eleven, just like Zane said.

The man stands and puts his hands on the table. "You're a lucky little girl to have made it back here. Most of those kidnappers don't take kindly to little girls." His grin makes me shiver, and I wish him out of the room right now. He walks around and to the door, opens it to exit and closes it behind him, leaving me all alone.

Normally, quiet doesn't bother me. For some reason, in the room I'm in, quiet makes the walls seem like they're moving, like they're going to squeeze in on me and flatten me into a breakfast pie circle.

The quiet lasts for too long, and I reach up and slide my

finger against my ear while tucking my hair back. At least I can listen to Delta Street people talking. Except, despite keeping my hand on my ear for a moment, expecting the sound to mellow, I hear nothing.

Not a blip of anything.

I tap at my ear again.

Nothing.

A third time.

Still, not a sound.

Well, that stinks. Slinking back against the plastic molded chair, much like the one in the commerce center's security office, I can't get comfortable. Slouching hurts my shoulder. Leaning back strains my lower back. Leaning forward on the table with my arm makes my shoulder ache, so I rest the injured one on my lap and lay my head on the other, on the table. It's not comfortable, but it's better than nothing.

The door opens, and I jolt up. "Brought you a meal replacement. It's all we have here right now. Better than nothing, right?" He sets it on the table and walks back out.

I grab the bar and tear it open on my lap. The first half falls straight to the floor. As I lean over to get it, a noise hits my ear, and I straighten again.

"Delta Street one, this is Delta Street two, location?"

"Delta Street two, this is Delta Street one, District Twenty-Six. Barrier."

"Delta Street three, this is Delta Street one, location?"

Static greets me for a second, before three answers in Twenty-One and ends with Barrier. The location check goes on and on and on as I grapple with the second half of the bar, attempting to free it from its package, but the wrap is too tight, and the bar won't come out. Giving up, I lay it on the table. Instead, I reach for the bottle of liquid.

"Delta Street zulu, this is Delta Street one, location?"

I hold the bottle in my right hand and twist with my left. The cap comes off much easier than the meal replacement package opened.

"Delta Street zulu, this is Delta Street one, location?" The voice is more insistent. Hesitant at the same time. "Delta Street ninety-nine, this is Delta Street one, *location?*"

No response comes.

"Dammit, Zane, where are you?"

"No names over non-secure channels!" another voice chimes in.

"Delta Street zulu, this is Delta Street one, *location!*" The question is insistent and loud.

There is no answer of course. Zane is obviously Delta Street zulu, and since ear piece is in my ear, and his comms unit, or whatever it is he said he lost, is gone, they'll never know.

He's as silent as I am alone.

"Delta Street zul—" The voice is cut off and my earpiece produces no more sound.

I bring the bottle of water to my lips but pull it back before drinking. Zane said they put stuff in the food and in the water.

But he lied about a lot of things.

He also said he shared all his lies.

Which is exactly what a liar would say.

What if he's right, though? What if they do mess with our heads, and if I drink this and eat that bar, I'll be a zombie like everyone else.

Like Cam.

What have I done?

Lowering my head to the table again, I push the liquid bottle and bar to the side and close my eyes. Maybe if I fall asleep and wake up, I'll find out all of this was a dream. That I never went to registration, or saw my sister, or found my dad, or met Zane.

My heart flip-flops in my chest.

If I keep thinking about it, maybe I'll come to a solution.

On a big yawn, my lids close.

Maybe, though, my first idea would work best.

Sleep. Wake. All of this will have gone away.

◦═━═◦

"Miss Keating," someone says in a soft whisper. "Miss Keating, wake up." Something nudges my shoulder.

My sore one.

I snap up and blink, over and over, trying to remember why my head is on a table and I'm sitting on a plastic chair in a dark room.

"Miss Keating, it's time to go," the person says.

Time to go. Right. Because that wasn't a dream. I have to go back to my District. To registration.

"Miss Keating," the female voice says with more insistence.

Turning toward it, I'm greeted by one of the nameless, faceless people—as I came to think of them during registration—covered in head to toe white. They have no identity and could even be non-human, except their eyes show.

"Sorry," I say. "I must have fallen asleep."

"Yes. You did. You need to follow me." She goes to the door and walks through it, as I stand, my stomach grumbling the whole way. "You should have eaten."

Should have is right. I want to go back for my other half of the bar and the liquid, but my guide will probably disappear on me if I do.

"This way." She steps through a hallway, like the same ones I came through when I first arrived within the red house. White halls, white doors, white-covered people. It's all so sterile. Everything about registration is.

Was.

Is.

"Please keep up, Miss Keating," she says.

I shuffle along behind her, exhaustion weighing heavy on me. My shoulder still aches, and the cat nap has left me more groggy than refreshed. Worse, I think I injured more than just my shoulder in the accident. Both my legs ache, as does my head. Given how we flipped, it makes sense, and since a few hours have passed since the accident, *all* my adrenaline has worn off.

We pass through another two empty hallways and out to a set of white stairs. White. White. White. Fifteen steps. Sixteen. Seventeen. On the twentieth, I want to drop to the floor and curl up in a ball—that's how bad my muscles hurt.

At thirty-one, she pushes open a door and brings us both out into the night.

Into the cold.

A tram waits under a single spotlight.

"You will enter the tram. It will take you directly to Eleven. From there, the administration will handle the remainder of your case."

Case? I'm a case now?

As I step out into the dark, lady-in-white closes the door, herself inside, me outside. No one else is around. Not a soul. On the tram, I count at least three people.

With a deep breath and a sigh, I make my way toward it. The doors open, and up I go, another three steps.

The doors close behind me, sealing off the cold, and me inside.

In total, absolute and complete warmth.

There are, in fact, three other people on board. One is

dressed all in white. *How surprising.* One person looks more like me—tattered, battered and worn out, with his, or her, head against the tram window. There's the controller, too.

"Have a seat. We'll be heading out soon," the controller says.

I plop into the first open seat, which, with at least twenty other rows, leaves plenty of space for anyone else who might need a spot. Like what I assume is the only other candidate on the bus, I lean into the cool, solid window and close my eyes. If I can get another couple of hours of sleep, I might have enough energy to deal with whatever's going to come my way.

On a screech, the doors open and close, letting in two more people, one dressed all in white again and another kid-looking person.

This repeats at least ten times, but I keep my eyes closed throughout the rest because I know it doesn't matter who's joining. We're all going to the same place—and if not—it doesn't matter. I just need to be told where to get off again.

Voices pick up in volume, but quiet again at a buzzer that sounds throughout the cabin. "Candidates are to remain seated throughout the journey. We will arrive in District Eleven in three-point-five hours." The voice is robotic and not even as friendly as the announcer on the first day of registration. "Until we arrive, no candidates are to speak to one another. All activities will be monitored and recorded for your protection."

My protection. Zane would laugh at that, I know it. My smile comes out without thought, and I force it down. I can't think about Zane, or June, or Cam. I have to focus on me.

Of course, a tram like this one is where Zane and I first met. *All set up to happen, of course.*

With his goofy grin and calling me by my dad's nickname. I should have known he knew something about me.

"Candidate F two zero five three four two five," a voice calls out and takes my attention from my inner thoughts.

Raising my hand, I say, "That's me." I want to add ma'am, or sir, but I'm not sure if I should, given the speaker is one of the ten people in white with no faces.

White-person marks something down on a tablet and calls out, "Candidate M one one three six two one."

A voice says, "Yes," in a deep masculine tone.

A crackle in my ear suggests my Delta Street people are about to speak, and fearing someone can hear it in the quiet tram, I lean into the window a little harder.

Another burst of sound comes through, before I hear, "Delta Street one, this is Delta Street one zero bravo."

"Candidate F six six six six seven seven seven?" the proctor says. I have to call her that to give her some sort of role other than scary-person.

A sob comes before a, "Here," in a soft cry. I wouldn't want that ID number, either. Everyone knows triple seven is bad luck.

Back in my ear, more static crackles, and, "Candidate is aboard transport vehicle to District Eleven. Confirm action," follows.

Did Delta Street suggest they're watching *this* transpo?

My eyes dart to the side, but I force myself not to turn, not to even suggest I've heard something.

The proctor continues confirming names.

"Delta Street two, zero, alpha, confirms rendezvous at District Eleven."

Who are they waiting for? What are they waiting for? Why?

If Zane is out in the cold with June and can't even communicate the information, how would they know to watch for something on this tram? Can I even act like I know? Of course I can't, because I'm not supposed to know.

The abrupt stop and lurch forward forces me awake. After watching the passing lights, night lulled me into a sleep, and I find myself at the end of my trip.

Back in District Eleven.

Back home.

As lights illuminate the tram's interior, I blink, adjusting to the lack of darkness. The controller rises and moves to the door. My heart beats in my chest at a fast and furious pace. I'm almost there. Almost back to where everything started. Where I want to be.

"Remain in your seats until called," the controller says.

With the lights on, the windows only reflect what's inside. Without cupping my hands over my face, I know I won't be able to see whatever's going on outside. Rather than risk an obvious show of curiosity—though it probably doesn't matter if I do peek—I sit in my seat like a good little girl and wait.

Waiting is interminable. The longer no one comes back to take us inside, the more I wonder just how long it will take.

A squeal in my ear makes me cringe. "Rendezvous reached," someone says.

Here? Surely not. I lean against the window anyway and, with my face against the cold plastic, try to see outside, wondering if anyone's out there talking and who it might be.

The door to the tram opens with a sucking pop, and a white-suited person boards. They walk straight up to me and point. "You. State your name."

"Uh ..." Why I've stumbled, I don't know. "Erianna ... Keating."

White-suited person moves on to the others, asking the same thing. When she gets to the last one in the back, she tells him to rise, which he does, and pushes him all the way to the front and out the door.

No one says another word.

At a commotion outside, everyone in the tram stands and moves to the right side windows, hands cupped around their eyes. All except me, of course. Curiosity consumes me, but not enough for me to leave my seat.

What do they see? What's going on over there? I want to ask, but I know I shouldn't. Good girls just sit and wait.

A shadow appears in the tram's doorway, and I glance toward it.

An urgent finger curl suggests someone should get up and move. I glance back, finding everyone else in the tram still riveted to the windows.

The finger curl gets more urgent. *Is that motion a signal to me?* Someone else? I slide my way to the edge of my seat, still not getting up.

The finger doing the curling becomes a hand, motioning faster.

If they want me, why don't they show their face? Why don't they just ask for me?

The top of a white-hooded head pokes around the edge and a white-covered face appears. The curling finger turns to a point, right at me.

Me? I mouth it, staying silent.

The head nods.

I step to the aisle, and since none of the other passengers are paying any attention to me, I walk to the front. I open my mouth to acknowledge the person, but he, or she, puts a finger to their faceless lips and motions for me to follow.

Into the cold night air I go, while outside, people race about in the holding lot, chasing after the boy they took off first.

Why'd he run? Why is he still running? Does he not want to go back to registration?

A hand grabs my arm and yanks me forward to a set of double doors and pushes me through.

The light is flicked on, and standing there in the warmth, without the sunglasses, my sister's face stares back at me. "What the hell are you doing back here?" she asks.

I want to ask her the same thing.

15

"Come with me." Her voice is stern, like Mom's is when she's mad at me.

"No." I don't want to go with her. I came back for me, not for her.

"What?" Shock fills her uncovered face. "Yes!" She says it as if that should make me choose to go.

"Not until you tell me what's going on. Why you're here. What you expect of me."

She raises an eyebrow, just as she's always done—or at least from what I remember of her. "You want all those answers? Fine. But you'll only get them if you come with me."

Mia jerks left, and, with little other choice, I go with her. Her feet move fast down a hallway that's illuminated only by her flashlight. We make turn after turn, until my head spins with knowing I'll never get back to where I once stood. I wonder what that means for my chances of getting back into registration once again.

After what feels like an hour, but is probably only a few minutes, she opens a door.

To a closet.

With an insta-potty.

Gross.

She goes in, her back to me, as I stare at the closed-top

bucket thing and follow. The door shuts behind us, the light diminishing to what can fit through a small crack between door and frame, leaving just enough to see shapes but not what Mia is actually doing.

"Why are we in here?"

Her silence doesn't answer my question. After some rumbling and shifting of stuff, she turns with an empty cup in her hand.

"What is that?"

Her gaze darts to the container before meeting mine. "What? This? A container."

"Yeah, but why are you showing it to me?" It looks like a bodily fluids sampler, and the shake of my head comes involuntarily. "I'm not peeing in that, Mia, if that's what you're expecting."

My sister throws her hands up in the air. "Of course not. What do you think—never mind. I know why." She unscrews the cap and digs inside it. "You must really be tired, if that's why you think I brought you in here."

It's five in the morning at my best guess. It seems, over the past three days, I haven't gotten more than four hours of sleep, maybe six one time, but everything keeps happening at night, when I'm exhausted and can't think straight. So, yeah. I'm tired.

"I asked you for answers, Mia, not to be brought into a closet."

She turns with whatever she dug out of the container, goes straight to a rack, and pulls off a white garment—the same kind she's wearing.

"What's this?"

"You, my dear sister who doesn't listen to a thing, are going to proctor candidates at the five a.m. session taking place in about five minutes, in place of someone who's taken an emergency leave. And immediately after that's done, we're getting out of here." She shakes out the suit and holds it up to me. "This'll do."

"But ... I'm not a proctor. I'm a—"

"Oh, Oz, Eri—"

"Anna," I say, more determined than ever to use my new name, not my old. "And I'm not a proctor. I'm a student. I'm going back to registration."

"Anna," she says with a soft lilt. "Look ... I nearly got caught two days ago and had to get to my post and shut down all comms, until I could be sure they weren't on to me. But I can't miss this morning because it's my last group to save. So, either you stay here in this closet with this insta-potty until seven, or you take this group—"

And do what? I want to ask.

"—you stand in front of the hundred or so people—"

A hundred? No way I'm doing that.

"—you let the Facilitator do his job—"

Okay, I could do that.

"—and then you use the tablet to run a report."

"No." *I can't run reports.*

"No?" Mia shakes her head at me. "How can you say no?"

"That's not why I came back here."

Her head does that little jerk, and her eyes narrow. "What do you mean?"

Steeling myself under my sister's glare, I say, "I'm going back to registration."

"Like hell you are."

Shock has me stepping back.

"It's not that hard. I'll show you what to do." She rummages around again.

"Mia—"

"Shh," is her only response.

Frustration ebbs from me, though I'm sure no one will ever see it. Especially not my sister. A moment later, she turns and holds out a comms unit.

"What's this?" I ask.

"Your job today."

"But—"

"No buts, Er—Anna. Just do this, and I'll ... I'll figure something out about you getting back into registration." Her statement ends on a seriously sad tone.

I thought I'd already figure out what I needed to figure out, but if she's agreeing, the least I can do it trust her. "What if something doesn't work with this? Who do I call? What if a candidate has a question? What if—"

"Haven't you paid any attention? No one, or very few, in white suits talk. They are all proctors. Monitors, for lack of a better word. The people who talk are in business attire."

She's right, at least from what I remember in the short time I went through registration. "You promise I won't have to do anything else?"

"I never promise. But, yes, I'm sure you won't."

"And if something happens, you'll come get me?"

Mia rolls her eyes. "Yes. And better yet, as soon as instruction is over, I'll come get you, and we'll get out—I'll figure out what needs to happen next. Now, put this on."

⚬━✦━⚬

Mia drags me to a teaching room with a gazillion empty seats. Okay, not a gazillion, but standing in front of row after row, after row, after row, I have to wonder why anyone would want to be a proctor. Facing all those empty seats is bad enough. The fact that, soon, candidates will fill them makes me shiver from toe to head—maybe more than usual because I should be in those seats, not up here.

Of course, Mia left, too; she didn't just show me the room, explain everything, and wait at the back. She told me, in no uncertain terms, to stay inside, do exactly what every other white-suited person does, listen to the man, or girl, in a suit, and, at the end, wait for her.

I expect, when this is over, she'll help me get back in officially. Of course, I should have told Mia 'no' and actually meant it, and did what I had to do, but she's my big sister. She's here to take care of me. Right?

The silence of the empty room is oppressive. There's a light floral fragrance that has dissipated since I took my spot at the front, replaced by something woodsy I can't identify. It's weird because all the seats are plastic, or some synthetic material strong enough to hold butts of various sizes—none of which would have a smell like that.

Blinking and staring out at the ocean of spaces, I wonder at how the registration organizers have managed to prepare and adjust for all the different candidates. All the eighteen year olds. All the hormonal injustice. Mom said I skipped that part. That I went straight from nine to twenty-nine. I don't know how given I can't make a single decision for myself.

Even now. I came back for me, and I'm doing stuff for Mia.

A creak and a slide precedes the outer door opening, and two white-suited people file in. I stand from my slouched position at the front table.

"You're early," the first—a girl—says.

"Couldn't sleep." My response is so easy because it's a ninety-nine percent not a lie.

The second moves on past and stands just to the back of the

educator's area—that one place where the proctors and facilitators stand and talk, or stand and wait, or present, or whatever. Since the first white-suit takes the right, and the second white-suit takes the middle, I opt to head to the left, directly in front of the doors that have closed again since they came in.

Both of them stand, hands behind their backs, feet shoulder-width apart. I mirror them, still trying to be someone I'm not. Disappointment and fury fill me with angst and anger all at the same time. I'm not mad at Mia this time. I'm mad at me. What's the point of being a grownup if I can't even make my own decisions?

I clench my fists in an attempt to let out my fury before anyone realizes I'm not who I am. To be here, I have to just be some complacent girl dressed all in white, waiting for candidates to walk down the path toward their non-future.

If only they knew what happened over the last couple days. If only they understood what the A.U. did to people without even telling them.

What do I know?

You'd know more if you stayed with Zane.

Forcing myself not to shake my head, I close my eyes—still hidden behind a curtain of white.

Another swish and the door opens, a stream of girls coming in, one by one, down the path, each one turning at the farthest available row and filling it all the way to the end. Behind them, a group of boys. Followed by another group of girls. Each line completes a row before the next comes in.

Is that how Zane and I looked to the proctors when we walked into the room? Like mindless drones doing exactly what everyone asks them to do? When, too, did five a.m. become the time of choice for class? On day one, we were told to report for breakfast at seven, and to start our sessions at eight. Five a.m. just seems too early.

While bodies move in tandem, and each spot is taken, one by one, the sound in the room barely increases.

Drones. They're all drones. Robots, perhaps.

Worse than before. Worse than when I was inside, just days ago.

These kids—because that's really what all we are—have no personality. No color, even. They've all been dressed in grey. The same grey suit I was given.

As the last of the people trickle in, a guy in a business suit follows, a tablet held in his left hand, his right swinging with each step. He nods at me, at the middle proctor, toward the one on the far side, and steps up to the empty table.

"Good morning, candidates," the man says. "Welcome to day six of registration." He holds up his tablet and taps on it. Around the room, blank comms units alight with images. "Today marks your final day of studies for your profession as Social Engineers, or, as we like to term it, Life Coaches."

My head snaps round. I was supposed to be a life coach.

"Today, you will see just what you're up against in this new society. The wave of social injustice that has become symbolic of the U.S. has found a way to trickle into the A.U., such that we have experienced many, many new inequalities among our people." He taps, and the images on the wall turns to a man on the street, barefoot with what looks like snow on the ground. "You see this man?"

Heads nod around the room.

"This man needs our help. He needs to be cared for. He needs to be rehabilitated and given a good job, one that pays for all his needs. He must have his blisters healed and his health managed. He needs you to take care of him." The man taps again and the image changes, but something about that previous one didn't sit right with me. "You see this woman?"

Those same heads bob.

In the image, it's a woman holding a baby, and in the background is a room with what is probably a divan, kitchen and office rolled into one. It looks like my mom's space.

"This woman can't take care of that baby by herself. She's all alone. She's helpless. She needs you to intervene."

Why? I want to ask. I really, really do. She's even smiling in the image, and it's one of those, 'I love my life' smiles, not the fake ones models give that are supposed to be real. Doesn't that mean she's happy? Mom's happy. Oddly enough. She is. She's told me. She doesn't care about not having more. She never cared about material things, just always about Mia and me learning and becoming independent.

The image switches again and again, all with what seems like someone being singled out for their situation, but in all cases, I don't see what the facilitator is showing. I see satisfaction. Freedom. Independence.

"These are the people you must save from themselves, that you must corral and ensure they are either under the direction of the A.U., or deported as traitors."

Oh, Oz.

They don't want me to help people, they want me to tattle on them.

They've been training an army of people like the ones they've shown, flukes, the poorer sort, to infiltrate our own kind and remove them.

Zane knew. He understood. He tried to tell me. To show me.

I take a step forward.

The facilitator turns toward me.

Repositioning myself, I stand straight again. *Be more careful, Anna.*

"Now, for your final survey, we'll determine just which ones of you is truly prepared to take on this role. The rest of you will be dismissed from service."

My hands itch to go to my mouth. Dismissed from service? Does that mean they aren't going to pay them? Aren't going to give them the one job they've been told they could handle? Taught to deal with?

The facilitator nods toward me and the other two people in white. They take off their lapel clips; I do the same. They walk to the head of a row; I do the same. They swipe the clip over a tablet; I do the same.

The first one blinks green.

The second is green.

The third is red.

The kid in the seat tilts up to me, blankness in his face, in his eyes, in everything about him.

Did I look like that?

"Proctor number three, move on," the facilitator says.

I do, and in the same row, receive two more red lights.

Moving up and down and through the crowd like the other two, at least ten other candidates blink red.

Each of them have that same emptiness about them. Like their soul has been sucked out of their bodies.

As the other two file down the rows, I do the same and re-take my spot, forcing my body to prevent the shaking I know is brewing.

"Now," the facilitator says, "those of you with green may depart in preparation for your first course of the day. Breakfast will be served promptly at seven, with tardiness marked as of oh-eight-hundred." He turns toward the three of us and faces his tablet as those with green lights rise and make their way out the doors.

In the room, at least two dozen remain.

Once the doors swish closed, the facilitator turns. "You lot will be escorted momentarily away from the facilities and to another." The man taps on his tablet and walks up to the doors, where he glances back. Without another sound from him, the doors open, and he disappears through them.

No sooner did he go than people in black suits appear. People just like the ones that came off from Cam's transpo. The Cleaners.

I want to yell and scream at them to wake up! To run! To not let these people take them anywhere. That they have to be free. They have to stop letting their minds be wiped and messed up by whatever the A.U. is feeding them.

I don't, though.

Not a sound leaves me, though my heart pumps hard in my chest because I know, not a single one of those twelve will exist, at least not in the same form as they are today, from this moment forward.

Silence accompanies the candidates as they rise and filter between the men, each one of them smaller than the presiding guards. Executioners, I should call them, knowing that while some of those people might not die, they will, probably, die on the inside.

As the last three rows file out, the kid who got the first red light, the one who faced me with an unsaid plea of nothing glances back my way, and all I can do is suck back in the tear that wants to fall.

∘━✦━∘

The other two proctors leave, and I follow, though if Mia isn't in the exterior hallway, I won't know where to go. The barrier shuts behind them, leaving me in the education room, and I plop down onto the first seat in row one and drop my head into my hands.

Why didn't I do something to help these kids who don't know what's going on? What could I have done?

This is obviously why they made everyone get up so early— to weed out the undesirables. It's a sad state that our country has found a way to decide who is worthy and who isn't.

Would I have been worthy? Would I have gotten a green light and been told to continue on my day? Or would I be making my way to the Cleaner?

The door swishes, and someone in a white suit walks in. He or she stops. I don't get up. There's a silent stare down happening, though neither of us can see the eyes of the other.

"Why are you still here?" he asks.

"I-I—" I don't know how to answer. "Stomach ache. Giving myself a minute."

"Oh." He nods. "When you are able, we need extra hands loading the cleaner transpos."

Everything inside me goes numb. Help them send people away? Is this what they do to candidates everywhere? How did I not know this? Why don't these people stand up and say something? Why don't they stop it?

Is this what happened to Cam? Did she get a red light on her comms unit?

"Well?" he asks.

I wrap my arms around my stomach, which does hurt, just not for the reason he probably thinks. "I'll be out there soon. Need to let this settle."

"Okay. If you find anyone else wandering, send them out, too. Main deck A."

I'm left alone again. Vomiting seems like the right next step, but that won't fix anything, since I'm not ill, just sick.

The door swishes open yet again, and, yet again, I turn and stand.

"You ready?" Mia asks.

I shake my head. I don't want to be expunged. I don't even want a green light. I just want ... *something that doesn't exist in the A.U.*

"What's wrong?" Mia asks.

I can't tell her. I yelled at her in the closet about staying. I have to see it through.

Mia steps toward me. "Anna ... I don't believe this place is for you, but I'm not here to tell you what you can and can't do with your life. It's yours to decide."

Tears fall down my cheeks at her words. The words I've wanted to hear for forever.

"I don't want to stay."

"Good. Let's go," Mia waves me forward. "Right now, while they're filling up the transpos. Everyone's focused on that."

"You know about that?"

"Of course I do."

Of course she does. Why did I even ask? "When is the ... you know ..." My voice has pitched low like I don't want to ask but must.

Mia covers my mouth with her hand. "I'll explain later. But right now is *not* the time if you want to get out of here." She takes her hand off my mouth. "Now follow me, do exactly what I say, and don't talk to anyone. Even me."

16

With Mia guiding me, the departure from registration comes with no more danger than me tripping over my own two feet. She did, however, have to nudge me several times when all my energy just left me like some deflating, oversized, white balloon.

After what had to be an hour of walking inside, we strip off our white suits, fold them up—Mia jams hers into her bag—and exit to a cold morning with a sky tinted orange and pink and the sun beginning its rise. I stop and stare at it as if I've never seen the colors so vibrant. As if by seeing the morning start anew, everything I went through overnight, or in the last week, is no longer an issue.

We trudge along, me wrapping the flimsy white suit around my shoulders like a blanket, my attempt to keep warm failing miserably as the cold pounds against all exposed skin. Very few people are out among us, businesses are still closed, and even the few transpos that go by seem to do so at a slower-than-normal pace.

"You can talk now," Mia says.

Eyes on the ground as I continue forward, I say, "The trip to the U.S. ... will it still happen?"

In my peripheral vision, I see her shake her head. "No. It'll have to be rescheduled. If it can be." Her sigh is audible, and her shoulders drop.

"Do you ... know where he is? Like ... do I need to tell you?" I probably should have right when she found me.

"We found Zane just fine—if that's who you mean. He's already back. Probably. Which, by the way ... what were you thinking?"

My head pops up. "What was I thinking? What do you mean? About what?" Is she about to yell at me for wanting to go back to registration? If so, I don't want to hear it. I just want to get somewhere warm.

Mia stops. "Why'd you go with Zane, traveling all around the A.U. for the last day and a half, two days, whatever?"

Oh. That. This I can handle, but we have to keep moving, or I'll freeze in place. "How do you—" I can't even begin to understand how she'd know. Of course, Zane did have eyes and ears on himself, so maybe he told them. Why would she be mad at me, then? "You told me to trust him," I finally say.

"Fair enough." She starts walking again, while the cold continues to pummel my bones. "And do you?"

I shrug. "In a way. Can't we take a transpo? It's freezing out here."

"Not yet."

Rubbing my hands along my arms to add some warmth helps a little. My mind returns to the fact Mia knows, knew, where Zane is—was. Did he even need me to go back to Registration at all? There have been so many secrets, they're really starting to irritate me. I need to know how she knows. "Um ... how did you ..."

"Know about the accident?"

I just don't get these Delta Street people. They know what I'm thinking before I even ask. "Yes. And how did Zane get back faster than me if the wall was up?" And if he could do that, why did I have to go to registration? Why couldn't I have just gone with him and then found a way to Mom's?"

Mia's lips curve up. "I thought you didn't want to do all that. Thought you wanted to stay at Registration."

"Okay, let's assume I didn't, how did you know?"

"Same reason I know about the piece in your ear."

She knows about *that*, too?

"Have you received any communications from it lately?" she asks.

"I-I … no. Not since I was on the tram."

"Good."

"Good?" I ask, shivering as we continue on. The sun rises farther into the sky, doeing little to warm the air around us, as a few people exit the buildings we pass.

Mia guides us down an alley, the wind dying as we enter. "There's so much you don't know, Anna."

"Ya think?" A pang of guilt runs through me for speaking to my sister that way. Grabbing her arm, I stop us. If I don't get some answers with a few less vague comments, I'm going to scream. "Stop talking around whatever is going on. How did you know about the accident?"

Her eyes narrow for a moment. She straightens and crosses her arms over her chest. "Okay. I can see you want to know."

Throwing my hands up seems appropriate, but I don't.

"I know about the accident because Delta Street has an in in District One … as you know. So I knew the moment the walls went up, and knew what district you were in because Zane had checked in about five minutes before with a location. Given the timing, we had a general proximity for where you were. So, we sent Mr. Perez out looking. He's part of Delta Street, if you haven't figured it out. He called in, and alerted us to that, as well as to the fool plan Zane had you go on."

"Does Zane know all that?"

"I don't know what he heard, or didn't, since you have his earpiece, and his voice is missing, but he's being debriefed now."

"How do you know about me having his stuff?"

"Because the sensors are bioidentified. When the earpiece went from Zane to you, it set off a sensor that traced your DNA in our system. Once it figured out it was you, it continued to work. Had it not, it would have shut down immediately."

"How did you know about the whole trip?" Seems like a stupid question, given what I've learned, but I just need to know. To hear it from her.

"Zane kept us informed. By duty."

Which is exactly what I figured. "Do you know if he's okay? He had some bruising on his face."

"He's probably being yelled at by a medic for the face injury, and dear old dad for making that trip with you because you weren't supposed to leave the living quarters." She really does know everything.

"Zane said he needed to show me."

Mia crosses her arms over her chest. "And did he? Did he show you, and did it change your mind about anything?"

Did it?

"Exactly," she says. "You see, Anna ... changing people's minds takes more than a whirlwind trip around the A.U.. You have to *want* to believe. You have to—" She taps my chest at my heart. "—want to believe in *here*."

Do I?

"And I think you do. Otherwise, you would have stayed in Registration."

She has a point.

"C'mon, kid. Let's keep walking. We can catch a transpo in

about three miles. If any are even running anymore."

∘══╼══∘

Frozen. That's the only word to describe my hands, feet, nose, lips, everything about me, as we step off the transpo and into the lobby of Delta Street headquarters, also known as Dad's place. The thirty minutes on the transpo, one only Mia and I rode, did nothing to defrost me. Or to release all the thoughts jumbled up in my head.

Mia does a shake like a dog, sending little droplets of water from her pure black hair. "It's so good to be home." She grabs my hand and yanks me toward the risers.

Standing straight, I find my sister is taller than me, maybe by an inch. She's beautiful, too—something I didn't see when in registration so many days ago. Her eyes sparkle, and there's a glow about her that I'd have to call complete and utter confidence. She's always been like that. I should have tried to be more like her instead of less like her.

Squaring my shoulders, I stand a little straighter, but even with the new haircut and permanent facial enhancements, I'll never be Mia Keating.

You shouldn't be, either.

At the light ding and stop of the riser, Mia exits and pulls me with her. We head straight through the hallway, back the same way Zane and I left, and into my dad's living space.

Zane and June both sit on the divan with a tablet between them. Their heads lift and turn, as we appear. Zane jumps up and races to me, hands sliding to my cheeks, blue eyes boring into mine. As he moves in closer, the warmth from his palms seeps into my skin, heating it like nothing else did on the trip home.

Leaning his forehead against mine, he sighs. "You're freezing," he says after a short silence. "And you're exhausted. And you're probably starving." He spins toward Mia, letting me go and taking the heat with him. "Did you feed her?" I presume he's asking Mia, though why didn't he ask me?

"Nope," Mia says from inside the kitchen area. "She didn't even drink the Kool-Aid." Mia walks back in holding a red apple while crunching on a bite. "Probably ought to make her something with a kick, while I go check in with Dad." She nods once and moves away down the hall.

Zane holds out his hand to me. "Can I make you some breakfast?"

My stomach grumbles as if on cue. "No, thank you."

"I'm just going to go ... in the other room," June says. "I'll check on Cam."

"*What?* Cam's here?" I can't believe it.

June nods. "Zonked still. In the back bedroom."

I start that way, but Zane stops me. "Take care of yourself first," he says. "Then you can check on Cam."

Staring back toward where June rolled and Mia walked, I want to follow. Every molecule in my body says 'go after them', but I face Zane again, and all those inner emotions turn to 'stay'. It's not like Cam's going anywhere, and if she does, someone will tell me. I hope.

"Just breakfast, then you can. Please," Zane says, emotion filling his voice.

"Okay."

Ten minutes later, Zane and I sit at the counter eating scrambled eggs, toast with honey, and drinking orange juice that comes from the fridge, not the powdered kind Mom and I buy since it can be stirred into plain water at any temperature. It's weird that we're sitting here eating, when the world—or at least my country—is about to come to a screeching halt. It's like everything is normal, except it isn't. Like me. I changed my hair and my face to be someone else, but I'm still me. Erianna Price Keating. I have a best friend named Cam, who is in some sort of coma. I have a sister who's disappeared, reappeared, disappeared again and reappeared a second time. A dad who's back, but isn't, and a mom who knows I'm in my formerly dead-dad's world now.

All the same, yet completely different, too.

"You know what the best thing is about this breakfast?" Zane asks after I've been quiet for a while.

I shake my head as I chew my toast. Same toast. Same method of eating it. Different place.

"There's not a chemical inside it. No brain numbing, mind washing, degenerative stuff inside. Just food. And as tired as you looked when you walked in, you already look better."

"I feel better," I manage behind a hand—hiding my full mouth. Pushing the rest of my eggs around on my plate, I scrape my fork against the ceramic.

"Anna ..." My name trails off on his lips.

Lifting and making eye contact, I wait.

"Before my mom died," Zane starts without further prompting, "she used to come in my room, even when I didn't want her to. She'd sit on the edge of my bed and say, 'Zane ... if you bottle it, it'll explode like an uncorked champagne bottle shaken for an hour. If you share ... everyone else can enjoy the champagne with you'. Now, no one can drink champagne except in the French Republic, but hey ... I see her point."

So do I, but I have no idea what that means to me. "You missed your trip."

Zane bobs his head a little. "Yes and no."

"What do you mean?"

"No one made it. With the barriers up, we had to postpone

the whole thing."

"But you still missed it." I stir the crumbs on my plate.

"Anna." He says my name the same way he did before.

Facing him again, I say, "What?"

"I know you're mad at me."

Do I have 'Anna is angry' written on my forehead, or something?

"And you have every right to be. I should have just gotten you through registration, shouldn't have tried to put so much on you. I—I'm truly sorry and hope you'll forgive me."

He meant *he* needed to unload. Not me.

All Zane's done is try to answer questions in the only way he can. He didn't have anything to do with the walls going up. He didn't have anything to do with anything, except exactly what Mia told him to do.

"Asking questions is a good thing, Anna. But I shouldn't have made you ask them and get answers on my terms."

"About that."

He cocks his head to the side. "About what?"

"Anna. My name. You can call me whatever. I was Eri until I thought I'd come here and try to be something I wasn't. Which is obviously the—"

Zane stops me by grabbing my wrist and holding it still. "Don't ever question who you are. That's what's in your heart. Everything you've done for you is important. What I've done isn't. Do you know what Anna means?" He moves around the counter, holding me the whole time.

Shaking my head, I stare up at him.

"It means grace. It means … 'God has favored me', where me is you, you know." Zane still doesn't let go, his gaze serious and directly on me.

I'd like to argue with him about the whole God topic, since he's brought it up again, but like all the constitution and governmental stuff, I'm sure he'll have something profound to say to me that negates whatever I'm thinking, so I don't.

"Anna ..." he says, so close the heat from his breath hits my cheek, eyes bright and focused on me. "I—"

"Cam's waking up." June's voice interrupts, but I don't tug free. "If you want to go talk to her, or something," he adds.

17

On the bed in the second bedroom of my dad's living quarters, Cam sits, cross-legged, still dressed in the frumpy jumpsuit, with her blonde hair falling around her shoulders in waves. She's always been pretty, and even in the grey, drab clothes, she's still Cam—that girl I grew up with, who I thought I knew.

"Cam?" I ask, standing in the doorway.

She turns toward me so slow, I'd swear someone had to crank her to get her to come around. As her gaze meets mine, a twitch of recognition comes into her eyes, lighting them up just a little. Her lips move as if they might curve up, but stay in a line. "Where am I?" she asks in a flat monotone.

Moving closer, I come to the edge of the bed. "At my dad's house."

Her brow furrows as if the answer can't be right. Cam always thought my dad died, too, so her expression makes me wonder if she's processing, or just outright confused. "My dad's house?" There's a slight inflection to that question.

I shake my head a little. "No, mine." Sliding onto the mattress, I hike up a knee onto the surface so I can face Cam. "Do you know who I am?"

A very slight nod follows without words.

"Do you know who you are?" I really don't have a clue what the zombie drugs do, so who's to say what she remembers and doesn't.

Another very small nod gives me an answer but I'm not sure it's the right one.

"Tell me your name." I take her hand between mine. The rings she wore on her hands are gone.

"Five-Five—"

"Your name. Not your registration number. Or your social identity number. Tell me your name." *Give me something that proves you're you.*

Her hands rise to her throat, where she pushes down on the collar. Cam always hated shirts that touched the front of her neck, and the button-up one that's on her is closed all the way to the top. "I like pink."

"I like pink, too," I say, wanting to stick with her line of thinking, or at least try to keep her engaged. Of course, I have no training in this sort of thing, and my career selection obviously wouldn't have been to help but to get rid of her, so I'm probably doing everything wrong. The scent of food hits me, and though I've eaten, my stomach growls. "Would you like some breakfast?"

She nods a little again.

The girl before me is definitely not Cam—not my Cam—the loud and boisterous friend I've had since level one educenter, when our facilitator put us together to read Winnie the Pooh, and Cam told the lady that classics were for old biddies, and she shouldn't have to read anything except what came on her screen. I happened to love that story, and until just last week, I thought our friendship to be more like Pooh and Tigger's than Pooh and Eeyore's.

"Okay, come on, then." As I rise, she grips my hand, tightening around my wrist and pulling on me.

Her eyes close, face cringing. "Pink," she says. "Pink."

Sitting again, I wait, her hand still on me, holding me in place.

"Pink. Pink. Pink!" Each repetition is more frustrated, as if memories are surfacing, but she can't get them out.

"Her brain's—"

Cam and I both jump

"—trying to rewire," June says from the open door.

"Pink," Cam says again, facing June.

"What other shades are like pink?" he asks.

"P-pink," Cam says and beats her fist to her forehead. Given that, I'm guessing June's right about the rewiring.

"How can we help her?" I ask.

"Normal food. Water without zombie salts. Time." He shrugs like those answers are simple. "You gotta get her back to a diet that isn't a hundred percent preserved and artificially enhanced with mood altering chemicals."

Food, I can do. With Zane's help, of course. Taking Cam's hand, I tug until she moves to the end of the bed. "Let's eat."

"Your name is Cam." June rolls backward, opening the doorway wide for us.

I glare at him. I'd wanted her to tell me. Too late now.

"Zane's got enough food for ten people. If she eats some, it should help."

Step by step, we make our way to the door. "Do you need to use the bathroom?"

Her blinks come, followed by a head nod.

"That's a good sign. Get the stuff out of her system." June scoots back a little more, as Mia exits our dad's room dressed in a teal shirt and gorgeous denim pants, with her hair pulled up to the top of her head, sending a cascade of black down her shoulders. She had it up before, but to reach so far down, it must be really long.

"Need help?" she asks, walking closer, her bare feet sporting red-painted toenails.

I shake my head. "Cam just needs to pee. In a real bathroom."

Mia's chuckle makes me smile. "I'll help her. Why don't you freshen up in Dad's and meet us in the kitchen in a few?"

"I don't have any clothes other than these, so I'm okay."

One of Mia's eyebrows wings up. "We have plenty to spare. In the second closet. Seriously." She takes Cam's other arm. "Go. For the moment, this girl doesn't know you from Adam, so take advantage of it."

Take advantage of it?

"Go, Anna. Shower. Change. Take a minute, or two, for yourself."

❦

Standing there, staring at myself in the mirror, I remember one major flaw with shorter hair—one I'd tried to avoid for years, and is probably why I never asked my mom to cut it.

Short hair sticks up in the morning. Or at night. Or any time one's head has been down, unmoving, on a table, or arm, or tram's window for an extended period of time.

Why didn't anyone mention the mess on my head?

You look exhausted, Zane had said.

Freshen up, Mia had said.

Maybe that was the signal. Why not just tell me outright that I look like a homeless banshee? Strands go everywhere. Up, around, over. Running my fingers through it gets a few pieces back into place, but doesn't really fix the problem. What I see before me is totally blush-inducing.

Searching for a comb, or something to get the rat's nest tamed before I jump in the shower, I open the cabinet beneath the sink. It holds cleaning supplies and clean-up paper—at least twenty containers of it. If my dad lives alone, why does he need so much? Moving to the over-the-commode cabinet, non-regulated remedies sit on two small shelves, but a little blue box grabs my attention.

With a chewable dental tablet working to clean my teeth and refresh my breath, I close the cabinet.

Curiosity has snagged my attention, though. The box reminds me of the one Cam and my so-called friends gave me, with the necklace that turned out to be stolen.

Glancing back at the door, as if someone might come through, I take the box from the shelf and hold it in the palm of my hand. It's not heavy. It's not slick. It's just a blue box less than two inches high in all directions.

What could be inside? A ring? A necklace? Something shiny? Something my dad owns? Something he gave? Something someone gave to him? For fourteen years, I didn't see him, and on the day I find out he's actually alive, he left me again. I deserve to know more about him. Would whatever's inside tell me something new?

Tapping my toes against the tile floor, I contemplate whether to open it—to see—to know.

Is it that private, if it's in a bathroom?

Can't be.

With my thumb and middle fingers holding the top, and my other hand securing the bottom, I lift my gaze to my reflection in the mirror. I'm not frumpy. I'm not the plain Jane I was last week.

I am Erianna, though. I am me. Snooping has never been me.

Don't do it.

It would only be a peek. It would only be a second.

The knock on the door bobbles my hand and the box tumbles. Falling.

Toward the water.

As if in slow motion, as if not controlled by me, I reach out and catch it with my good arm as it bounces off the seat.

My heart hammers in my chest.

"Anna?" Zane asks.

"Be right there." Heaving air like I've run a marathon, I hold the box to my chest.

"No, it's okay. I just wanted you to know, Lucie brought some clothes over for you. Since you didn't pick anything out. And I know you won't because they aren't yours, so she's forcing them on you. I'll leave them just outside the door."

The blush comes fast. Thank goodness I'm behind a closed door.

"I'll be in the kitchen, if you need anything. And you can take the earpiece out now."

Hand to the door, I whisper a thank you, and promise myself I'll never consider opening someone else's stuff again. Turning away, I spin the handle on the shower spigot, ready to wash off the grime of the last three, four, however many days it's been, and start fresh.

⌇

Loud, serious voices draw me down the hallway, each getting deeper and louder as I approach. Not only have Mia and Cam found their way there, so, too, have June and Zane, as well as Marlena and Lucie.

It's Lucie who turns first, who comes to me, arms outstretched, and wraps them around me.

"My, my, you're a breath of fresh air on a cloudy, pollution-filled day," she says in her drawl. Holding me at arms' length, she makes sounds like *Mmm* and *Hmm* and taps her lips. "This is the perfect color on you, darlin'. Just perfect. Better, even, than the blue. Don't you think, Marley?"

Marlena comes over, too, as the rest continue their conversation. "Perfect. How's the ..." She wiggles her finger toward my shoulder, but I know her question isn't about how I'm still holding it at a funny angle. It's about the tattoo on the back.

I can't help the smile. "Just as pretty as when you put it there."

Lucie claps and hugs her sister. "I knew you had it in you, kid. And once we get ourselves to the U.S., you're gonna be a star." She bumps fists with Marlena and walks back to the table.

Marlena holds out her hand, and I lay mine against her palm. "You okay?" she asks.

"I'm fine."

Her head tilts a little. "You know that's the number one lie women say, right? And you know that I don't believe you for one minute." She glances toward the group and back. "Come with me." Trailing after her, we end up on one of the divans right next to each other. "Tell me what's wrong."

What's wrong? What *isn't* wrong? "I'm just a little overwhelmed."

"Is it your friend?"

I give her a small nod.

"Is it that you had to stand in as proctor and learned what they're really going to do with life coaches?"

I jerk back.

"You think I didn't know? Darlin', I'm part of Delta Street, and I'm part of your life. Girl, I know what's happenin'. Maybe that's the problem. Maybe that we know all this stuff, and you're just learnin'." She wags a finger in my direction. "That it?"

"How do you know all this stuff?"

"It's Delta Street's job *to* know." She takes my hand. "Remember when we were getting to know each other, and I told you about your job and how you'd have to look and act, etcetera?"

"Yeah."

"Honey, I was tellin' you that because I was trying to prepare you. We all were. *Are*. Everything Mia, Lucie, Zane, me, and even your Daddy, have done is in preparation for this moment."

"This? Like right now this moment?"

"Well, sorta. I mean you finding out and figuring it all out and being able to properly assess what you want to do with yourself." She closes an eye for a second. "You don't still want to go back to registration, do ya?"

"No." That I've said it so quickly and without thinking must mean it's true. "No, I don't. I-I don't want to ruin people's lives. I want to make lives better. I can't put people on a transpo, only to have them disappear."

Her lips curve up. "I knew you couldn't do that. You're too goodhearted. And I knew it would just be a matter of time before you figured that out."

"What happens next, though?"

She runs a hand down my cheek. "That's the one question I don't know the answer to. All's I can tell you is, we're waiting for orders, and until we get them, we have to sit tight."

I pause for a few beats, debating whether to ask her, or tell her about what I really want to do.

She eyes me like she knows I'm thinking.

"Can I . . . can I ask you something that's just between us?"

"Of course." Her lips pull up in a small grin.

"What if—" I glance toward the kitchen door opening.

"What if . . . if I just want to go home."

Her head shifts a little. "But you are home."

Closing my eyes, I take a deep breath. "Home-home. To my mom."

"And stay in the A.U.?" she asks in a deep whisper.

I nod.

"You don't want to go to the U.S.? You don't want to be a part of our lives? Because you know if you go back, that's what will happen."

A pang hits my chest at what I'll be giving up, but I know it's right for me. I may have figured out that Registration wasn't, but staying here is still right. I give her another quick nod.

Her hands go to her chest and up toward her neck in a V-shape. "Well . . ." She exhales, long and fully. "Well, if that's what you know in your heart is the right choice, then no one here is going to stop you." She does this little headshake thing, like she's forcing herself to say the words.

"Would you be mad at me?"

Eyes wide, she says, "Of course not!" and lays a hand on my knee. "Darlin', we in Delta Street get what freedom is about. It's about choice. It's about doing what's right *for you*, and finding your place in society, so that you can be both a contributor, as well as find peace and happiness—at whatever level that is. That's the whole premise behind the U.S.'s success. People are empowered to choose for themselves." Her hand goes to her ear for a second, but she lowers it just as quickly.

"Did you hear something? Did someone say something? Do you have one of those ear things, too?"

Her nod comes with her saying, "Just some noise, is all. We get that every once in a while." Waving it off, she adds, "Now, I do have a question for you. On this topic of staying here."

"Okay."

"Zane."

"That's not a question."

She grins at me and leans in. "You know what I mean." With a shrug, she says, "What do you think about him?"

"Um …" I get that she means something other than 'is he a nice guy'?, but what does she expect me to say? We've only known each other a few days.

"I know you've only known him for a few days, but …"

My high alert buzzer goes off in my head, not that she's read my mind somehow, but the way she's said it, like there should be more to him than what I'm thinking.

"… he's smitten with you."

How would she even know that?

"And I know that because …"

Oh, good Oz.

"… well …" She gets even closer, if that's possible. "… He's known about you a lot longer than you've known him, and I've known him even longer, so I know how to read him a little. I probably shouldn't even be saying this, but I think, even though he'd support you, one of two things will happen. If you don't go, he won't go."

The mini headshake that I do is just an attempt to process what she's said. He has to go. It's what he's always wanted. I haven't been in his life that long for me to be such a factor.

Marlena rises. "Choose what's right for you, knowing all the facts, and that …" She points toward the kitchen where Zane must still be. "… is a fact. That boy's been waiting years to meet you, and I know he won't let you go easily. So, if you want to stay, be prepared for him to be right by your side." Her nod precedes her departure.

"Anna!"

At Mia's call of my name, I jump up and follow Marlena

to the kitchen.

Everyone, except Cam, stands in front of the windows. She's sitting at the table like some well-disciplined child. Mia signals for me to join the window crowd, and I do, right between my sister and Zane.

On the ground below us, safety and security transpos roll along the street. A people-deserted street.

"Where is everyone?" When we'd been on our way to Dad's place, I thought the early morning hour kept people inside. Of course, at eight a.m., people would have been going to work, and I should have recognized that, which means something else happened, and Mia didn't know about it, either.

Why did the transpo run, then? How were we able to get on it and make our way here? Mia didn't seem nervous, or weirded out by it, or anything.

"Mia," I say, "What's going on? Where is everyone? Why—"

"They're preparing," she says, fists balled at her sides.

"Preparing for what?"

Zane turns to me. "War."

We're in the city center, miles from the border, yet security forces and armored transpos file down the street right in front of me.

"I seriously thought we had more time." Zane's fists bunch at his temples.

Turning to him, I tug his arm down from his head. "War? Why? I thought it was just upset people."

He swivels to me, eyes intent and serious. "The walls don't just go up for protection but to prepare."

"Why?"

"How do you think *this* district will react when the people here are given no credits for screen time? Entertainment. Or for a single non-essential? Or when it gets so bad, not even for food. No credits, no funding, no input means no output. It's over, and this is telling us that it is." He runs a hand through his hair. "All that work lost."

Mia moves around me and pats him on the shoulder. "There's nothing you or I could have done. Your uncle. My dad ... all of Delta Street. We all tried."

Marlena and Lucie both take big deep breaths and flank Zane. "Time is just as big a commodity as credits," Lucie says. Marlena nods, adding, "And once it's gone, there's no getting it back."

I don't even know what to say. I don't understand how we can just run out, how a gigantic country made up of millions of people can just be creditless. Surely, people will have enough credits for food, or we'll be able to continue to provide food, but the way they're talking, that doesn't seem to be true. No matter how many times Zane or Mia have said we were running out of credits, I figured they meant a long time from now.

"Did you know that aside from District One, Nine and Eleven are the two richest Districts?" Lucie asks.

I live in the *richest* District?

"And despite that, despite all the influx of credits, ninety-nine percent of the population lives from one dwindling deposit to the next," Marlena says.

"Which means, what we're about to experience is going to be phenomenally bad." Mia turns back to the window, and everyone else does the same, me included.

"If they don't get their deposit tomorrow, there will be riots right here." Zane points beyond the window, down toward where the security transpos have parked.

"They won't, either," June says, reminding me of his presence.

"They won't what?" I ask.

He wobbles the tablet in his hand and points to the screen. Though he opens his mouth, words don't come out. Instead, he turns the tablet toward us, a graph with a big red line on it in the middle.

"What's that?" I have to ask, since no one else has.

Mia's hand pulls me in close to her in a weird hug. "That, my sister, is the end."

It looks like a line on a screen to me.

Zane turns to me, too. "It means, what your dad tried to get China to do failed. They're no longer going to give us credits to add to our debt ceiling, and we can't advance anymore to our own citizens because our systems are gridlocked, because what China already lent us is gone, and they've called in the debt."

Whoa. Staring at the floor is a better option than looking into their eyes and showing them I have no idea what that means.

"To put this in layman's terms," June says, and I bite my lip to stop the smile, "China is no longer going to support us, and we're on our own. But not only that. All that we've borrowed from them so far, we owe it back. Right *now.* And everyone who's not been living under a rock knows that, if you've accepted even one dime from our government, your name is on the list, and China can swoop in and take back their credits from *you* directly."

"What the heck?" No way. He can't be serious.

"It's true," Marlena says. "You. Me. Well, not you. Me, though. If you study the laws and the agreements the CEO made with our allies and enemies, you know that anyone who lent money, once they call it in, it means they get to take over and come and get it. So, China can take it right from me. In any way they want."

I whirl to Mia. "This can't be true."

She shrugs and closes her eyes.

"What about Dad?" Panic makes my chest tighten. "He's on the administration! Does that mean they'll go after them first?" Mom's like me, so if they don't know about me, they won't know about her. Right? "Does Mom know about this?"

Mia shrugs. "She might not know about it hitting tomorrow, but she's known this was a possibility. Just like Dad does."

That has to be why she was so determined to stay off the grid, and why, because of her stubbornness, she'll be safe from whatever's coming. At least knowing that, I can breathe a little easier. For once in my entire life, I'm glad she's a fluke.

"People in Eleven and Nine ... they won't wait a few days to react," Marlena says.

"Oh, it'll be tomorrow. No question." Mia taps on the glass. "That's probably why they're sending in security forces now."

So, we have a day. One day until whatever is coming will actually begin. Only a day, though.

Swallowing, I peek toward ground-level. Security forces continue through but at a slower pace.

"Do you think there's a way we can overcome this? I mean ... what if we find a way to pay it back?" I ask.

Mia and Zane glance toward each other on either side of me. "How do we, in the A.U., earn credits?" Mia asks me.

"Um ... by working?" I know it's not a question, but it definitely comes out as one.

"I mean the people who pay the workers. How does our government earn money?" She crosses her arms over her chest.

"Well ... like any business, people buy ... stuff ... from ... us." Even as the words come out of my mouth, I have no idea if it's right, but that's how Mr. Milton earned credits—people bought his food, and he earned from that.

Mia's lips curve up. "And what do we sell?"

"I-I— everyone sells something different." I have no idea if I'm answering right, but I get the feeling I'm not.

"You have no idea, right?" she asks. "And that's because," she continues before I can even answer, "we don't produce anything that people around the world want. Nothing. Not a thing. Which means, all we're doing is funneling our own credits through our own systems, but we're not earning any new credits. More mouths to feed and people living longer means we've had to borrow from other countries, China in particular, because they, unlike us, produce *everything*."

"Private enterprise. That's what we need," June says. "The way it's supposed to work is simple. Someone creates a product people want. A business is born from that. That business hires people. Those people make and sell the product. People buy the product, and that cycle continues. With each purchase, a portion of the cost is taxed. A government only earns from taxes. But what has happened here is that the government took over every aspect of the economy—the creation, hiring, production, etc. So we have no real income. We're done."

I like the way June explains things.

"Tomorrow, most people will be confused and ask questions. A few will have known what's going on from the start. Within a week, riots will be across the entire country," he says.

Zane inclines his head toward June. "And in a month, unless we agree to be taken over by China—"

"The A.U. will collapse." That comes from Mia.

A grinding sound has us all facing the windows again. Below, several huge transpos have stopped at the corner of our building. At least a dozen men exit the transpos, covered in dark gear and helmets, carrying stuff over their shoulder. Bags. Long metal poles. Guns. Big ones, even from my vantage point. They walk, or more like stalk toward the building, knees bent, the weapons in their hands sweeping the area, until they all disappear, and Mia, Lucie, Marlena and Zane all grab their ears as if an ear-splitting sound has just come through their heads.

"Go!" Mia's yell has me spinning. "Now!" She pushes me toward the center of the room as Zane grabs my hand.

Lucie and Marlena take off, waving June with them toward the door.

Not knowing what's going on, but with my heart beating frantically in my chest because it can't be good, I follow, but stop. "Cam!"

"No. We have to go," Zane says, tugging on me.

"No!" I pull free from his hold and start back toward her.

Mia stops me with both hands to my shoulders. "I will not let you be caught by security forces, Anna. They're coming here for Dad because he went AWOL. Which means, they know about his allegiance. You have to get out of here."

A gasp leaves my lips.

My sister stands firm. "If they catch you, they'll classify you as a traitor, by virtue of you being here. And if they find out you're related to Dad, you'll be hauled off and locked up before you can think straight."

Tears well in my eyes.

"That is, if they don't ship you off to the looney bin first, where you'll be processed, sterilized, and delivered as an insane sex toy to some third world country."

I can't help the shiver that goes through me. "I-I— what about Cam?"

Mia puts her hands on my shoulders. "I'll get her secured, if you promise, *promise* me, you will stay with Zane and do whatever he tells you."

Once again, I'm in a position of weakness.

Zane tugs on my arm. "We gotta go, Anna. Now. We have to."

"Please, Anna." Mia holds her hands clasped out in front of her. "Please go. Please trust me. *Please*, because if you don't, you're going to condemn me and Zane to your own fate, since neither of us is leaving you."

I jump forward and hug her. "Be careful," I say.

She squeezes me tight in return. "You have less than sixty seconds. Go."

We do.

Zane leads me out to the hallway, around to Marlena and

Lucie's living space and inside, through the door, and to a back closet.

"Ready?" he asks.

"For what?"

"Just hang on tight." His arms go around my waist, and a second later, he jumps.

The floor beneath us gives way, and my scream dies as he clamps a hand over my mouth.

Sliding. Spinning. Whirling. Those are all the sensations that play through my mind as we fall. Down. Down and farther down. I want to ask when it will end, when we hit something, my knees buckle, Zane's grip on me releases, and I roll away, landing at the toes of a pair of black dress shoes.

My stomach churns as it rights itself. All the breakfast contents I've just eaten spew from within me, and I lean right to avoid throwing up on the shiny shoes.

A hand touches my back. "Let it out, Windy. Let it out." The voice sounds so much like my dad.

Breathing in and gagging, my head spinning, a bucket finally appears in my line of sight.

"Sorry, Anna. I didn't realize that would get you." That comes from Zane.

Zane and my dad? How is that possible?

Leaning up and blinking through tear-covered eyes, I stare at my Dad.

The hand he keeps on my back reminds me so much of his comforting caress from way back when.

He lowers to me and runs a hand over my head. "Hey, my windy girl." His smile is one I'll never forget.

Scrambling, I launch myself into his arms and hang on tight. "Don't let them take you." Burrowing my face into his jacket, one that doesn't smell like plastic, I cling, wanting everything in the last five days, or fourteen years, to go away. For us to be at home. Me, Mom, Mia and Dad—all together, in our little shack. Happy. Not running from imaginary people during registration. Not sliding down hundreds of feet to get away from my own government. Not with a country that's in financial ruin. Normal. Just every day normal.

"Anna . . ." Zane's voice penetrates my inner thoughts. "We have to go."

I shake my head against my dad, his arms still around me.

Dad's hand goes across my head again. "You have to go, baby."

"But I don't want you to be in retention. You're not a traitor. They'll hurt you." I sound like some sniveling two-year-old.

"I know, but you have to trust me." His arms don't let go; they don't even relax their hold on me.

"If I can get up to my place before they do, they'll have no ability to take me. And if you go, I know Zane will keep you safe."

I peel myself away and tilt up to him, though we're so close I can't focus on him. "But—"

"I don't have time to explain right now. I shouldn't even be down here with you, but I didn't want to pass you on the way and not get a chance to see you." One more hug passes between us, before he releases and holds me at arm's length in a mostly dark room—not that it matters since I've had my eyes closed for a while.

"I don't want you to . . ." *leave me for another fourteen years.* ". . . go."

"I'll see you again. Soon." His gaze goes toward Zane. "I need you to get as far away from here as possible." He tilts my chin up as he straightens again. "It's not safe here, Erianna. It won't be for a long, long time. So I need you to go."

"Go where?"

"With the team. They'll get you to safety. You—" He reaches into his jacket and withdraws a white note chip. "Use this if you need it." The chip looks just like the one I found on the seat of the tram, when Cam and I went to the commerce center way back when.

"But—"

"No buts, Erianna. I want you safe, so that while I'm still here, I don't have to worry. Understand?"

I nod, not really understanding, but wanting to do exactly what my dad tells me. To make him proud.

"I'll keep her safe, sir," Zane says, reminding me that he's standing right behind me.

"I know you will." Dad holds out his hand, and Zane's shakes it. "I'm counting on you." Gaze back to me, Dad says, "I love you Erianna. I always have. Everything I've ever done has been because I love you. And Mia. Please know that." With a kiss to my forehead, he disengages from me and walks straight to a red light in the far corner. One arm extends outward, and a second later, Dad vanishes.

"Where'd he go? How—What just happened?" I ask.

"It's a transport tube, like the one we jumped down through. It just sucked him up."

Blinking doesn't help, or bring anything else into my vision.

"Mia!" My eyes go wide as I turn toward Zane. "She's up there. Dad will—"

Zane touches my lips with his finger and points up with the other hand. "Shh," he mouths. "Company." That, too, comes across only as a movement of his lips.

Above us, the surface creaks. Around us is ninety-percent black, and breathing in, aside from the residual vomit smell, brings in the burn of wet earth to my nostrils.

Zane takes my hand. "Let's go."

My heartbeat picks up speed. "What about Mia? What about Cam?" Panic strikes me again at the thought of them still in my dad's space. I didn't even warn him they would be there.

"Really, Anna? You're going to worry about them now?" His tone has me backing away. "Hell, Anna, I'm sorry." He runs a hand over his head. "Look ... Cam's with one of the top operatives in the world. If Mia said she'd have it under control, she does. Now you need to, too."

Breath in deep, and let go. Follow Zane, and trust him. Dad and Mia do. You can do this. "Do you promise they'll be safe?"

"I don't make promises when I don't have control over every possible outcome."

"So, that's a no?"

"Yes. That's a no." At least he's honest. "Now, come on, because we've got a ways to go to."

1 9

"Zane." I whisper his name in the pitch blackness.

"Shh," is his only comment back.

Step by step we continue through nothing, a solid wall of emptiness, through which I have to close my eyes, because I'm afraid a claustrophobic panic attack will hit if I don't. It's been at least five minutes in the dark, moving at the pace of a human-sized snail, my hand tucked against Zane's, walking blindly into an abyss.

The terrain hasn't sloped, at all, but stayed flat. We've hugged the wall at our right, and nothing has touched my left side, but I don't know how wide the space is. There's no moisture in the air, which I would expect of a cave-like structure. No sound, either. There is a chill, though; sometimes, it goes warm, then cold again.

Zane stops. I wait. He adjusts his grip on my hand, tighter, thank goodness.

"Z—"

"Shh."

We wait more.

Seconds pass.

Minutes.

I want to yell out his name, to make sure he's still alive, but the warmth from his palm tells me he is. I also want to ask him to get us out of here, but I know that's just what he's doing—in the oddest, creepiest way possible.

A swish sound happens, just before a pinkish light appears in front of Zane.

I guess I had my eyes open, after all, since I can see it.

Zane turns to me, his face in shadow, head and shoulders silhouetted by the light stick. Before I can even inch back, his cheek is next to mine, lips at my ear. "From here out, I need you to stay absolutely silent. We have to cross under a street, and sound vibrations can be picked up by sensors. Once we pass, we'll be okay to talk."

I nod against him and breathe in the scent that is him. The clean, fresh something that has surrounded him since the moment I met him.

"Anna?" he whispers, still at my ear.

"Hmm …" My response is as close to silent as possible.

"Nothing. Let's go."

The small pink light is our lead, and with Zane's back pressed against the wall, I do the same. It's smooth, like an interior living space wall, not like the rock I expected of an underground passage. It reminds me of the wall we passed on our way down to registration from the red house.

Each step Zane takes, I mirror.

Each moment he stops, I do, too.

Our hands remain linked, fingers entwined.

One by one.

The passageway narrows, and I reach out, bumping into the opposite side inches beyond my toes.

A bubble of panic rises inside me.

Zane moves another step.

I can't, and our arms stretch out a little.

What if the wall behind me collapses forward? What if all

of it in front of me does? What if the walls are moving, and Zane's been walking me through a trap, and the next step I take will simply squeeze the life out of me? I don't want to die! I want to be with my dad. I want to be with my sister. I want—

Zane tugs me to his side and wraps his arm around my shoulder, the light stick illuminating the wall just in front of us, no more than a shoe's width away. He angles his head toward it, and I stare at the wall, at the inscription. At the words on the smooth rock, inscribed into the hard surface in a jagged pattern of clear letters.

Eric and Belle.

My mom and dad.

Zane stops me with a squeeze, and I recall what he said about sound.

A rumble overhead makes me tremble. Have they found us? Did I mess up? Zane tugs on me, and we shimmy through the opening and into a space much wider than the tunnel, with plenty of room to spin around in. My heart does a flip-flop of happiness, though Zane still keeps us to the edge and continues on through the wider space toward a door.

A simple, wooden door.

I point to it, but don't say a word.

Zane nods, and a grin takes over his face—a lifting of his lips that brings out my own.

We made it.

His hand raises, to knock, I assume, when the door slides open a crack, and Zane yanks me to the side, into the darkness again and smothers the light, his hand over my mouth this time.

Voices fill the area where we'd just been. Male voices. Deep ones. None that I recognize.

Zane inches us back, one tiny movement at a time, until we

pass through something soft, and we're wedged between the door's frame and more rock, with me against him, my chest to his, his arms around me, holding me tight. That same panic consumes me, and I want to cry out, but I know if I do, whoever Zane's just saved us from will know we're here. The fact his grip on me has tightened and he hasn't said a word, that even his breathing hasn't regulated, suggests whatever came through the door is not good.

The men get louder, as if they've entered into the space, calling out to one another to sweep the area.

I shiver in Zane's hold, trembling from fear of being found, and knowing, clearly, that we do not want to be.

Light breaks over us, but doesn't stop, and two seconds later, someone says, "All clear," as they file back through the door, and all light, sound and movement ceases.

Under my ear, Zane's heart pounds a ferocious beat. His arms stay tight around me. I say nothing. I barely breathe, in case someone is left out there, waiting for us to appear, to be snatched up and taken away. How is it that every simple task for me turns into something unexpected? Why can't I just have a normal life like I planned?

Because normal doesn't exist anymore.

I have to remember that.

Zane's hold on me loosens a little. "I think we're okay," he whispers right at my ear. "Stay here, while I check."

I nod against him, and he slips away, easing himself from me and leaving me in pitch blackness. A second later, he's back, light shining in the space where we'd hid.

"We're clear." He holds out his hand and guides me to the anteroom—the place where we'd been waiting, expectantly, to continue on our journey. "That was really weird."

"What do you mean?"

Zane scratches at his head. "The only people who know about this passage are Delta Street members. It's considered a safe passage to get from downtown to … out."

"So, if they came down here, do you think up there, or wherever, has been compromised?"

He shakes his head. "I don't know."

"What do we do?"

"I don't know." That's a first. Ever, in my experience with Zane.

I shuffle closer to him, chills racing through my body. "What if we just go back? To my dad's place, that is. Maybe whatever he had to do is done, and it's safe again."

He doesn't say anything, just paces across and back through the small space.

I stay mute as he meanders by me a few more times. If I had to think so intently about what to do, I'd want silence, too. "Do you hear anything?" My question comes out before I can stop it.

He shakes his head again. "Comms were cut off, to prevent any accidental conversation."

"How are we going to know what to do? How are we going to—"

Zane's hand on my cheeks stop me. "It'll come back on. You trust me, right?"

Every nerve ending in my body says *yes*, while my mind screams *no*. "I'm just scared." I almost can't believe I admitted it, but maybe that's what's been holding me back from trusting him completely.

"*Do* you trust me, though, Anna?"

"Yea—"

"Good. Let's go."

On a whirl, I follow Zane back to the door. He presses a button, and it opens, revealing an empty space just big enough for three, or four, people. In we go, he presses another button that closes the door, and without a sound, we begin our way up.

A riser.

We continue for what seems like forever, Zane holding my hand, me standing next to him, waiting, waiting, and waiting more as the riser jiggles and shimmies in a constant upward climb. All manner of possibilities fill my mind as to where we're going. Will we shoot out of a glass roof, like on the old film *Charlie and the Chocolate Factory*? Or will we plummet back to the earth once we reach our destination? If we do get where Zane's taking us, who'll be on the other side of the doors? Someone? No one? Some*thing*?

We keep going, still in silence, until all at once, we stop with a slight lurch.

"Ready?" he asks.

Why do I always have to be ready? For some reason, I nod, and Zane presses that button again, opening the doors up wide.

A dark hallway, a dark *empty* hallway, greets us in silence. Unlike beneath the surface of the earth, some light illuminates from underneath two doors on the right, two on the left, and a red emergency beacon at the far end. Zane's head swivels left and right, before he pulls me with him down the corridor, to a third door on the right, which I hadn't seen because it has no light beneath it. He lifts a flap and presses numbers onto a pad, laying his entire hand on it afterward. With an audible click, the handle releases, and with my hand still in his, we pass through.

To stairs. I groan in silence.

"Just two levels," he says, as if he heard me.

By the tenth step, my thighs burn, telling me I haven't taken enough time off exercise since Mia took me up the stairs this

morning. At the second level, though, Zane presses more buttons, places his hand on the pad again, and when the door
unlocks, he pushes it open one inch at a time, his face pressed
against the widening crack.

Releasing me, he holds up one finger and throws open the
door the rest of the way.

No one approaches.

"Come on in," he says.

The room is nothing like down below. It's open and bright
and white, but not clinical like registration. Better yet, it's a
hundred percent empty.

There's not a bit of furniture anywhere. Just an empty, open,
square room with two doors and a wall of windows.

"Where are we?" I ask, as we step inside and Zane closes the
entry behind us.

"It's one of the Delta Street safe spaces." He moves in front
of me, to another door on the left, opens and closes it, shifts
to the right, does the same and turns back to me. "All clear."

"Why are we here?"

"To let me regroup. To think." He walks over to the floor-
to-ceiling windows. "You see that tiny building over there?"

All I see is a field of buildings and roads, and everything that
makes up a city from way far up. "Which one?"

"Over there." Zane points. "Like, look right past where my
finger is pointing. Through the towers."

Even squinting doesn't help. I have no idea what he's trying
to get me to see.

His hands land square on my hips and guide me forward
and to the left, his warm cheek hitting my nape, sending a chill
down me. The tip of his finger gives me an angle to follow, and
I try hard to see what he's seeing, but I really don't, and I shake
my head, mostly because I'm not really sure what to say with

him pressing up against me. I also don't want him to leave.

His chin presses into my shoulder. "Don't worry. That's where we need to go, and I'll get you there."

"Where is there, though?" I don't pull myself away, just stay put and stare out the glass.

"It's the U.S., Anna."

Surprise has me spinning. "What?" My hands go to his chest. "The U.S.? But I just thought ..." I don't know what I thought. I don't really want to even think.

I just want to stay right here and not move.

A light in the corner of the room blinks, and as a small tweet fills the air, Zane goes rigid.

"What?" I ask in a whisper.

"Someone's coming." He drags me over to the left door, which he opens, and shoves us both inside.

The room contains nothing more than sink, mirror and closed commode, and really only has room for one person, not two.

Zane holds the door open a crack as silence fills the room again. He says nothing. I keep quiet, my calves pressed up against the ceramic rim. I would sit, but fear if I do, I'll want to stay there and never move.

Time ticks by, how long, I don't know. I just keep breathing, as silently as I can, worry, fear and frustration all mixed together. Thoughts run through again about registration and had I stayed, but even I'm tired of thinking about the what ifs. 'What if' never got anyone anywhere. Or is it that 'What if ...' did get people somewhere and 'What was ...' didn't? I don't know anymore and just want to get somewhere I don't have to leave.

A creak comes from the outer door, and my body tenses. Zane hasn't relaxed—not one bit.

When he does, and he opens the door wide, and I fall forward, left with nothing to support me since my hands were on his back. Thankfully, he whirls and catches me, a wide smile on his face. "Sorry about that."

As he rights me, I glance out through the open door. "June!" Following Zane, I race toward June and wrap my good arm around him, squeezing him in a hug.

He pats my back and laughs into my shoulder. "Now, that was a nice greeting."

Pulling away and hiding my sure-to-be-red face for a moment, I say, "I was worried."

"You and me both." He rolls on past us, toward the windows, which he faces for a moment before spinning back. "You guys picked this as a safe space? Two stories above the riser." Head shaking commences.

Zane slaps his palm to his forehead. "How'd you get up?"

"One step at a time, man. One step at a time." Curling his arm, June shows off a bulging bicep muscle. "Told you I could handle anything."

"How'd you know to come here?" I ask.

"Marlena and Lucie suggested it as a first stop."

"Why weren't you here before us?" I ask.

He rolls closer to where Zane and I stand in the middle of the empty room. "They nearly caught us as we left the Delta Street building. The twins went on when I told them to go. They didn't want to leave me, but I—" He shrugs. "I figured it would be better if I met up with you, if you made it. So they said to start with this building, and I positioned myself near the riser waiting to feel it engage. But the vibrations, as they came up the first and second times, were too heavy for just you two, so I waited longer. I also noticed that it went up floor by floor. Did that a few times and then went silent." He inches himself in closer. "And then it came up again and went straight up. All the way to the top, non-stop, so I took a chance and followed."

"And here we are." Zane reaches out a hand, and June shakes it. "Glad you made it, man. We almost got caught underground."

"Do you know what happened with Mia and Cam?" I ask.

June shakes his head. "They stayed, right?"

Zane says, "Yes."

I don't even want to think about what might happen if they get caught with Dad, or what has happened to Dad. A shiver runs through me, and I force myself to still.

"Comms are down," June says. "And right after I got my own devices, too."

"Yeah, mine, too." Zane presses on his ear. "I thought it would be temporary, but I'm hearing nothing, still."

"What's that mean? If no one can communicate?" I ask.

June and Zane face one another, and for a moment, their silent standoff sends a wave of worry through me, until it just ticks me off.

"Someone just tell me."

Both of them turn to me, June's lips curving up. "If comms are down, there are just a few reasons why that could be. First, it's been shut off as a precaution. Second, it's been compromised."

"Third," Zane interrupts. "The raid in the A.U. is even bigger than we thought, and everything on the grid has been shut off to prevent exposure."

"That wouldn't surprise me." June shakes the tablet he's had with him since our adventure began. "I can't get any comms on this to the A.U., to Delta Street, to the U.S. ... anything, and I have my own power source and private network for it."

"So, they *are* shutting things down." Zane taps his chin.

"Why?" I ask. "Who?"

"To weed out the rioters. If they can't talk to each other, they can't collaborate, except in small batches," Zane adds.

June taps his chin. "Or to circumvent any possible coup. To find traitors. To enslave the population, by getting them to stop what's coming before it well and truly hits."

"Huh?" I can't help myself.

Zane faces June. "That's probably why they've gone after the top-level candidates." He spins to me. "Why they came after your dad. They suspect and need to deal with them first. Which also means my Uncle." Zane taps on his ear a few times. "I wish I could hear what's going on!"

Me, too.

He starts pacing again. "That was step one when the A.U. and the U.S. split, too. They took down the top-level administration. Then they built the wall to prevent us and *them* from communicating. Since the wall isn't going to stop anyone this time, step two is to systematically shut down services, until the people are so broken, they'll give in to anything. You want food? Stop rioting. You want clothes? No more protests. It's happened before in poorer districts. Districts that are the poorest today, actually."

"Really?" I ask. "They do that? That's just ... cruel."

June nods. "No history book will confirm it, of course, because *our* history is flawless to the minds of an unquestioning population. But it happened. On a much smaller scale, and it worked."

Zane points toward June. "What he said. Now they're just taking it up a notch. Covering the entire district, probably the entire zone, or even the country. We knew the possibility was there."

The two guys look to each other again, and a moment later,

Zane comes to me. "The country is going to fall, Anna, and if we have any chance of a life worth living, of the freedom your dad fought for on the inside, of not being poisoned by our own leaders—"

By my own family.

"—we have to get over the border wall. Our direct opportunity is gone—the planned mission, which was actually organized with our U.S. Delta Street operatives, is over. Now it's flight or fight on an individual basis, and I don't think I have fifty years in me to try and fix things here. Not right now."

"So that means flight," June says and holds out his hand toward Zane. "I'm in."

Zane takes it and turns to me. "Anna? You in?"

I thought I already agreed when my dad told me to go, so I guess I have no choice. Do I?

He reaches for me and runs a hand down my cheek. "Anyone that's caught trying to leave when the country goes into a nanny state is subject to incarceration, and safety and security is actually allowed to shoot on the spot."

I glance toward each of them in turn. "You're lying. You're trying to scare me into going." Not like I have a choice.

He gets closer. "I promise I'm not."

"But my mom ... and Mia ..."

Zane slides his hands down my biceps, my left one singing the song of not having healed fully yet. "For right now, we have to think only of us. You. Me. June. Just us. Us against our own world. Your sister told me you were tough, but I didn't see it before. I do now."

June rolls to the windows, facing out.

"What's that mean?" I ask. "That I had to prove to you who I am? What I can do?"

"Yes." His eyes go wide. "No! That's not what I meant." He

waves a hand. "I didn't trust me to know how to trust you, to trust us getting anywhere." He palms his forehead.

"Huh?" June and I both say at the same time.

I bust out laughing. Zane has never, in the time I've known him, been unable to formulate a complete, absolute and perfect sentence.

"I just . . . I needed to know how much you could deal with, before I asked you for the ultimate sacrifice."

"That would be death, Zane. Not a trip to the U.S.."

He and June share a glance.

"Are you seriously trying to tell me I could die?" I poke him in the chest, wanting to know more. "Answer me."

"I told you they have authority to shoot. And it means to the death. If we make it to the wall and get past, we're home free. If we don't, because of the way the A.U. is operated right now, then yes, we could die."

I don't know what to say. Except I do. I turn to Zane and look him straight in the eyes. "You asked me if I trust you, so now I want to answer you. Truthfully." Stepping to him, keeping my gaze on him, I say. "Can you get us out of here? Can you get the *three* of us to the U.S. without us dying?"

His face remains fixed, a storm brewing in his eyes. "I don't—I don't know."

Twice now, he hasn't been that stone wall of knowing everything. For that, a bit of my heart breaks, and at the same time my faith in him builds. I hold out my hand and wave June over. He smiles and rolls up, placing his hand over mine. Gaze locked on Zane's, I say, "Take us to the U.S.. Take us to freedom."

With a nod, Zane's hand drops to mine and June's.

20

Standing in the safe space room, staring out the giant window, I can't help but wonder at the quiet below. No one has broken out into fights. People aren't running through the streets, set on vengeance and violence. They aren't doing any of what I thought would be happening by now. It's like I'm waiting for it. Waiting for the shoe to drop, as my mom says. For the moment when what Zane and June predicted will come true.

Their mumbles grow louder behind me, and turning from the window, I walk over to the only two people I can communicate with in this world. My two newest, and only, friends.

Dropping to the floor, since there isn't a lick of furniture in the place, as June likes to say, I look up at him in his medical cart. He smiles at me before readjusting his focus to the tablet he and Zane have been staring at for hours. They've been searching for the fastest way to the border. Fastest way to one particular spot on the border line, I should say—one only Delta Street knows about, apparently.

The sun is still up, and according to Zane, it would be best for us to travel at night. To make sure no one sees us. Listening to Zane and June, who could talk for hours and hours, I think, has lulled me into an old habit of just sitting and not moving. Cam used to hate that I could do that, but neither Zane nor

June have mentioned my stillness.

Over their voices, my stomach grumbles, and both their heads pop up.

"Sorry. Didn't mean to interrupt." Breakfast, has, of course, long since been over with.

"We should eat," Zane says. For a guy who's hungry all the time, the six or more hours it's been since we arrived seems like a long time to go between meals. His focus must have really been on whatever he and June have been studying.

"This place is empty, right?" June asks. "Like, no secret rooms, or hidden doors, or concealed food?"

Zane nods. "Yeah."

"For a safe place, it seems kinda anti-safe without any edibles." I can't believe I said that.

"It wasn't expected to be used." Zane stands and stretches out his arms, the bottom of his T-shirt riding up and showing off a well-toned abs and hipbones.

Heat creeps into my cheeks, forcing me to look away. "So, what do we do?" I pick at the soft flooring.

Zane cracks a few joints, which sends a ripple of ick through me. "Well, we have two options. One—" He moves over toward the window. "—we beg from someone in this building. Two: We sneak out when it gets a little darker and head to a Delta Street supported location, which will take credits off the system so we can stay off the grid. Or, three: we eat the carpet and walls." He spins until he faces me, a broad smile across his face. "Which would *you* prefer?"

"What's the closest Delta Street option?" I ask, hoping he's joking about the flooring as food. That's not possible, right?

June taps his tablet for a minute. "There's a pizza place about eight blocks from here."

Mmm. Pizza.

"Eight blocks isn't bad." At least, I don't think it is.

"Yeah, but you have no coats. Again," June says.

Why do I keep forgetting that? Oh, yeah, because when I'm in a warm room, I don't need one.

"I'll survive," I say, as Zane does the same. Meeting his gaze, we both smile.

June whips his jacket from the back of his medical cart. "This is what planning ahead does." He winks at me.

"So, eight blocks, pizza, we work off the debt, and then what? Back here?" I ask.

Zane shakes his head. "I think we should start out toward the next stop."

"Which is where?"

He points to June.

"At the edge of the city, there's another safe place. It's a walk though. About five miles."

A chill races through me. A walk that long without a coat is not going to be fun.

"Maybe we'll just borrow a transpo," Zane says, adding, "And who says we're going to work off the debt? This is a Delta Street supported loc—"

Standing, I firm my feet to the ground and stare at him. "I will not eat at someone's establishment without a credit to my name and not repay them their kindness, no matter who they are."

June holds up both palms. "I'm not going against that," he says.

"Anna." Zane steps toward me.

"Don't *Anna* me. I hear that tone. It's the *you don't get it* tone that you use all the time when I don't just agree with you. Is that how you paid at the pathway side farmhouse where we had breakfast the other day?"

Zane stands still, hands in his pockets. "We support each other, so we can get through this mess." He waves his hand at me like that's supposed to answer the question. "I've already told you this isn't a credits thing. No one's going to charge you for food, or clothes, or anything."

Not backing down, I say, "You said we got into this mess by giving away too much for free. For not being required to work, or prove our need. So, did you lie to me?" Fury and disappointment run through me. "Did you pay those people before?"

He closes his eyes a moment, and when he lifts them again, I see clarity. "You're right. You're totally right. We'll go. We'll explain, and we'll ... clean dishes."

"Or sweep," June says.

I cross my arms over my chest. "Or whatever they want us to do."

Zane nods. "And yes, I paid the bill before because I had credits. Because I'd planned ahead. Because I'd been prepared and not rushed." Another head bob comes my way as he slides his hands out of his pockets. "This time, I have nothing but the non-working comms unit in my ear. So we'll do whatever you think is right."

⌐═╼╾═⌐

"There's a commode in the back that needs a scrub," Mr. Timbre says, as he pushes an eighteen-inch pizza onto the table in front of us and checks the comms unit on his wrist for the fourth time since we've entered. "Can't get anyone else to do it, not even those who work for me." He thumbs over his shoulder in the direction of the kitchen. "And last time I went in there, I couldn't deal with it, either, on account of my back."

"I'll handle the restroom, sir," I say. "Zane and June will clean the dinner dishes."

"That's awfully kind of you." He scratches at his temple, glancing left toward a wall of black and white imagegraphs. "Never had anyone offer that. Not even a single ... *Delta Street* ..." He whispers the name. "... member. Not ever." Straightening, he says, "Now, enjoy that pie, and let me know if you'd like anything else."

Zane and June dig in before I can even get my hand near one piece of crust. By the time I've eaten my first, they're both finished with a second, heading to a third. None of us has spoken since the food arrived, clearly in need of sustenance.

There are a few other people in the place, but not nearly enough to sustain a business, especially at the dinner hour, though, we're at least an hour early. The walk here had been uneventful—a first in the time I've known Zane.

That fact also leads me to believe that what they suggested about the pending problems may not be as true as they think. Maybe, in the past, our people have reacted poorly to the news of shortages, or changes in direction, but we're more refined now. We know better, and everything will be just fine.

Maybe if we go a little slower than Zane thinks we should, we can just let this ride out, stay in the safe place on the edge of town, and once we get notice, we can go home. Not to the U.S..

Of course, now I wish I had a comms unit, too, so I would know when the right answer reaches us.

"Last piece. You or me?" Zane asks.

I lift my head, having been lost in my own thoughts. "You can split it."

"Wait." June holds a hand out over the slice. "How many pieces have you had, Anna?"

I shrug. "Enough."

Zane stares at me, his eyes narrowing. "How many, Anna?"

"Why does it matter? I'll be fine. You guys nee—"

"Eat it," they both say.

My eyes widen. "Geez. Okay." Slipping piece number two to my plate, I take a bite.

"Now," Zane clasps his hands and lays them on the table. "We're going to take no more than one hour each to help here, because that's over and above the minimum wage to cover the fees for one pizza and some drinks."

That's fair, so I don't argue but continue to savor the melty cheese.

"I'll bus tables because I can get around—" Zane's head whips toward June. "I mean, I can get around easier in between everything. Not that you can't, or —"

"It's okay." June waves Zane on.

Zane gives a deep exhale of breath. "And maybe you can work the dishwasher in the kitchen?" He points to June. "And you offered to take the bathroom, which I still can't believe."

Because you've lived a life of privilege.

"So, we'll handle those three things and call it even. Then it should be dark enough to start out toward the edge of the city and keep our cover."

Finishing chewing, I wave a hand. "Even in the dark, aren't the cameras going to pick us up? And aren't they monitored?" *And didn't we just walk through them on the way here?*

Zane nods. "Yes, but the cameras all work a certain way. When we start down one way, we'll time their movement left and right. They always sweep on a specific schedule." He scoots up closer. "Did you notice, on our walk here, that every two blocks, I stopped for about thirty seconds?"

"I did," June says. "I was wondering about that, but just figured it was transpo traffic, not that there was much."

I'd noticed, too, but didn't think anything of it. If I get what he's saying though, this means he really does know how to get around the cameras. Just like he said.

"So," Zane starts again, "we just need to time our movement, to avoid the cameras. It won't mean a whole lot if we're caught on one, or two. We're just three people moving about the city like everyone else."

"But ... if they trace our entire path, they'll know where we're going." June palms the table. "Right?"

Zane points a finger at our new friend. "Exactly. So we stay above ground and figure out the path with the least number of spotters, and go from there."

"How far is it, exactly, to the border, where you want to go?" I wipe my lips, once I've finished the slice.

Zane's head bobbles left and right. "Depends on how many alternative routes we have to take, and if we can get some sort of transpo."

"Yeah, but how long?" I hold my napkin on my lap under the table. "Distance, I mean."

"Couple hundred miles."

I jerk back. "What? How did you expect me to see a building a couple hundred miles out from where we were before?" Not just that, but how are we going to get there on foot?

He shrugs one shoulder. "I guess I can picture it in my mind's eye."

"How? If you've never—" My gasp comes out before I can stop it. "You've been there before. This isn't your first trip." Did he lie to me again? No, he never said he hadn't been there. He just said he would be going.

The headshake confirms my suspicions. "Yes, I've been there. My sisters live there, remember?"

I'd forgotten that.

Which also means, if he goes, he's really going to stay. I'd want to stick with my family, too. Still do.

June does a silly bow toward Zane. "I'm humbled to be in your presence, if you went *and* came back."

Zane's shoulders fall a little. "It's not like I had a choice. My uncle is here. He had custody of me because of my parent's deaths, and he wanted me to be here with a father-figure, not that he's been around, at all."

My heart falls for Zane just a little. His uncle and my dad— absentee parents of the century. Yet, my dad came back. Why didn't Zane's uncle?

"Where's your place, Zane? You never did say. I mean, we went to Mia's and to my dad's, but you never showed me yours."

Only his eyes lift up toward me. "The next safe place is mine."

Oh.

Even more reason to get there. To give him a place where he can let go, just a little.

I stand and lift the pizza pan. "Then, let's get these chores done so we can start walking."

Zane's eyes brighten, as June rolls backward from his spot at the table. "Dishes it is." June reaches out and takes the pan from me. "I think you drew the gross straw."

"Straw?" I ask.

"It's a game ... I'll explain it some other time." He maneuvers out and back toward where Mr. Timbre waits with a huge smile on his face.

I pass Zane, but he grabs my wrist before I can get far. As I turn back to him, our gazes meet, but he doesn't say anything for a moment. Offering a smile, I slip free, and continue to the back of the space, prepared to pay for the two slices of pizza I ate.

The restroom isn't dirty; the commodes only needed a little scrub. Why anyone would complain it's a job they can't do, I don't know—unless they think they're better than everyone and don't use the same facilities as everyone else. Which they do. We all do.

Ripping off the apron Mr. Timbre gave me to protect my clothes, I run the water one last time into the sink, to get the bubbles to dissipate, and stare at myself in the mirror.

Once again, the day's activities have blown my hair every which way, but at least I didn't sleep, so the strands have fallen back into the right place. Mostly. Adjusting my shirt and fixing my jeans, I realize just how much Marlena and Lucie have a magical ability to pick out clothes for me. For the second time, they've given me something I truly love. Glancing over my shoulder, as if someone would come in the door, I ease the collar off my shoulder and turn sideways to peek at the tattoo Marlena put there.

The colors have grown more vivid over time. She'd said they would as they blend more with my own skin. What once exhibited a paleness is now rich and bold—the butterfly coming alive on my shoulder blade.

"Anna—"

As the door swishes open, I spin and jerk my shirt up.

Zane stands there, head cocked a little. "What were you looking at?"

"What do you mean?" I tug at the hem of my shirt, trying to even it out on my shoulders.

He moves to me with just one giant step. "Are you hurt?" His hands go to my arms.

I shake my head.

"But you were looking at something."

Flames lick at my cheeks. "Yes, but it's nothing, and no, I'm not hurt."

"You're sure?"

I nod, shrug my shirt up a little more, and grab the apron. "I'm done in here. And thanks for knocking." Walking around him, I hike up the side a little more.

Outside the restroom, June sits in his chair, talking to Mr. Timbre. As I come around, his gaze meets mine. "We're all finished."

Mr. Timbre turns and holds out his hands, coming at me. He manages to get them around me before I can sneak away, a light beeping sound coming from behind me. "You are so helpful. I want to thank you once more." Letting go, he opens a closet and withdraws two coats that are old and battered but totally wearable and probably ridiculously warm. "I know you're on a mission, so you must stay warm, or risk catching cold." He tosses one behind me toward Zane. "Here. Wear it." Holding it out to me, I can't help but slip my arms inside, though after having cleaned the entire restroom, the heat is way too much.

I hold it closed against me, anyway. "Thank you, but—"

"No buts. You did not even eat half of what they ate, and you did double the work, so I gave them extra, since this one said you would be angry if I offered and you did not earn it." He glances back over his shoulder, toward the door, something he's done a lot since we arrived.

I will always be grateful for what he's given us. "Thank you, Mr. Timbre."

"You are welcome. Now, I've also packed a small to-go box. This is on the house, and I will not take no for an answer." He pulls three white boxes from the counter and hands them to Zane. Probably safer that way, since he'll accept without question, and I would probably try and offer to do something, but the heat building up in the coat is getting to be too much.

Another tiny beep sounds.

Glancing down, I realize it's coming from his wrist-comm. "Now, you must go." He points toward the back, where I know there's another exit because I threw the trash bag out that way. "Right now."

The hurried exit seems a little pointless, given no one else is there, and Zane and June haven't shown any signs they've gotten word of a problem. Unless he's waiting for someone.

Mr. Timbre flips off the light to the hallway we're in, cloaking us in darkness.

I turn and step forward as the front door dings—the same sound it made only a few times while we ate, and only a few times while we cleaned. Glancing back shows a series of men in black jackets filing in, one after the other.

"Shoo," Mr. Timbre says, pushing me. "Do not pass in front of the building."

Zane grabs my hands and tugs, while June pushes me from the back, and Mr. Timbre walks away from us, saying, "Mr. Osso, it is so good to see you."

I freeze. Osso? *The* Osso? The one who started all the problems and is at the helm of this sinking ship we call the A.U.? My family? He's at a little pizza place on the outskirts of town? *Today?*

I whirl back, because I just have to see, but Zane all but drags me into the darkness outside.

Yanking myself free, I say, "I'm going back in there."

"Like hell you are." Zane paces the small space between the building we were in and another.

Light from a road lamp fills the space, enough so I can see

Zane and June and their expressions. June's is serious as he faces his tablet again. Zane is furious.

"He knew. He knew that man was coming here, and he let us stay." Zane's pacing has grown faster. "And you—" He spins and points a finger at me. "You wanted us to clean."

I back up a step, eyes wide. "Don't you go there, Zane Warren. Don't you dare. It's you who put us in this position of having to run from the very people inside that building. It's you who thinks our society is falling apart, and yet doesn't feel the need to pay people when they do a service for us. It's you who listens to whatever's in your ear, instead of looking at the world through the two eyes that you have. Open them, Zane!"

21

The walk to Zane's place is done without an word between the three of us. Zane leads, carrying the boxes, gesturing only with his hands. I'm in the middle, as if he doesn't trust me to stay with them, and June's rolling behind, tapping on the tablet, saying nothing.

For over five miles, we walk that way, stopping every three lights for a period of sixty seconds, while Zane checks his wrist unit—on which only the time works.

The entire time, no one exits the buildings we pass. No one enters any, either. No trams, or transpos, pass on the pathway. For as large as the city is here, in District Eleven, I can't believe no one is out.

As we stop at a building, Zane lifts a panel and presses numbers.

"Wait!" June says, breaking the unbearable quiet.

Zane's hand hovers over the enter button, but doesn't depress it.

"It's on lockdown. We're in twenty-four hour lockdown."

I whirl to him. "What does that mean?"

June palms his forehead. "It means if Zane presses *Enter* to get us into this building, the A.U. is going to know someone entered this place, at this time, on this day. Not exited, but entered, which means we weren't in place at the time of the lockdown, and thus, we either have no place, or we're just the people the A.U. is looking for."

"They're searching for traitors by who goes in and who goes out of their buildings?"

June nods. "It took me a while to figure out why there wasn't anyone out. The lockdown came right before Osso walked into Mr. Timbre's pizza place. We wouldn't have heard it because we don't have comms, and our ears aren't working."

"And Mr. Timbre doesn't have a screen unit in his restaurant." *And I kept us there longer than I should have. And then I yelled at Zane.* Guilt slices through me. "He knew they were coming. He kept looking at his wrist unit, and he pushed us out really fast." Trying to help? Yes, trying to help. That, I can't question.

June points to me. "At that moment, they shut everyone in, or out. If you're out, and you go in, they will come looking. If you're out, and you know there's a lockdown, you have to go to the main commerce center for review and overnight stay." He turns to Zane. "What are we going to do?"

Zane's lips curve as he presses the Enter button, anyway.

June and I gasp.

"What have you done?" I can't believe it.

Pulling open the door, Zane waves us both in. "You're forgetting that this is a Delta Street building, and there are some things not maintained, or at least bypassed, by the A.U. security. One of those is entry and exist. Well, not completely, but the A.U. won't know we came in *today*."

I follow June inside. "And you knew that the whole time, didn't you?" My tone comes out harsh, but I probably deserved his omission for yelling at him before.

Zane nods. "Yes." As he pulls the door shut and presses buttons, the locking mechanism resets, and a soft green light reflects from the inside. "We're up on the tenth floor, so follow me."

"What about your uncle?" I ask. "Will he be here, like my dad was at his place?"

The answer comes in a shrug. "If he is here, that's fine. If not, fine, too. Just come with me."

We both do, me slipping off the hot coat as we round a corner and come to a set of risers. One is already open, and Zane marches straight to it. June and I follow. Again.

All three of us face the doors, no silliness like before in my dad's place when Zane and I rode up. The ten-flight ride, like our walk, is also taken without words.

Mia used to give me the silent treatment when we were kids. I, though, hold the world record in silent, or so Cam has told me. She even made a little plaque for me on an old comms unit that I had. 'World's Best Quiet Girl', it read.

At a small ding, Zane leads us onto a floor that reminds me eerily of my dad's space, and into living quarters that I'd swear are an exact replica of my dad's, though the decor is different, with bolder colors like reds and blues on the walls, instead of the pale neutrals of my dad's. A swirly accent rug lays between two black divans. At my dad's, what I considered fancy actually makes me think he didn't plan to stay. Everything had a 'I live here' quality, but not a 'this is my home' type of vibe.

Zane's place is a home—as much of one as Mom made in our little ramshackle place.

"Wow," June says from behind me. "This space is seriously tricked out."

"My uncle's idea. Everything in here is his, really." Zane flops onto the left divan, throwing his coat onto the other side, where someone could have sat. He drops the three boxes on the short table between the two pieces of furniture.

June rolls up to the edge of the table between the two divans. "Seems no one is, or has been, here in a while." He wipes a finger across the table.

"Maybe not to tidy, but I can guarantee there's food in the kitchen." Zane thumbs toward the same place that my dad's kitchen would be. "Or we could eat this." He points to the boxes.

I take a seat opposite Zane, holding the coat in my arms, squished against my knees.

"I could use a restroom," June says.

"Same place as in Mr. Keating's."

His confirmation that the two are laid out identically makes me think all buildings might be. They'd be easier and faster to put together that way, at least.

June rolls away, leaving Zane and me in a room filled with nothing but unknowns. Neither of us faces each other. Neither of us meets the others' gaze.

"I'm sorry." I'm the one to break the oppressive silence.

Zane's head whips my way, his brow creased. "For what?"

"For ... yelling at you." It comes out a whisper, though it is true. I am sorry.

A grin blooms on his face. "You think I'm mad at you?"

"Well, um ... yeah."

Zane grabs his coat and tosses it over the far arm of the divan. "Come here. Please." His added 'please' is genuine, so I do as he asks.

He faces me, one knee on the divan, elbow on the top of the back, head resting against his palm. The other hand he holds out, and I place mine against it, mirroring his position. On a deep sigh, he said, "I'm not mad at you. I'm mad at me."

"Oh."

"See, normally, I know everything." His grin grows wide.

"And ... I have to admit ... I don't much like being wrong."

"But you weren't!" I say too fast. "We missed the lockdown warn—"

"No, we didn't. *I* did. I was seriously shocked to see an Osso there, at a Delta Street supporter's business, and it reminded me that you're technically an Osso, and that June's Grandma even recognized that. And you're right that I need to look at the forest and the trees, you know, just beyond stuff." He shrugs. "But who likes being told that? Reminded that one of our fundamental missions in this country is to not be like our own officials. And I was doing exactly ... and I mean *exactly* what Osso is doing, just on a smaller scale." He heaves a breath. "And that freaks me out. It sucks that you saw through it so well." His hand squeezes mine. "But it also amazes me, because you saw it before me. So really, I want to thank you for having your momentary breakdown, or whatever you want to call it. Because you did ... you opened my eyes."

A yawn builds in my throat, and I turn and use my shoulder to cover my open mouth.

"And you're exhausted," he says. "Come on. You can sleep in my room."

<hr/>

"Higher, Daddy, higher!"

The swing lets me fly, soaring into the air, my feet rising higher and higher, as I try my best to touch the clouds.

"Higher, Daddy!"

I giggle as pressure from behind propels me forward, upward, closer to my goal, to the ceiling of white fluffiness.

"Higher!"

Back and forth I go, until the ropes holding my swing wiggle, and I grip them, hoping I won't fall off, that they'll hold me, and that I won't go all the way over.

As if he can read my fear, big hands grip me from behind and slow my descent. "That was a little too high, I think." Dad's deep voice booms through the warm, humid summer air.

I scramble out of the seat and into his arms until wrapped in his embrace and the safety of being understood.

◦═╾═◦

My eyes pop open to a dark, warm room. I'm not swinging. I'm in bed. *Just a dream.* A dream I've had ever since my dad left so long ago.

Recognizing that I'm not with my dad, not in his place, but that I'm not alone, I breathe a sigh and let my lids drift closed again.

◦═╾═◦

I climb onto the swing.

"Higher, Daddy!"

He pushes me once, and my little legs kick out.

"Go higher. Let Mommy see!"

"Erianna, come inside now." My mother's sing-songy voice calls for me, but I don't stop swinging.

"Higher!"

"Oh, Eri, look at you. Mia's on her way. Come down now."

"Higher!" My legs reach past the top, into the blue sky.

Mia appears from nowhere and shakes a finger in front of Mom's face. Without a word, she storms out the door, slamming it against the frame.

I reach out, the swing falling away from me, yelling, "Mia! Come back! Come back!"

"No! Eri! Don't let go!"

As I grab the ropes, they wiggle within my grip, shaking as

if they're about to break loose from the structure.

"Press the buttons and hang on!"

Around me, I search for buttons, but there aren't any.

"Press the buttons, or you'll fall!"

Nowhere are there buttons. My swing keeps going higher and higher, my feet reaching up to the blue sky—to a sky that turns purple as I get closer to it, red as I go backward, purple as I go up, and red again as I return to the ground.

"Push me higher, Daddy! I want to go higher."

Up and up and up I go, until the swing is nearly even with the top of the frame, and the sky changes to that pretty purply-blue. I want it to stay that color, to not turn red, to not look like it's bleeding.

"Higher! Higher!"

No, don't go higher, I try to tell myself. *You need to be safe. You need to do what Dad told you to do.*

"Higher! Higher!"

Up. Up. Up. The sky's color deepens the closer I get to it.

"No! No! No! Not higher. You're going to fall! I'm going to fall!"

My little self keeps asking for more and going, going, up and up.

The swing arcs.

It's going to go all the way around.

I'll fall out, and the sky will turn red, and people will die. I will die.

"Higher, higher, higher, daddy!"

No one pushes me, yet the swing keeps going.

"Higher, higher!"

No, not higher!

"Anna."

Purple. Red. Purple. Red.

Sky. Ground. Sky Ground.

"Let go, Anna."

Zane's face appears as I go up. Dad's, as I fall back down. June. Mia. Mom. Cam. Zane. Dad. Back and forth, back and forth, and I can't stop any of it.

Screaming, I let go and grab my head, squeezing my eyes shut to make the swinging stop, and tumble into nothingness.

"Help!"

"Anna, I got you."

⌐══╾═○

Light streams in through uncovered windows—ones I'd have sworn were set for night privacy before I crawled into Zane's bed.

"Morning." Zane's voice flows from across the room.

I blink and blink, only to realize he's sitting in a chair across the room.

Hugging the blanket tight, not that I'm naked, or anything, I ask, "What are you doing in here?"

"You had some bad dreams. Or I figured they were bad."

I hate those dreams. The whole feet to the sky thing makes my stomach queasy just to think about. Pressing my fingertips to my temple, I force the embarrassment of someone else knowing about my dream away. "How . . . how did you know?" A shiver races through me.

"You were calling out *higher!* and *don't let me fall.*"

Oh, Oz. Heat fills my cheeks. In the last week, those dreams have come any time I've managed to really fall asleep. They always happen the same way, with some of the same scenes.

"The first time I came in, you were sound asleep. I left, got halfway comfortable—as much as I could on the divan, since I gave June my uncle's room, and you did it again. Came back, and you were quiet. Decided I'd just sit here, and ended up falling asleep."

I wish I didn't remember my dreams. Especially the one where I swing with my dad, asking him to push me higher until I think the swing is going to flip all the way over the bar at the top. That's usually when I wake up—right as the seat, and my entire body, is about to fall off.

Zane shakes the blanket that's around him, and with a quick throw of his head right and left, the bones in his neck crack.

I cringe. "Eww, don't do that!"

"Going to have a crick in my neck for a while, I think." He stretches to each side, a smirk mixing in with his grin, and shifts so he's sitting with his elbows on his knees, turning his head with his hands.

"Come up here," I say, sitting up and running my hand along the bed's surface. I owe him for everything he's done to help me.

His head pops up. "What?"

The temperature in my cheeks rises again. "Uh ... my mom says I give really good shoulder rubs. I can massage your neck."

"Really?"

I almost regret suggesting it but force myself to nod.

He slips from the chair and climbs up, facing me.

"Turn around." I motion with my finger, like he can't figure out what I want him to do by what I've just said, which is, of course, stupid and sends flames back to my cheeks again.

Zane does as I ask, luckily without further commentary. Leaning forward, I lay may hands on his shoulders, slide them up to his neck, and knead.

Zane hums a sound that has to be happiness.

"Good?"

A deep sigh follows.

I continue massaging the stress and kinks out of his muscles for a few minutes, the tips of his dark hair tickling the back of my hands.

The muscles in his upper shoulders tighten. He leans his head to the left, stretching as I rub there. Out of nowhere, he breaks free of my hands and spins toward me. His eyes, so dark, yet with speckles of light, bore into me. My heart pounds in my chest, and my palms go damp as he stays silent.

"Did that help?" I ask when he hasn't said anything for an unusually long time.

"Yeah." His voice is breathy. "It did."

He's still and silent for a long time, his eyes dipping down and coming back up to meet my gaze repeatedly.

"Dibs on the shower," June says, rolling by

It breaks the stare-down Zane and I had going, and Zane slips from the bed. "I'll make breakfast."

Left alone, I curl the blankets within my fists, trying to understand just what happened between us.

Awkward doesn't begin to describe what's running through me, as I join Zane in his kitchen. The space is painted a bright, sunny yellow, with the sun itself streaming through the glass. Like the living area, with the exception of the color and furnishings, it's an exact match to my dad's place.

Zane stands at the stove, mixing and stirring while something sizzles, sending whiffs of good smells into the air. "Just sit at the counter," he says, his back to me.

Whatever he's preparing has my stomach in knots, but in a good way—in anticipation of being able to indulge. I clasp my hands on the black and white surface of the counter. "What are you making?"

"Just a casserole. A mix of stuff that was in the ice box. We actually don't have much, I guess because my Uncle hasn't been here."

I nod though he won't see it. "How long did you live here?"

He stirs for a moment then says, "Three years. I went with my sister initially, like the first month after my parents died, but as I said, my uncle wanted me here with him."

Yet, if today is anything like the past three years, his uncle didn't spend much time with him. "What educenter did you go to?"

He shakes his head. "I did all my coursework on my own."

"What? How?" I'm sure, if my mom knew we could do that, she would have kept me off the grid even more.

Zane ladles something onto a plate and turns to me, sliding it onto the counter. There's a mix of greens, reds, yellows, chunks of something, and a heavenly smell that tickles my nose. "When your uncle is a high-ranking guy, you get the benefit of choice." He spins back around and dishes more out onto another plate, before coming back and sitting at the counter with me. "That's probably why I know so much useless information. My instructors didn't really teach. They just told me what I had to read, and after I read that and got bored, I read more and more of whatever I could find. Stuff your dad gave my parents, stuff my uncle left out on his desk. That kind of thing."

We eat in silence for a moment. He points his fork my way. "You know, now that I think about it, I don't know why my uncle brought me back. I mean, he left me here by myself most of the time. And yeah, I'm grateful for the space, and all, but my parents were really the ones involved with Delta Street. My uncle only joined in once they died." His voice grows raw with emotion, and he scoops up more of his breakfast as if for distraction.

"I'm really sorry about your parents."

His response is a repeated nod.

"What's cookin'?" June asks, joining us. "Actually, never mind. Doesn't matter what it is because it smells like food."

"Dig in." Zane pushes vegetables around his plate.

As June rolls over to the sleek, round, glass table, the sun truly takes over the sky through the floor-to-ceiling windows. I jerk my head to Zane, and we shift from the counter to the table, to sit with June.

On the pathway below and beyond the window, there's no

sign of security forces—or anything actually. No one walks outside, though, and no transpos travel. The only moving things are the birds, which swoop down every so often toward the ground, as if by having no traffic, they're free to take over every open space possible.

"So ..." June starts, bringing my attention back from outside. "... how do we get from here to over there, without getting caught in a world where nothing is moving. It's going to be pretty obvious we're not doing what *they* want us to do."

"Have you found out anything new through your tablet?" I ask.

"Not much." June extracts it from the bag at the back of his chair and lays it on the table. "The twenty-four-hour curfew ends tonight at six, but they could implement another one that starts at the same time."

So, we'd still be as obvious as the birds flying around the city below us until dark. "Are there any tunnels like at my dad's place?" I ask.

Zane shakes his head, his focus still on his plate.

"Does that mean that, unless people and transpos are allowed back out, we're going to literally be stuck here?"

He shrugs.

I turn back toward the window and stare at the masses of buildings just a little shorter than ours, but with nothing obvious going on. It still amazes me that a lockdown can keep people inside. If what Zane and June said about the rioting from the other districts happened—the more rural ones—how did they make an uneasy peace happen in the city? Or is it only me who has that sense of unease running through me?

Compliance just doesn't come that easy.

Unless ... I touch my palms to the glass of the window. "Is everyone in the city drugged, Zane?"

"Probably."

Whirling back to the table, I stare at him. "How is that possible?"

He points toward the sink.

The water. Everyone needs it. No one's not going to drink it. Would something get into the system that fast, though? Within hours? Or minutes? Or do they target specific areas? Places they suspect, maybe.

This is registration all over again, but on a grander scale. It's not that my country doesn't care about its people—though, it doesn't—it's that they want complete and absolute control.

Give everyone the opportunity to think for themselves every once in a while, but take it away when convenient. Like Cam and the cleaner, though she was obviously drugged.

"They could also be engaging the tracking devices—the chips," June says.

I jerk so hard a headache takes over, and I close my eyes to will it away.

"You okay?" Zane asks.

Rubbing the back of my neck, I say, "Yes," through gritted teeth. Breathing slowly, to force the ache to subside, I stare into Zane's blue eyes. "Tracking devices? Chips? What's he talking about?"

Zane releases a deep sigh, one that tells me he's read way too much about this subject, too. "There was a period of unrest about thirty, forty years ago, but it was during that time that they started filling the water with tasteless salts meant to calm the riots. Yeah, this was in twenty ninety-five ish. But because they couldn't pump it through fast enough, they opted to add a chip, just a little chip, to the back of the brain stem, to all newborns."

My eyes open wide.

"This chip could then, when activated, trigger certain reactions. Actions that you wouldn't know you hadn't chosen, but did anyway. That continued on for about thirty years, until right before our decade, actually."

"You're telling me that people have devices embedded in their heads to stop them from doing ... stuff?" I just can't believe it. "That would have made world news! That would have been inhumane! It *is* inhumane!" I know there's not one in me, but I still reach back and rub the back of my head and neck. The headache no longer affects my skull as, instead, a creepy sensation takes over.

Zane's lips curve up a little. "When were you born, Anna?"

"In fourteen, like you."

"Thirteen for me," June says.

"Which is about the time they stopped," Zane says.

"Why?" I ask. "Why stop using them, if they were serving their purpose?" The back of my neck still tingles at the thought of having something implanted there.

"The chips started to degrade, and they started shorting out, or not working at all. Turns out they were the cause of quite a few deaths from suicides, where people couldn't figure out what was wrong with them because the chips were messing with their minds, the electrical stimuli being too much for people's hearts, or disintegrating, and parts would flow through the blood stream and cause a heart attack." He shrugs as if it's no big deal, which I can tell from the clenching of his jaw it definitely is.

June waves his tablet in the air. "If the powers-that-be activated even half of the chips, and they randomly worked, those people with them would have gone home as demanded, taken their families with them. Gotten their coworkers to abide by the law, etcetera."

"Those who didn't follow the rules would still be out there."
I glance over my shoulder and still find no one outside. *This can't be true. Mom would have had*— "My mom," I say and face Zane. "She was born when these chip things were happening. How did she—" Just voicing it has it all falling into mental place. *My grandmother.* She kept my mom out of the Osso mess. She must have known, have understood, separated my mom from it. "My dad—he—he'd have the chip, wouldn't he?"

Zane nods. "He did."

Which is another reason why my mom wouldn't have gone with him. Wouldn't have taken a chance at being back in the administration's grasp because she'd have had to fake it, no matter what, on top of her own principles. *"Someday, you'll appreciate everything I've done for you."* You have no idea, Mom, how fast that has happened.

My heart aches, knowing my grandma and mom both sacrificed their futures for me and for Mia—and what did we do with it? We both went to registration. We both broke away.

Why didn't you just tell me, Mom?

Because you never would have understood, I say back for her in my head.

She's right, too. Had Zane not done everything he's done this week, I would have been like everyone else at registration, and everyone else out here in this world—compliant to a government with complete and absolute control.

"How did all of this happen, Zane? How did we get like this? Why—"

Zane scrambles up and leaves the table. "Be right back."

I stare at June, my brow furrowed. June's face is a mirror to what I expect mine looks like to him.

Within just a few second, Zane returns. Holding a red box in his hand, he opens the top, revealing a set of white rectangles with black dots.

"What are those?" I ask.

"Dominoes."

June rubs his palms together. "I love this game."

I just sit there, waiting for an explanation.

Zane dumps the box out onto the table, making clacking sounds echo through the space. "Sorry." He starts turning over any that are showing the black dots.

June joins in until the entire area is covered in little rectangles of white.

"Pick five. Any five." Zane waves me forward. "And don't let us see the dots on the other side."

I do as he instructs. June and Zane do the same.

"June, you want to start?" Zane asks, pushing the other pieces aside.

"Sure, because I have double six, anyway, so I'd get to." He grins like a kid about to get an ice cream cone and places the piece in the center of the table.

"Now, I'll go." Zane matches a six to June's six. "Now, you match to the six or the three," he says to me.

I have a three and do exactly that, adding a four, which June butts a piece up against, and Zane follows. We repeat until June and Zane have one piece left in their hands, and I put my last down.

Both guys stare at me.

"What?"

"You sure you've never played?" Zane asks, showing his piece to June who chuckles and grins.

"So, who won?" I ask.

"You did," they both say.

I figured that, but didn't want to presumptuous and let out my grin early.

"Now, that's one way to play. That's one of the many versions of the game." Zane stands and slides all the dominoes to the pile at the end he called the boneyard. "Now, this …" He stands one up on its end and places another about a half inch from it, repeating the action all over the table.

June joins in half-way through, until the entire set of dominoes stands tall like a little army of rectangles.

"Push the last one," Zane says.

"So unfair," June mumbles, smiling.

Zane punches him in the arm, but doesn't event get a grunt in response. "Let the lady do it. Especially since it's obviously her first time."

I can see what's going to happen. They're all going to tumble. *That* is obvious.

With a small tap, I push the one on the end, the one that started the whole trail, and watch as, piece by piece, the entire line of little white rectangles, a few dozen of them, clatter to the glass and create a small spiral pattern. Aside from the noise, it's kinda cool.

"So … what does this have to do with my earlier question?" I ask, picking up the pieces with Zane and June and starting my own little trail that follows the edge of the table. "You know, the *How did all of this happen?* And *How did we get like this? How does,* or rather, what do dominoes have to do with it?"

Zane smiles at me and sets up a set of six which he makes fall with a flick of his finger. "Remember when we were in the garbage riser, and I said all this was because of the domino effect?"

"Yeah."

"All these pieces were lined up earlier, and it took you, just one person, to push them all down. Every last one of them."

"Right." *So?*

"Had you not taken that one step, nothing would have

happened."

"Unless there was an earthquake, or something to shake it," June says.

Zane laughs. "Okay, there's that. But let's say that's not part of the equation. To start the change, there had to be a trigger. No change happens without at least one person, one action, one *something* starting the process."

"Right ..." I create another line, and Zane creates a parallel one next to it.

In this run, though, he places his pieces pretty far away from each other. "On three," he says.

"Okay."

"One ..." June counts. "two ... three."

Zane and I flick the last piece, and mine go down in a heap, his much slower, each tap from the previous one not enough to make the next fall fast, and on the sixth one, it doesn't even reach the next.

"Just because they're in line doesn't mean they will comply," he says to me.

"Okay." I seem to be the queen of one word responses right now.

"If we look back, and I think I told you this before, President Roosevelt—because remember, that's what a CEO was before."

"Yeah. I know."

"He started a chain that was like yours, using what were called Executive Orders." Zane starts setting up more pieces. "He did that to get stuff done ... *his* way. It was meant to help, but it backfired. Then later, like my line, there was a break, when it looked like things would swing the other way, or stop, but then new presidents were elected, presidents who were more progressive, though the very nature of being progressive was twisted. They didn't do what a majority wanted, they did what a minority wanted—what *they* wanted. They didn't bring the country together, they tore it apart by siding with one, and only one, group. This was in the late nineteen hundreds. And it went faster through the early two thousands ..." Zane stands up more dominoes really close to each other. "... and faster and faster until ..." He flicks the first one really hard, it bangs into the next, and they all fall. "... catastrophic failure ... and the U.S. split into two."

"So, you see, Anna," June says taking my attention, "dominoes is a very, *very* future-ruining game and should never be played by amateurs." At his wink, a laugh spurts out from me.

"So, Osso isn't really at fault here, then."

Zane joins me in another round. "He alone isn't. It's just all those before him set him up, and he has fallen right ... in ... line." He smacks a domino on the glass at the end of the line. "He could have fixed it."

"Fixed what?" I ask.

Zane knocks down his current row. "Way, way, way back when, we had three equally powerful branches of the government. The judicial branch, which upheld the laws, the executive branch—also known as the President's branch—and the Legislature, which had people in it like our District Representatives, who are supposed to work *for the people.* But over time, they became the richest people in the country, and they either lost their spot, or gained it, based on how loyal they were to the Executive rather than through populous voting."

"Up in the one percent of the population for credits, by the way," June says.

Zane and I both look toward him.

"What?" he asks. "I had a lot of time to read, too, and you met my Granny. All my books were historical."

Zane's lips curve up. "So ... with power came greed, and

with greed came corruption. Some in Congress, that's what it was called—"

"And what the U.S. still calls it," June adds. "Though, they do everything differently now."

"With each election, the divide in the country grew wider and wider until, eventually, the leaders who wanted to split had the momentum they needed and did it."

"And what is now the A.U. fell into a dictatorship," June says, "because the people who didn't go pledged their allegiance to the king—I mean Executive." He winks at me again. "It's as if we never left Europe in the first place."

"So, what's so good about the U.S.—I mean, yeah, we obviously have problems here, but every country does, right?"

Zane gives me a little nod. "In the U.S., the laws prevent any change to the constitution, and all branches of government are equally in place and, get this, those that serve, they are servants. They don't get paid anything more than the job they gave up to serve, and they can only serve for three years. This means their leaders aren't in the one percent, doing everything they can to keep their jobs. They're in the *eighty* percent, like most everyone else, doing what they should—amongst the people."

"So, how does this game play into it?" I ask, still wanting to know why he brought out the dominos.

Zane shrugs. "It's just an illustration, and I told you a couple days ago, I wanted to show you it since you'd never played it." He moves on to setting up another run, with June this time.

The calm surrounding us is nice, serene, and I wish it could last forever, but I know it won't. When the change comes, though, I want to be ready. "Um ... I was thinking about taking a shower. Do you think I could borrow the bathroom?"

Zane stares at me as if I've just asked the world of him.

"Or ... not?"

He shakes his head like he hasn't heard me. "Yeah, yeah, sure. There's a box of my sister's stuff in the closet. You could pick something out, if you want. They won't miss it, I promise. They don't want it, won't miss it, all that stuff. Really. Free to good home. Use. Whatever." His eyes twitch like something's zapping him.

"You okay?" I rise from the table. A glance at June shows nothing new.

Zane says, "Yeah. Fine. Go shower. You deserve it."

Passing them both and walking toward the exit from the kitchen, I glance back and find June and Zane face to face, whispering.

That's weird.

And none of your business.

Reminding myself that he'll tell me if he wants to, I put the moment out of my mind and decide clothes and cleanliness come first.

2 3

Zane and June sit on the divan together, June's tablet between them, as I enter the living area. When neither of them
acknowledges my presence after at least a minute of being in
the same room, I say, "Hi!"

They both lift their heads, Zane's eyes widening for a moment. June's lips curve up.

"What?" I ask, weirded out again by the stares.

Zane's shoulders relax. "You look like someone who just
totally enjoyed a hot shower."

"I feel like one, too."

"Would you like some lunch?" He stands as if I've already
said yes, but my breakfast hasn't even fully digested.

"I'm okay. You can go back to whatever you were doing."

June and Zane face each other again, just like they had in
the kitchen before I left, but neither says a word to the other.

"Okay, spill whatever's going on that you're too afraid to tell
me." I figure that has to be it. Showers do more than just clear
the dirt and grime, but refresh the mind, too. Especially when
overtaxed by one of Zane's history lessons.

"Why would you think something's going on?" June asks.

I raise an eyebrow. "Let's see. Zane acted like he got zapped
in the kitchen, then you were head to head for a moment, and
now you're not really talking. You're acting like everything is

fine and trying not to tell m—" A moment of panic hits me. "Did-did you hear something in your earpieces?"

Their faces stay blank.

"Did something happen to my dad? My mom? Mia?"

"No!" June and Zane say at the same time, and June motions for Zane to continue. "Not at all. But you're right ..." He turns to June for a moment and gets a nod. "The comms came back up."

"In your ear?" *Well, duh.* "I mean, what have you heard?"

"They've confirmed everything we've suggested," June says.

"Like?" I can't believe they're going to make me ask.

"The chips were activated," Zane says.

"The boundaries are in place," June says.

"Credits are empty."

"China is taking over, unless the U.S. will accept the debt and reintegrate with the A.U."

"Mia got Cam out," Zane says, he and June adding one fact after the other. A huge sigh of relief escapes me.

"The twins found a trucker who willingly took them to the border, and they convinced authorities to let them enter," June says.

Marlena and Lucie are safe.

"And my Uncle is a traitor."

My gasp comes out before I can stop it. "What?"

Zane nods as his muscle work at his temple and jaw.

"What do you mean? Like, are they going to put him in rehabilitation? Will there be a trial? Do—"

"He's a traitor to Delta Street. He gave up your dad."

My dad. "What happened to him? My dad, I mean. You said he was safe, but—"

"He is. He's actually ... um ... with your mom."

A moment of pure bliss passes through me, until I remember

that Zane's probably going through hell about now, knowing his own uncle, the one who brought him into the whole mix, isn't really one of us.

Us. Did I just think that?

"What ... what do we do ... about your uncle, and all? Anything?"

"We pretend he never existed."

"What about your ear things. Doesn't he have one?"

Zane nods, as June says, "They went off air once they figured it out, and they just got everyone back on. That's actually why they went silent, not because everything was cut off by the A.U.."

"Oh." *Oh.* "Is there anything I can do?" I clasp my hands to keep them from shaking. "Maybe ... uh ... food. You ... want me to make you a pot of noodles?" I offer Zane a small smile all while my insides are trembling. "It's my specialty."

"Noodles?" A grin alights on his face. "Just noodles? Or is there some magical ingredient in them?"

"Well ... uh ... you know, so ... no." *It takes imagination to taste the magic.* Or at least that's what Mom always said when we had noodles for dinner, lunch, or whenever.

"And you'd make noodles for me?" Zane asks.

"Yeah. Like I said, it's my specialty. And pasta is good for the soul." Mr. Milton always said that to me, when he gave me the leftovers from a pot on days Mom and I had the credits to eat there.

I don't understand why Zane's not madder, or sadder, or something other than his neutral self about his uncle. Except when he told me his uncle went the wrong way down Delta Street, he hasn't shown much emotion. Shock? Fear? I can't read into him. "I'm going to make noodles." I have to do something other than sit here and wonder.

With the biggest pot carried over to the sink to fill it, I place my hand on the faucet to start the water, but stop before twisting. What if it's tainted?

Back at the ice box, I find dozens of bottles of water. Grabbing and opening at least ten, I use that water to fill the pot.

These are the times I wish myself home, with Mom and Dad. I can't help but think that, somehow, with them together again, things will be okay. That we'll all be together again soon.

It takes a long time, because, well, a watched pot doesn't boil, and I search for spices, or something to add, since sauce doesn't seem to exist, nor do tomatoes to make any. Not that tomatoes are in season. One cabinet has a rack of spices, and adding basil, oregano and a bit of salt to the water, I hope it will give the noodles enough flavor to make lunch something other than plain.

Voices rise from the living area, but I can't make out the words, and I tune them out as I continue my search for extras to go into my silly little meal. With three plates set nicely on the table and some forks to go with them, I grab three more bottles of water. If I'm not going to cook with the tap water, we probably shouldn't drink it, either. Of course, I'm assuming the bottles aren't tainted.

Ugh. What if they are? Since Zane's uncle hasn't been around, maybe these are all old enough to be normal. What's even normal anymore?

As the water bubbles over, and the timer on the heater clicks off, I strain the noodles, steam rising to the ceiling, bring the pot over to the table and stand at the far seat.

"Lunch!"

Noise from the living room reaches into the kitchen as June rolls over to the empty spot, and Zane stands in the doorway.

"Don't you want to eat?" That let-down feeling begins to grow inside me.

"You actually cooked?" Zane asks.

Let-down is replaced with ticked-offedness. "Yes. I'm not a good cook like you, but I said I'd make noodles. And I did."

"You *actually* cooked." At least he doesn't ask it in question form.

"*Yes*, Zane. I *actually* did. And you have to use your imagination a little, since it's really all we have, but yes, I made noodles."

"You cooked for me."

What in the world is going through his head?

"And for June," I say.

Zane comes closer, by just a few steps, his eyes tracking the table where the noodles still steam. "You cooked." He sounds so sad, yet not. I can't figure him out. As his gaze lands on me, I turn away. "Anna."

When I glance up, Zane's at my toes. His hands reach for me, and before I can stop him, his lips touch mine.

A moment of panic erupts within me, but it's drowned by the softness of his lips, of the taste that mirrors the scent that has been so Zane—so guy, yet so Zane. He presses a little, releases and touches my lips again. "Thank you." Letting go, he sits in the other seat and doles out pasta onto each of the three plates, while I still stand in the same spot, rooted like some statue.

"You're not going to expect me to do that to get pasta, right?" June asks with a high level of sarcasm in his tone.

I slowly sit and face June, shaking my head.

My first kiss. In a kitchen. Because of plain noodles that we'll have to imagine taste better than they will.

Noodles, and my first kiss.

Was not expecting that.

I'm sure Zane has no idea his kiss and my first happened at the same time.

⁘

As soon as he finished eating, Zane helped clean the dishes, and he and June moved back to the divan to strategize, leaving me sitting at the table in a bit of stunned excitement.

The pasta lunch with imaginary sauce went over well enough, though while they talked the whole time about stuff I paid not one bit of attention to, I kept thinking about Zane's lips on mine.

On mine. Like really there.

Sure, I'd imagined that with RK a long time ago, but something held me back then, and that turned out to be a good problem, given how awfully that relationship ended. Before RK, I didn't really have a boyfriend, so what I pictured in a first kiss did not include sauce-less noodles.

He did kiss me, though.

A smile creeps up on my face. Biting it back doesn't do any good. That kiss is going to stay on my lips forever and ever and ever. The only thing that kinda bugs me is that I have no one to tell. No Cam or Mia, or even Mom, for that matter.

No one. Not even June, since he saw it all happen. Not that he'd want me to tell him. Or that he'd care.

Zane did kiss me. Right on the lips.

Head in hand, I don't force the grin away. Eyes closed, I picture Zane coming toward me in that slow-motion walk, his hands extended, wanting to commit it to memory.

A sigh escapes, and I realize I've been sitting at the table for a good long time, all by myself. A bird flies down past the windows, catching my eye. So does the transpo on the pathway ten stories below.

I jump up.

Not just one transpo, but a couple of them. Normal ones—not military. People.

"Zane! June!" Standing there with my hands to the glass, I can't help but think that, if transpos are allowed on the ground again, we have a shot at borrowing one to go the rest of the distance.

Both guys join me in the kitchen a moment later, and with me waving them to the windows, they, too, face toward the ground.

"Either the lockdown has been lifted, or people are just going to go," Zane says.

"It hasn't even been twenty-four hours, though," June adds, concern etching his voice.

"Do you think it's been lifted, or are we watching more people break rules?" I can't believe how whiney I sound and cough into my hand.

Zane shakes his head. "Don't know. I haven't heard anything about it through comms, so you could be right that people are tired of being cooped up."

On one hand, I'm surprised at how little people can deal with, but on the other, based on what Zane and June have repeatedly told me, people in the A.U. have no other way to react.

More transpos fill the street, all heading in the same direction.

"Why isn't anyone—"

"Coming into the city?" Zane finishes for me.

"Yeah." It does seem weird that not a soul is going the other way—toward us. They've been traveling in the same direction as the birds: away.

June taps his tablet, but both he and Zane jerk back.

"Something in your earpiece?"

Zane nods and closes his eyes. June stops whatever he did on the unit on his lap.

I wish I'd been fitted for one so I can hear, too. Comms must be popping in randomly, though, for them to jump with each message.

Just under ten seconds of silence pass before Zane says, "We gotta go." He whirls and grabs my hand, spinning me around.

"I need my shoes!"

"You have three minutes. And don't forget a coat."

June rolls by us, heading toward the back bedroom.

"Hurry, Anna. We don't have—"

A click sounds from the other side of the room. From the entry door.

"Go to my room, get in the closet, and don't come out. Got it?" Zane stares down at me, his eyes serious.

I nod and run that way on tiptoes as Zane races into the living space. In his room, I slide open the closet door, tuck myself against the back wall, and slide it closed again with my toe until only a smidge of light passes through. No way can I go in total darkness. Not after being in the dark on the riser. Not after being blinded by a lack of light. No, I just can't. I can, though, be silent. That's *my* specialty.

The door to the bathroom, which shares a wall with the one I'm up against, clicks with a sound I know is a lock.

Mumbled voices travel in from outside. They aren't raised. They aren't anger-filled. They're just . . . normal. When a third fills in the empty space, one of two I don't recognize, I have to wonder who's shown up. Zane's uncle? Someone from Delta Street? A neighbor? A responsible tenant? Security? Who?

Footsteps carry through the floor, vibrating a little as they get closer. One set of footsteps, I realize. Is Zane coming to get me?

They carry on past and stop.

The stomps start again, heading the other way. "... the Osso family, why don't you share your ..." the voice comes in and goes out like the Doppler effect, and I don't get to hear the end.

Mumbles continue until I almost can't take it. Actually, I can't. If I've tracked the movement properly, there are three people, and they're all in the kitchen. The wall by the head of the bed is shared with the kitchen. If I can get closer to it, I might be able to listen in. Of course, if I had an earpiece, I could probably hear more, but it is what it is.

Easing open the closet door, I peek inside the room and find the outer door open just a crack, too. Crawling up and reclosing the closet, just as I had it, in case someone peeks inside, I scramble over to the far side of the bed and shimmy underneath—the joy of being small.

Sounds reach me from the kitchen with a relative level of clarity, but I have to concentrate to pick up all the nuance.

"... plan is to undo everything ..." That comes from the third voice I heard before.

Undo what?

"... could really use you ..." That comes from the second voice—a little higher pitched than the third.

What if they're strangers and have broken in? My heart races a little before I remember Zane didn't start screaming for help, or anything.

Calm down, Anna. Making up stories isn't going to help. And now you've stopped paying attention to whatever they're saying.

Focusing again, I listen.

"... and security detail will pick you up at oh-seven-hundred tomorrow," voice two says.

Who is the other voice?

"I'll be ready," Zane say.

Ready? Ready for what? They must be part of Delta Street, and they know how to get us out of here. Will that apply to us all? Surely, it will. If so, why hasn't Zane come to get us? If they aren't Delta Street, who, then?

Chairs push back and scrape the floor.

"Can you believe those people think they can leave?" the first voice asks on a chuckle. "We give them transpo access, and they flee like birds. Where are they going to go? The borders are closed. They have no credits." The man huffs. "I'll be glad when all this is over, and we can wave them all away as traitors and restart everything our way."

Restart everything? Who is that guy? No way that's a Delta Street person.

"Glad to have you with us, Zane," the same voice says. "Your Uncle here says you're the right person for the job. The Chief is looking forward to hearing what you have to say."

Chief? Is he talking about Osso? Zane's going to talk to our CEO? And his Uncle is recommending him.

"How great that you got out of registration, so we could have this chat and your support on this." That is voice two, which I'm guessing is Zane's uncle.

He wouldn't. Zane wouldn't be going with them.

Would he?

24

It seems like forever passes before I hear, "You can come out now," in Zane's voice.

I scramble from under the bed, June exits the bathroom, and we all regroup in the living space.

"Your uncle and Osso Junior?" June asks.

Zane nods.

"He sounded like was expecting you." June's brow is creased, eyes narrow. It's not a happy face. "Were *you* expecting *him?*"

"No." Zane stares straight at June. "It was totally a coincidence. I don't know what he thought exactly, but I did *not* plan to meet him here. I didn't know anything about him coming here."

"Your uncle could have been covering for you, since Osso was here, and if you weren't supposed to be, then Osso might have suspected something," I say.

Both guys turn to me, awe in their eyes.

"What?" I shrug. "I can put two and two together, just like you." *Slower, maybe, but I can.*

"You could be right," Zane says.

"So, does that still make him a traitor?" June taps on his tablet. "I mean, we heard that through the earpiece, but maybe *that* was just a cover, too."

Zane stands and paces, running a hand through his hair.

"Maybe. Maybe you're right. But if they turned off his earpiece, then, that usually means—"

"Cover is blown," June says. "Not that he's a traitor."

"So, it could all be one giant misunderstanding."

I'm sure that's a huge relief to Zane, to think his uncle might not be the bad guy he thought, but I'm not convinced. "If the earpieces are undetectable, though, why would they turn his off?"

Zane shakes his head. "What do I do now? Who do I even trust?" There's a hint of worry in his tone. "How do I know what *to* do now?"

"We trust only us," I say.

Zane stops and points to me. "That. That's right. There are only two people I can trust right now, and that's you both. And you're here. And … yes. That."

"So, what do we do?" June tilts up to the still-standing Zane. "Either you go with them tomorrow morning, or we have to get out of here, like, right now. Of course, if you don't wait for them, Osso's going to know something's up."

I know how he feels. His uncle shows up in his life for five minutes, and all of a sudden, Zane's going to be the bad guy if he doesn't follow along. If he's right, he's wrong, and if he's wrong, he's still wrong.

Zane's finger pointing begins again. "We have to leave." He spins and walks toward the door but comes back. "He didn't know I'd be here, so he had to just be covering for me."

"But then they'll point back to your uncle, too," June says, stopping Zane's motion. "But maybe then, he'll cover for you again. I mean, what if he isn't a traitor?"

Zane's face pales. "… if I don't go with him tomorrow, they're going to know *I'm* not one of them. And then if my uncle's legit, he'll be caught because of me."

My throat tightens. "But if you go, you …" The heads whipping toward me stop my flow.

"Keep going," June says.

After a cough to clear my throat, I say, "What if you go, like they expect, and you dig in and find out what they're doing, and you keep your uncle's cover *until* you know. For sure, I mean."

"Where will you both go?" Zane asks. "You can't stay here, because they could come back. Or my uncle could. There's also no more food. You can't use credits, and you can't work your way through all the Delta Street locations. You don't even know where they all are—or at least, not the ones who'll help you go to the U.S.. And you have to go to the U.S. We all have to." Zane's voice speeds up as he talks.

Loyalty is a tough pill to swallow. Does he stay with me and get me where my dad told him to take me, or does he go with his uncle and ensure his uncle's life is safe. Maybe. What do I know about what they actually do to traitors?

I stand and move to Zane, and take him by the arms, like he's done to me so many, many, many times. "June and I can go to my Mo—"

"No. That's the wrong way. You have to go—"

"Give us three stops." June holds up his trusty tablet. "Three points that we can get to over, say, two days, that if you can't get your answers and meet us by that third stop, I'll signal Anna's dad to send Delta Street operatives to get us out of here."

"You'd do that?" Zane's gaze meets mine as he asks.

Would I? Leave with June, but without Zane? Closing my eyes, I nod—as much as I don't want to.

He tilts up my chin. "Promise? Promise me you'll get out of this country. Promise, or I won't go with my uncle."

Now I'm the one in the middle. If I don't promise, I know

Zane won't go, and his uncle will, or won't, be found out. Why does that always happen to me? "Yes. I'll—I promise."

Zane moves forward. For a moment, I'm expecting another kiss, but instead, he holds up his pinky in front of me. "Pinky swear."

"What?"

June chuckles behind me.

"Pinky swear," Zane says again, his little finger held high.

"But—"

"Oh, just do it, Anna." That comes from June.

"But what for?" I have to ask.

Zane grins at me. "To promise you'll go. For me."

"But I just sa—"

On his exasperated sigh, I wrap my pinky around his, and he tugs us super close, so near his lips are about an inch from mine. My heartbeat speeds up.

"Thank you." One nod later, he lets me go. "I have an idea."

"What's that?" June asks.

"My transpo. It's in the holding lot, on level three. I can go down there and setup Anna's credentials to operate it."

"Won't you need it?" I ask. After he figures out what's going on, he'll need transportation himself, in order to make up time to meet us.

Zane cocks his head my way as if to say 'Duh, Anna.'

"I'm with her," June says. "Won't you need it?"

Finally. Someone agrees with me.

"If my uncle is on our side, he'll give me a transpo to get out. If he's not, a transpo here, on the edge of District Eleven, when I'm in District One is not going to help me. It'll basically be a useless piece of machinery if you don't take it, and make your trip easier."

"I can't operate a transpo." I never have, so putting me in

that position is not a good idea.

June waves a little. "I can."

Zane's lips squish to the side. "It's not feet-free."

June's eyes widen a bit. "You? You don't have the latest and greatest technologically-advanced transpo?"

The chuckle from Zane makes the tension building up in my shoulders release. "It was my mom and dad's. So it's really old."

"Like Mr. Perez's ... what was it ... a truck?" I ask.

"Kinda, yeah, in that it requires credentials to run. Aside from the energy consumption, that's the only upgrade I did. So it will be slower than most transpos, which means you'll have to stay to the right because everyone is going to pass you."

Something confusing whirls in my brain. "Isn't that going to make us stand out a lot?"

"It would, if it wasn't registered. I have a license for a classic. If anyone stops you, or intends to, they'll record the plate, and the plate will tell them it's registered for historic purposes— which means, if it's out, it's being shown on purpose. Better yet, it's been rented to show."

June grins. "A rental. Doesn't matter who's in it ... could be anyone."

Zane's lips curve up, too. "My parents' idea a long, long time ago."

"What about the walls? How will we get through those?"

The raised eyebrow suggests I should know better. "District Eleven's wall will have a pass through for transpos with credentials for other districts. I'll give those to June. Eight, on the west side of Eleven, will only have a fence line. Use the credentials again. Twenty-One, to the west of that, is so far out, the guard will probably be there, but he may not be if you get there in the middle of the night."

I definitely wouldn't have known that.

"What about what your uncle said, or Osso said ..." I can't remember who said what anymore. "... about everyone leaving. They won't get through the border."

"That's right. *They* won't. Delta Street has a way, but only from that far post. Trust me on that. Unless you're in Delta Street, you'll never get through a closed border."

"Even if the guard isn't there?"

"Even if," Zane says.

"But *we* will? How?" I can't believe he's going to send us without telling us.

"Trust me, Anna. You'll know. Now back to my transpo ..."

"Maybe if I take a look, we can find a way to make it work. For me, that is." The smile on June's face says he's totally down for a challenge.

"Yeah, we could. Anna? Want to go with us?"

"Into a cold holding lot to work on a transpo? Uh, no. I'll just stay here."

⁂

"Anna."

My name rings through my head, but I can't grasp who's saying it.

"Anna, wake up."

"Zane?" I blink a few times, bringing in the light of the bedside table, the closed window coverings, though lamps from outside brighten the spaces between the weave. "What?"

"You were asleep."

I blink more. "Huh? What time is it?"

"About eight."

"Eight?" I sit up fast. "That's, like, five hours ..." from when I snuck off to Zane's bed. The last numbers I saw on the clock were 6:50. I must have fallen asleep, while he and June did whatever they had to do with the transpo.

"Yeah, I didn't want to wake you when I came up an hour ago." He sits on the bed, squishing the edge down a little. "Figured you needed it."

Rubbing my eyes and, in reality, needing more sleep, I say, "Please tell me it's eight at night, and we didn't miss your uncle."

Zane laughs. "It's the eight o'clock that's past dinnertime, and June and I ordered pizza."

"Again?" Why do guys like to eat pizza so much?

He chuckles. "Yes, *again*. Because there's a pizzeria right next door that I could go and get it from and bring it back. And they're Delta Street supporters. And—" Both his hands go up. "Before you tell me about cooking or cleaning for them, I have a credits account from my uncle. So, I used that."

"June and I will pay you back."

Zane shakes his head. "You said someone had to pay, not that we have to pay our own way. So, no. I paid. That's done."

"But—"

His face goes all serious with a building frown.

"Okay." I cover my mouth realizing I haven't used a dental tablet in at least twenty-four hours, and the last one would have already outlasted its usefulness.

"So ... get up and come eat, 'kay?"

I nod, not wanting to waft nap-breath his way.

He rises and heads to the door as I slip off the bed and go to the bathroom. "Oh, Anna?"

Hand on the frame, I stop and spin. "Yeah?"

"I like the butterfly."

Heat flushes my cheeks as I pull my sleeve up over my shoulder. Rather than respond, I slip into the bathroom and let my smile free.

⚬━┥━⚬

"... around six a.m."

One steaming box of pizza and another, halfway eaten, one wait for me when I join Zane and June in the kitchen again. "What's around six a.m.?" I ask.

"When we should leave," June says. "I have the credentials now, and I've converted the signal lever to a hand control."

I reach for a slice, awe and wonder running through my mind. "You did that in five hours?"

"Three hours, two minutes and twenty seconds, to be exact."

"Wow."

Zane nudges my elbow. "This guy is a wizard with all things electronic."

Nodding in agreement, I chew and, after swallowing, finally manage to say, "That's really awesome."

"And this means ..." June points a finger at me, at himself, at me again. "... we can go straight to the border zone and skip the other two places altogether."

Zane holds up a hand above the table, and June slaps his palm with his own.

"We'll still wait for you, right?" I ask, hoping, at least, we can stay in the A.U. until Zane can catch up with us. Just because we'll be moving faster to the end-point, doesn't mean I actually want to be there.

"Yeah, yeah, sure," June says.

Zane doesn't even turn to me, so I do to him. "You're still going to meet us, right?"

He nods, but doesn't look at me while doing it.

Deciding to ignore him and his obvious hiding of something, I go back to my pizza. "So ... if we leave at six, that means we have to kill time the rest of the night, right?"

June picks up another cheesy slice. "After this, I'm going to clean up and get some sleep. I want to be fully rested for whatever comes tomorrow."

"I'm with June. I think we should all get some rest. We have a plan. We know what we're going to do. You leave at six. I leave at seven. We're all in the clear."

And we might never see each other again.

"I'll sleep on the couch this time," I say, wanting Zane to be fully refreshed.

He shakes his head. "No. Keep my room. June can take my uncle's bed, and I'll take the couch."

"Zane—"

"No." More head movement continues. "I need to be able to hear the door if anyone comes back, and if you're in the back, I can close doors faster than I can get you up."

He has a point, but I don't have to like it. "Okay." Of course, my mini-nap has caught up with me, and energy courses through me now. "Do you mind if I read one of your books?" There's a whole shelf of paper books in his room that I stared at, reading the spines without touching them before I laid down.

His lips curve up. "I don't mind, at all. Actually, there's a really good one I think you should read."

"What's that?" I ask, diving into a second slice.

"It's called Nineteen-Eighty-Four. By George Orwell."

"That's banned," June and I say at the same time. "You have a copy?"

June's eyes alight, and Zane's expression mirrors June's. "My mom and dad gave it to me. It's wrapped in a cover that says Two-Thousand Fourteen."

"Which means, what?" June asks.

"It's the year, from my research, where everything really fell apart. It's when the cold war sort of restarted. It's when we paid so much interest on our debt that we could have funded the entire military for the entire world. Or paid what used to be called Social Security for our over-eighties population. It's the year the idea of the split really started to take hold."

"But there's no book called that," I say.

"Of course not. Do you think people want to read what's happening right under their noses?" He shakes his head. "No, they don't. So, it's my way of hiding the old one, but reminding myself why I kept it."

"What's it about?" I ask.

"It's ... let's just say, what's happening now. If we'd written it fifty, or a hundred years ago, no one would have believed it. Probably. Well, Nineteen Eighty-Four was written in nineteen forty-nine. And while not everything in it happened, or so they thought back then, you might see some similarities to now. Government surveillance, mind control, absolute corruption, socialism, and totalitarianism at its best. A total failure. That kind of thing. Read it. You'll see."

◦━━◆━━◦

"Higher, Daddy, higher!"

As it always happens, the swing lets me fly, soaring into the air, my feet rising higher and higher, but this time, I know I don't want to swing. I need to get on the ground.

"Higher, Daddy!" my little self says, encouraging the pushes.

I don't giggle this time, though. I want down. I have to get down. I have to go with June. I have to wait for Zane.

"Higher!"

Pressure from behind propels me forward, upward, closer to the ceiling of clouds. To the top of the wall.

No! I scream in my head to stop myself from fighting with me.

I grip the ropes, hoping I won't fall off, that they'll hold me, that they won't send me over the wall. Up. Up. Up and over.

Stop!

My feet drag on the ground as I swing down, kicking up dirt into the air around me, covering me in a cloud of dust, but the swing goes up again, closer to the top, to the wall, to the point the swing is going to release me and fling me over the top.

"Higher, Daddy!"

No!

The little me and the mental me aren't connected.

He pushes me once, and my little legs kick out.

Feet drag.

A push from behind sends me up again, over the top.

Stop!

"Erianna, come inside now." My mother's sing-songy voice calls for me.

"Higher!" My legs reach past the top, into the blue sky.

No!

Mia appears from nowhere.

I reach out, yelling, "Mia! Come back! Help me!"

"Eri! Don't let go!"

My swing goes higher again, my feet reaching over the wall, into the wire that's on top.

"Push me higher, Daddy! I want to go higher."

No! No! No!

"Higher! Higher!"

No! No! No! No!

Up. Up. Up, I go, the sky deepening the closer I get to it.

The swing's ropes release, loosening as if I'm floating, stuck, hanging and just waiting to be thrown over into the U.S.

"No! No! No! I'm going to fall!"

"Anna. Anna, I got you."

Zane.

Gripping the ropes, I try to stop, but I can't. Even with Zane there with me—though I can't see him—I can't get a grip. I can't find the ground. I can't stop the flying.

"Anna, I got you."

Something tugs against me, pulling me off the swing, holding me, flying with me, my legs and arms outstretched as if I'm still going forward.

A pinpoint of light makes me blink. Allows me to see. To find my reality. The lamp. The bed. Zane's room.

Not a swing. Not outside. Not by the wall.

My heart hammers in my chest, and given how hot I am, I'm must be covered in sweat.

"You were dreaming again." His voice is calm and soothing at my ear, his body behind me.

I nod. It's the only thing I can do. I hate that dream. Hate it even more now that our border wall is showing up in it. Mom used to tell me the dream meant I had a need for independence, but if that held any truth, wouldn't I be more like Mia, instead of a confused little girl reading a two-hundred-year-old book?

A shiver wracks my body.

One second later, the blanket I'd kicked off, probably on a mental upward swing, comes over me. "I got you. Just rest."

With a slight motion of my head, I try to relax.

Zane's arms come around me, holding me tight. "I won't let you go."

I don't want him to, but I know he will.

25

Two days without Zane is going to be weird. I haven't been away from him for more than a few hours in almost a week. Thanks to his transpo, though, June and I are on our way to Delta Street location number one-two-three-four-five-six. I thought it a bit too simple a number for a secret op safe zone, but Zane reminded me, before June and I left, that sometimes what's right under the nose can't be found and is, therefore, the safest place to be. His words, not mine.

At least the sun is shining, the sky is blue—not the grey-black-red that pops up in my dreams—and June is operating the four-seater transpo—*uh*, car—instead of me.

He's been eerily quiet for the last hour, though.

"You okay?" I ask, wanting to break the silence.

"I am. What about you?"

"I'm fine." Am I really? Or is that my standard answer?

"I heard you scream last night."

Heat creeps up into my face. "Bad dream. Happened a lot when I was a kid." Happens more now.

"Before, or after, your dad disappeared?"

"Oh, befo—" Actually, when did it start? "Maybe after."

"Ever have it analyzed? The dream, I mean, not yourself."

"My mom did some research. I remember something about independence."

June shakes his head. "Every dream has some sort of theory of independence because by the very nature, your mind is working independently for you. Tell me about it. If you want, that is."

With nothing but pathways and transpos zooming by us, I figure *why not?*, and share a handful of the various iterations of the dream.

"So, you're going to go around, or over. Scary thought."

"Feels like it, too. My stomach gets all squirrely."

June chuckles. "I'll bet. They say that going around and around like that means you're confused. And that someone else is pushing you means you're not in control. That things are ... well, happening against your will."

That sounds about right in my life.

"But ... because you don't actually go over, and in this latest one, you've put your feet to the ground, I think it means you're exerting your own will into the scene. You want to stay rooted to the people around you."

"Like my mom?"

"Uh ... sure. Your *mom*. We'll go with that."

He doesn't say Zane, but, yeah, I figure that out on my own.

"Also, with you not going over the wall, it might mean you have a *little* control. Like you do know how to make change happen. But by letting it keep happening, you're not in a position to *make* the change happen."

A little convoluted, but I think I get it. "So, is there a way to make it stop? To, you know, not have that dream anymore?"

"I've read that you have to figure out the trigger in real life so you can find a way to let your mind stop bringing it up when you're asleep. Like ... if your *mom* is really your issue ... then you could make amends with her. Show her how you do have control of your life, and how you've learned from her and put her teachings to good use."

"What if it's someone else? I mean—" Coughing into my hand, I gather my thoughts. "What if it's not Mom, but ... maybe someone like my dad?"

"Then figure out what you have no control over when it comes to him. Or *whoever* it is."

We continue on without speaking for a while as I consider that there's really nothing there depicting my dad. Actually, anytime he's in the dream, he does exactly what I want. Pushes me when I say push and stops me when I get scared. Could it be Mia? She's been outside of my life for so long that I don't think it's her, and even with her brief appearance in last night's version, she's still herself and doesn't control me, except when she needs to.

"Um ..." I start after so long.

"Um?" June snorts a laugh. "Just spit it out, Anna. I mean, I know you can't live your life without me, so it's best to just say it and be done with it so we can carry on with our sordid romance and kick Zane to the curb. Unless, of course, the dreams are about him." The wink I get brings out my own smile.

"It can't be Zane, June. I've only known him for, like, a week."

He shrugs. "Who says that's not long enough?"

"Normal people."

"Who's normal these days?"

He has a point. "But a *week*, June. A week! It's not like I'm in love, or anything, so how can my subconscious be dragging him into my sleep?"

"The subconscious does what the subconscious wants to do. You don't have much control over that. Could even be your subconscious you need to control, and to that, I can only say *good luck*."

"That is exactly my problem." That's why my dreams are going to plague me for eternity. I have no control over them. Maybe it was mom way back when. Or dad after he left, Mia as I grew up, and now Zane doesn't help, that's for sure.

A flash of blue makes me gasp, and as I turn around, I find a security officer behind us. June slows the car, but the lights blip off, and the security personnel shoots off around us.

"Well, my heart's pumping hard now," June says.

"Mine, too. I guess Zane was right about what would happen. He's been right about a lot of things."

"Anyone who can quote, word for word—"

"That's what a quote is." I giggle and force myself to stop.

June eyes me with a mischievous smile. "Anyone who can quote constitutional laws from the nineteen hundreds has to know his stuff. I think he has an eidetic memory."

"A what?"

"Like … a photographic memory, though he has complete recall, too."

That would explain how he can remember all the camera placements and angles and movements. "That's … impressive."

"It is. It's incredibly unique and—" June's expression as he whirls to me is one of terror. "Oh, my—"

"What?" Fear grips me.

"Oh, my Oz. Why didn't I think of that before?"

"Think of what, June?" Worry fills me until I shake.

"He said they could use him in their discussion with the administration." June slams his palm on the wheel.

"He, who?"

"They need him because no one else on the council knows the history the way Zane does. Argh!" He hits it again.

"Who are you talking about, June?"

"His *uncle*. *Zane's* uncle. He's in on this. I know it. His uncle brought him back from the U.S., took him away from his sisters because his *head* would be useful. His mind would be useful. His brain would be useful to the administration."

"He's not going to tell them things he doesn't want to say."

"Like hell he won't." June's palm goes against this forehead. "They'll get everything out of him. Including everything about his parents, and—"

"That's not poss—" I'm stopped by June's quick glare.

"Do you know what they did to the males in registration?"

I shake my head as memories of my own medical procedures pop in, chilling me to my core.

"They hooked them up to these electrodes that could measure how pliable the brain was. How easily it would be to extract data from them. Oh, god! They were looking for the Zanes of the world."

"How do you know this?" I have to ask, since June didn't go.

"Zane told me."

"Well, then, he knows what they plan to do."

"No, he doesn't. He said they wanted to know how pliable their minds were, to see how easily they could be manipulated for their careers. He wasn't thinking about what they could be doing with the technology. They're going to hook him up and force him to share everything he knows. And his uncle is behind it, because he knows Zane has been in Delta Street from the beginning. He knows how Zane's mind works. I'll bet he even got immunity from Osso himself, if he could bring in *one* person to spill all the beans about everything Delta Street."

"Oh, Oz, no. We have to go back. We have to help him."

"How, Anna? He gave you his ear piece again. No one's talking, or chattering. There's nothing but nothing right now."

"Then, we make something happen. You said it yourself, I need to control something."

"I didn't mean right now. I meant—"

"I know. But ... we can't let him walk into a trap, June."

June shakes his head. "I know, but how are we, you and me, who don't know anything about the inner District and probably will get caught and tortured ourselves, going to help?"

He has a point. "We'll ... we'll *get* help. Just like I said I would two days from now if everything went wrong."

⚬━━━⚬

Standing in front of my mom's door with my hand poised to knock is about as nerve-wracking now as it was the last time. Yet again, I have a guy with me, though it's June and not Zane, and while I might think that's better, I'm sure my mom won't.

"Come on, Anna, even I'm cold out here," June says.

On a deep breath, I knock a couple times.

Movement sounds inside, and after a few seconds, the door opens.

"Erianna." My mom's wide eyes don't surprise me. "What are you doing here?" Her gaze drops to June. "Come in, come in." She waves us forward.

I go first, June right after me. As the door closes behind us, Dad steps from the hallway where the bedrooms are.

"Anna. What are you doing here?"

"Dad ..." I want to run and jump into his arms and let him do everything, but I'm not going to. I'm taking control of this situation.

Moving in farther, to give June room, I stand at the edge of the divan. "We need your help."

Dad's eyes do that quick-wide-blink thing that makes me think he's worried, but he doesn't show any other emotions, so I can't tell if I just thought he did it, or I wanted him to. Then again, that's probably how he's been trained—to show no emotion. Zane's a lot like that. "How can I help you?" he asks after forever.

"Zane's uncle showed up yesterday and convinced Zane to go to District One to talk to Osso."

There, Dad's eyes do move, and I know that means something's going on. The rest of his body language, though, remains stoic. "What did he say? Zane's uncle, that is."

"He said he could use Zane's input," June says. "I think he actually means his memory."

Dad nods. "Why did Zane go? We notified everyone of Bryan's allegiance."

"And I heard it, sir. So did Zane." June rolls closer to my dad. "But when Zane's uncle showed up, with Osso, he didn't rat Zane out. He covered for him. Or so we thought. He didn't react poorly, or negatively, so we thought maybe what went through our earpieces was also a cover."

Dad turns to me, his glare serious. "And you decided to find out for yourselves, instead of doing what I expressly asked."

I want to cringe. I want to cower. Everything within me does. Firming my stance and meeting Dad's gaze, I say, "We did what we thought best with the information we had. And …" My voice betrays me a bit with a warble. "… taking orders without thinking is how we all got stuck in this position in the first place. So, I'm here to ask you to get me into District One, so I can let Zane know what's going on and get him out of there."

Dad shakes his head. "It's too dangerous, and you're not equipped to handle it."

Turning away from my dad, I face June, my entire body wanting to tremble, and my eyes filling with tears. I knew he wouldn't help. Why did I even want to ask? "Let's go. We'll figure this out on our own." How, I have no idea, but June's smart, and I'm willing.

I head to the door, but it opens before I can leave, Mia standing in the frame.

"Mia!" Mom says, delight and fear in her tone.

"Looks like there's a party going on, and no one invited me." She steps in, slipping her coat off.

"Where's Cam?" I ask.

Mia raises an eyebrow. "You don't trust me, do you?"

"I—" *don't know how to answer that.*

"It's okay. I wouldn't, either, after what you've been through." She moves farther inside, to the ice box as if it's her own house, and takes out a bottle of water.

Bottle? Mom never let us have bottled water before. I don't remember ever being mind-bent, either, so maybe I've always had it. What do I actually know anymore?

Tipping it back, Mia swallows and says, "Cam's at home. I convinced her parents she wasn't a runaway from registration, that she got caught up in something bad and needed to be taken care of by *her family*, not the A.U." After downing the rest of the water, she adds, "And then I told them that if they told anyone I was there, I'd turn them into the authorities for having household help when this District isn't afforded that."

"So, they're going to take care of her and not rat you out." Though not a question, it sounds like one with the way I lilt up at the end.

"Exactly. And then, I went for this seriously long run to burn off energy and think, and I ended up over on Fifth Street and caught up with a friend of mine who also happens to be a friend of Zane's. She's an Intern for Osso, and they heard Osso was taking Zane in to District One for support. Now ..." Her fingers, still holding the bottle, half-point toward me. "... tell me how that could possibly happen. How Zane would ever agree to go to District One, let alone to Osso himself."

"Um ..."

Before I can say more, June spills the whole story.

"And then," Mia says, "*she* convinced *you* to turn all the way around to go after Zane?"

June nods.

"Huh." She taps her temple. "Well." Her one word exclamations are bizarre. From what I know of my sister, she's always incredibly eloquent and a lot demanding. "I'm impressed. Thoroughly. Didn't think you had it in you, Anna. Guess growing up has changed you. Let's go."

"No!" Mom's exclamation comes out loud and firm.

Mia and I both turn toward her. "Zane's like a brother to me," Mia says. "More than even my own sister—no offense." That last little bit, she aims at me.

I'd respond, but I get what she means, and it really doesn't bother me.

"If you're not going to help him," she says, "which is evident by your actions so far, then I am."

"It's too dangerous," Mom says, as Dad shakes his head and adds, "You can't."

Mia's shoulders go rigid, and the glare she gives Dad is one I remember from when we were kids. Never, ever, tell Mia Keating she can't do something. That's the sure-fire way to make her do it. "Once again, here we go. I'm not fourteen, Mom. Hell, I'm not eighteen, either, Dad." She swipes her coat from the divan. "Start remembering that. When are you supposed to meet him?" she asks me.

"How did you—"

Mia rolls her eyes. "Come on, Anna. If Zane went in, he had a plan to get out, or he has a plan, at least, to get to *you*. Or haven't you noticed he's totally into you?"

"She noticed," June says, turning away really fast.

Mia raises an eyebrow. "So, where and when do you expect to meet him?"

"In two days, at the final house," June says.

She gives one definitive nod. "Good. Then, come with me. We're going to—no, better not say exactly." Her glance is quick, but I catch it: right at Dad.

"How will you get in the District?" Dad asks, stopping Mia and me as we reach the door.

She turns, hand on the knob. "The way every other Osso does." She opens the door and steps out into the cold, and I follow.

"Please, no! Mia, no!" Mom's voice trails off, as I close the door and follow my sister toward whatever plan she has.

26

"Wouldn't this be safer if we—" My comment is quashed by Mia's absolute and intense glare as she glances back toward me.

She's been navigating for June, taking us through the District Eleven wall and into Nine in Zane's classic car. He really did mean it when he said this car would get us anywhere.

Facing the front again, she says, "Nothing is safe for resistance members right now. Nothing. And if they really do get Zane to spill his guts about everything, we're even less safe. Worse, he'll be killed, no matter what his uncle tries to do to save him after—if—he tries anything, which he won't."

"How do you know he won't? They're family."

"Because he's the one who turned Dad in," Mia says as if it's obvious.

Oh, Oz! I sent Zane there. I suggested it. I'm getting Zane killed! My heartbeat speeds up, that inner fear and desperation filling me. Maybe it's not true. Maybe Mia just thinks Zane's uncle turned Dad in. That could be it, right? "How do you know ... who turned Dad in?" I hate that my voice cracks when I'm super nervous.

She taps her ear, which I assume is my answer.

"Are you sure they'll kill Zane? I mean, since his brain is so valuable, maybe they ... maybe they'll do something else."

Mia gives me that same intense stare from before.

"How do you *know*, Mia?

"Because I've seen it happen. First person view. No second-hand information."

"You watched a murder?" I can't believe what I'm hearing.

"No. I watched them get what they wanted out of a kid. In the end, he was a good as dead."

So not really *dead.*

She continues, "I was in an interrogation of a registration candidate that they sent out on the first day. I saw the brain stimulation, I saw him fight to hold back, and I saw him get dragged away by security."

My heart flipflops, aching for those people, and for Zane, and the fact this stuff happens. If it really does. "But you *didn't* see them get killed, right?"

"No, but . . ." Her voice trails off as I register the 'no', which, to me, means we have a chance. Except, Zane's already been there for hours. There's no way we're going to get to him before he says something.

"We need to get to the center buildings and find out where Osso is," Mia says, while I'm lost in my own thoughts.

"Why Osso?" June asks.

"I mean Zane," Mia says.

Disbelief has me asking, "Why did you say Osso?"

A very small but audible sigh escapes her. "I just misspoke."

Mia never does that. "I don't think you did," I say. "So, why did you?"

"You're getting annoying, the bolder you get," she says.

"That doesn't answer the question!" I instantly regret the pitch of my tone.

Mia's eyebrow wings up, a small smirk on her face. "Let's just leave this as a need-to-know topic."

"He's not going to do any of the dirty work, right?" June

asks.

Mia shakes her head. "He'll be monitoring. Probably personally."

"Because it's Zane they are interrogating?" My heart does another jump.

Mia's head goes side to side, followed by an up and down. I don't know why she has to exhibit so many non-verbal expressions right now. "Look ... Bryan brought Zane in, or rather suggested Zane, and he's been in the gray area of loyalty for a while. Osso's most likely going to be standing watch over the whole procedure. Maybe even participating with questions as a test of Zane, but it'll really be more about his uncle. Your goal is to find Zane and get him out. Not prevent him from saying anything."

"Okay ... but won't that mean the bad guys will know all the good guy's secrets?" I ask, sounding stupid even to myself.

"They probably already do, so it no longer matters. Now, it's more a search and rescue." Something's up with her, but I'm not going to probe further.

"So, how do we do this? How do we get Zane out? How do we even get in?"

"Fastest way in is to prove you're one of them," June says.

"You intend to tell them who we are, don't you?" I ask the car, but I'm sure Mia knows I mean her.

"That'll give us some immunity, at least for a little bit." Her answer is deadpan.

"Is that why Mom and Dad didn't want us to go? Not because it's dangerous, but because we'll have to give up who we are?"

"Probably." She doesn't really sound sure. Or maybe she's answering so I'll shut up. Either way, I think I'm going to be sick.

Mia turns in her seat until she's facing me, mouth open as

if to speak. "You look green."

I feel green. Or whatever green feels like. Rather than speak, I just nod.

"Pull over for a sec, June."

The transpo—car—slows to a stop. Mia gets out and opens the door for me. "Breathe in. Deep and slow."

Sitting on the edge of the seat, head at my knees, breathing in, I can't help but worry. My mind spins as fast as my stomach tumbles. Everything is falling apart. People I've just come to know are being hurt because of me. People I've loved all my life are risking their lives for others. People I barely know have to hide.

Tears form and fall, but while I'm facing the ground, no one will see. I hope. I can't believe how stupid I've been all my life. A hiccup forces me to catch my breath.

"Are you crying?" Mia squats in front of me.

I shake my head, hoping that will be enough to ward her off.

"Okay, tell me why you're crying."

"I'm not—" The hitch in my breath totally ruins my lie.

Chuckles sound from the front seat.

A hand lands on my back and rubs. "So, girl-wonder finally breaks. I wondered how much it would take to reach this point. Me in Registration was my first thought. Dad was my second."

She doesn't have to know how I broke down in Zane's arms after she disappeared again.

"So, it's Zane that does it, huh."

I whip my head up and crack the top on Mia's chin. She crashes to the ground, hand on her jaw. "Ouch!"

I scramble to her. "I'm so sorry! So sorry!"

"Do you know how many times you did that to me as a kid? When we were little, that is." Tears fill her eyes.

"Bumped you in the chin?" I ask.

She nods as she sits up and rubs her jaw. "Yeah. Oz, you did it at least a dozen times, and every time it hurt like hell, and you'd run over to me and tell me how sorry you were." A crack of her jaw right and left makes my stomach squeeze. "It's like old times."

Except, we're about to turn ourselves in to people our parents have tried to keep us from forever.

She stares up at me. "And now that that moment is over. I can't make you stop worrying. If you did, you wouldn't be the Erianna Keating that I know and love. But," she says, rubbing at her chin, "instead of that stopping you, let's use it. It's instinctual, and it could help us."

"How can worrying help?" I ask.

Mia stands and brushes off the back of her jeans. "Use the skills that come with it: listening, thinking, processing and communicating with me. Between the three of us ..." She motions between me, June and herself. "Osso and his administration don't know what we look like, thanks to Mom. So—"

"Uh ..." June interrupts, "... I think that thinking is flawed."

"What do you mean?" Mia asks.

"Anna," June says.

A shiver runs up my spine. "What about me?"

"If my grandma can tell you're an Osso through her inch-thick specks, you think a trained operative won't? If you go in to any administrative building, there's a strong likelihood you'll be recognized. I mean, I know you're going to admit to who you are, but I think there might be another way."

"What way?" Mia asks.

"I'll show you," June says.

⁂

Five minutes later, we're stopped again in front of Osso's

latest sham of a distraction technique—a giant outdoor, advertising poster.

"Why are we here?" I ask.

"Because of that billboard." June points up through the front glass of the car. "I've been seeing them the whole trip."

The image is strikingly similar to June—a boy in a medical cart, but with giant letters that spell out: Don't let this happen to you.

Mia beats the dash with her fist. "A kid in a medical cart—"

"It's just a wheeled chair," June says, "not a cart and not medical. Yes, it helps us get around, but it's just our version of legs. You have yours; we have this."

"Sorry." Mia pats him on the shoulder. "I didn't mean to offend."

"You didn't. At least, not me."

"This is brilliant." Mia's tone is excited. "Osso's media has put focus on this." She points up to the image. "He's been vowing to eradicate certain diseases that have reappeared, and as long as we do everything he tells us, we will. Polio is one of them that's back. Or a strain of it is."

"It's been back for decades," June says. "To be completely truthful."

Mia nods. The smile just won't go away on her face. "Exactly. There is no resurgence, unless our executives let one happen by preventing the use of the vaccine. And Osso's using that right now to his advantage. Using the fear of possibility over probability. We know it's just distraction from the fact that there are no credits."

June nods. I can really only listen.

"Thing is, the administration isolates itself from everything, including disease. This is better than me, or Anna, would ever be at getting us not just through the border, but into the right buildings."

"So, you agree this idea is safer than calling yourselves out for who you are?" June asks.

"Yes." Mia says. "It's perfect."

"Why is this so perfect?" I ask. "What's the idea? I'm so lost." Oops, I said that out loud.

Mia turns toward me. "If we bring June, who actually *is* in one of these chairs, to the border, and people see him—like the guards and medical center administrators, and our executives—they will freak out. Right now, most people have only experienced *images* like the public poster. But we have the *real* deal. Our administration knows this isn't going to be a pandemic, but bringing June in will create mass hysteria inside their district, and take the focus off you and me. But . . . because we're with him, we'll be shuffled right along."

27

Uneventful. That's what I label the rest of our journey into District One. Thanks to Zane's car, we made it through the wall as if we had ambassador status. No one escorted us into, or through, the city, even though there couldn't have been more than a dozen transpos around—more than on the far side of District Eleven, but not nearly as many as I expected for city center in the middle of a workday.

Buildings jut into the sky like spears, sentries around The White House. We pass, still in the car, slowly making our way to the main gate.

"Are we going to The White House?" I ask.

"Yes."

"But I thought that was just a museum." At least, that's what they told us in educenter level one.

"The new one is a museum. The old one is still used by the Osso family," June says. "You know, a long time ago, this building was surrounded by green."

We turn and stop in line behind five other transpos. "Green what?" I ask.

"Grass. There used to be a huge, wide lawn in front. But as the population density skyrocketed, they repurposed all lawn in the city center for new buildings to house diplomats, ambassadors and other Administrative leaders. Can't have them working out in the Districts, you know."

I didn't know. "What about my dad and Zane's uncle? They have places out there."

"All just setup to look like their homes." Mia huffs. "It's pathetic really. Dad's place in District One is amazing. I mean .... It. Is. *Amazing*. And he hates it. So do I." She shrug-shivers as if trying to fight off something that landed on her shoulders.

"District One really is where the credits are," June says.

"Everyone here has more credits than they can count." Mia's tone is irritated. "They could probably fix the problems themselves just by sharing."

I can't believe what I'm hearing. "But aren't we—they—I mean, isn't everyone on a fixed credit system?"

Mia's laugh comes out strong. "We're supposed to be, but since when have you seen a member of our administration *not* put themselves on the highest possible pay scale?"

I haven't seen them do anything, so her question is kinda pointless.

She shifts toward me as the line shrinks, and we move up a little. "These are the highest paid people in the world right here. Do you know that if there's more than a ten-minute wait to get from the outskirts of the city center to inside, they tell you to work from your housing space until it clears?"

Uh, nope. Didn't know.

"That way, there's no stress upon entry to the office."

"It's like an enforced utopia," June says.

People walk on the sidewalk near the big white building, the blue sky sparkling above. Some have little dogs. Kids stroll with what I assume are their parents, or caregivers. It certainly looks fairy tale perfect. Kinda creepy, actually.

"Maybe everyone here is under a drugged spell," I say, wanting to find an answer other than affluence for why it's better here than everywhere else.

Mia's head goes back and forth again. "No way. Here, everything is fresh. Everything is clean. Food is brought in from farms certified to grow without any chemicals. So there's no way anyone will be influenced."

"Then, how? How are people just going about their business, knowing what's coming?" This doesn't make sense to me.

"They don't know any different." June moves us up to spot number two in line.

"Oh, they know," Mia's counter statement is profound. "They're protected from it all. That's why the walls around One are so high and still up. They're going to insulate themselves, no matter what happens on the outside."

"Even more reason to have Zane, then. To find the traitors and do away with them." June's grip on the car's steering wheel is so tight his knuckles turn white. "They'll leave everyone else to fend for themselves, won't they?"

"Until the drugs run out," Mia says. "But, by then, the few who are still fighting will just be corralled and shipped away."

We move to the first spot, and June turns a handle that brings the glass in his door down. "Pathway permission, passbook and registration confirmation, please," the guard says.

As Zane had told us, June pulls out a certification, along with his own identification, and hands them over.

"For the other two, as well." The man leans in, making eye contact with me.

I don't have any identification.

Mia spins to me. "Hand me yours, and I'll give it to the guard."

My eyes must bulge out of my face.

"Thanks," she says and turns back, reaching out with two objects in her palm.

What did she just do, and how did she just do it?

"Purpose of the visit?" the guard asks.

Mia nudges June. "Oh, I'm ... uh ... I have the polio."

The guard jumps back as if June might infect him right then and there. "Stay in place, please." He moves farther away and speaks to another guard. They both turn toward Zane's car, and their lips move for a couple minutes. Seconds later, they disappear into the little building at the gate, and a third person, a woman, I think, comes to the door with a white mask on her face, gloves on her hands, and the things Mia and June gave to the first guard in a plastic bag.

"You may proceed to the medical wing. Only the medical wing. Fourth left. Someone will be waiting."

"Thank you." June takes the bag and tosses it to Mia. With the glass wound back up again, he says, "That was rude."

Mia lifts a shoulder. "They don't know what we know about you, and if the propaganda has worked, which it obviously has, then they're freaked out by you. That's good for us because it means even nosy people will leave us alone." Her smile is wide. "It's the perfect way to get anywhere, and I mean, anywhere we want."

⊙━━━━⊙

The medical wing of The White House is a building in the far back. It's not really a wing, at all, but a completely separate building unit.

"Guess they really want to keep sick people out." June pulls the car into a designated holding spot and silences it. "Someone mind getting my chair?"

"I will." I jump out and move around to the back, where we'd stored his medical cart. Lifting it proves a little difficult, but I manage with only one scratch to the side of Zane's transpo-car-thing.

Mia stands at the front, stretching her arms up high. "You have no idea how awesome this is."

"What is?" I ask, setting up June's chair next to his door.

"The fact that June is with us. There is just nothing better than being undercover and completely out in the open. Nothing like it." She taps on her ear, I presume listening to something. "These went dead as we crossed into D-1. Might as well leave them in here, just in case." Both she and June stick their fingers in their ears, adjusting the earpieces, I guess. Mine hasn't made a peep since Zane gave it to me, so I don't do anything to mine.

With June settled and the doors to the car secured, we start toward the building, where two people dressed in white coats exit. Standing just outside the doors, masks on their faces, they wave our way, but don't walk out toward us.

I stay beside June as Mia pushes him, and he stretches out his left hand, palm up. "Put 'er there."

"What?" I ask.

He laughs a big hearty sound. "Hold my hand."

I place my palm against his.

"Be my girlfriend."

I jerk, but force myself not to move my hand.

June chuckles. "Not for real. For them." He nods toward the people we're heading toward. "No one in their right mind would ever even consider you an Osso, if you're holding my hand. So, it'll help keep your cover a little more."

"Why not? I mean why wouldn't an Osso hold your hand?"

"Because they'd never, *ever* affiliate with an imperfect."

I squeeze June's hand. "How can you say that?"

"Because I know it. You know why Granny said you were my ticket out? Because she thought I could use you. But you're different than everyone I've met, and yes, before you ask, I've met others from the Administration. You're compassionate. You're kind. You're thoughtful. You may be an Osso by blood, but you're not by spirit." A sigh releases from him. "And you're the only person, aside from Granny, who's ever called my chair my legs." His hand grips mine quickly in what I'd call a mini hug. "So, let's do this. Poster child, here I come."

Our trio keeps moving up the walkway, all the way to the medical-looking people dressed in white coats. Underneath the white, which reminds me so much of registration, a hint of pink and some blue peeks out—as if to say 'I am someone different!'

"Welcome to The White House Testing Facility." The one with the hint of pink extends a gloved hand toward June. "Juniper, is it?" she asks.

"Yes, ma'am." June's got his full southern drawl going.

Creases appear in her forehead as if she's smiling, but I'd never know, given the mask covering her mouth. "I'm Jaylene Hunter, and this is my research partner Arvonne Lattimer."

"Hello," he says in a super-deep voice.

Jaylene pats Arvonne on the shoulder and says, "We're here to introduce you to a few folks as well as to confirm your diagnosis and integrate your story into our activities. Won't you follow me?" She turns and walks through the door Arvonne holds open.

Glancing back toward Mia, I get a nod, telling me to follow, and I walk between Jaylene and June, with Mia in back and Arvonne behind her.

Jaylene spins around and walks backward, her hands clasped together in front of her. "A little tour, shall we?" She turns around again and heads toward a set of double doors. All in white.

It may not be registration, but it feels like it could be. As I think it, my knees tremble.

"This entire facility is dedicated to the health and safety of our le— our population, right now with a particular focus on the resurgence of Polio." She stops and faces us for the third or fourth time. I don't know why she can't just walk backward and talk, and stop spinning around.

"You, sir," she says, her gaze directly toward June, "can be cured. We're sure of it."

I don't need to glance over to know June's smiling. What I'm not sure of is if he believes her, or he's faking for the show.

Jaylene's hands clap once. "But, for now, we'd like to get to know more about you. Would you be willing to join me in here?" She extends a hand and what has to be a wall opens, since I didn't even see a door.

The wall-door-thing rotates once, and white disappears, bringing in rich colors and tones, browns and reds and blues, and lighting that's not stale or old but warm. Opulent. That word.

"Sure thing," June says, and I step forward as Mia pushes him toward the door.

Arvonne steps around and in front of us. "Juniper only."

Mia and I freeze. We both turn toward June.

"Sure thing," he says again, and with his gaze on me, he gives me the tiniest nod as if he's trying to say 'I'll be okay.' He does the same to Mia.

"You two will be escorted to a waiting lobby," Arvonne says, taking June's chair and rolling it forward out of Mia's control.

We both stand there as the door-that-is-wall-that-is-door rotates again and closes, leaving no sign it even existed.

This isn't registration. It's way worse than registration.

"This way, please," a young, female voice says, making Mia

and me turn. The girl, has to be female based on her stature and tone, is only about five feet tall and has the prettiest blue eyes I've ever seen. Like our greeters, she, too, has a mask over the lower half of her face and wears a white coat that covers any distinguishing features about her body shape.

We follow her down another white corridor to a see-through door that opens into a holding lot for people. The room is as stark white as the hallway, with grey seating along the perimeter.

Once inside, our little guide says, "This is just a precaution." She slips back out, and with a scratching buzz, the door closes and a shade floats down inside the glass, blocking our view to the hallway.

Mia jumps to it and pushes since there's no handle at all.

The door goes nowhere.

"We're locked in." Palm to forehead, she says, "I should have seen that coming. Dammit." Like Zane always does when he has to think, Mia starts the back and forth stepping of a nervous pacer. Back home, she stated that Zane was more brother than me sister, and I can see it. They have similar mannerisms—ones that she and I don't share at all.

Dropping to the grey, hard-backed divan—the largest seating in the space—which has absolutely no softness to it at all, I stare up at my sister. I have to believe this is a precaution, as the girl said. What else could it be?

Mia keeps up the pacing. Back and forth from the windowless door, to the opposite side of the room, which has absolutely nothing on it. Just more white.

A low sound echoes through the nearly empty room, and all at once, a mist descends from the ceiling.

Mia leaps back to the door and bangs on it with both fists, as I jump up, the spray coating my hair, dripping onto my nose.

"Cover! Don't drink it!" She hits the panel, but it doesn't open.

A single breath brings the liquid into my nostrils. I blow hard trying to keep it out, but another breath in sucks it in deeper. "Mia!" Panic compresses my chest as I try to avoid breathing in whatever the substance is.

Mia's hands cover her nose and mouth, and her unmoving chest tells me she's holding her breath, but at some point, she, too, is going to suck in air. Her head goes back and forth, shaking as the liquid falls beneath our heads, but it, at least, stops coming down from the ceiling.

Behind my hand, I take another breath, a sweet strawberry flavor filling my nose. It doesn't, however, make me drowsy or loopy, as I expected. It just smells nice.

After at least a minute, the spray dissipates fully, and we both remove our hands from our faces.

Our clothes aren't even wet—as if the mist didn't touch them at all.

Mia and I stare at each other. "What the hell?" She reaches out her hand, but there's no sign of liquid anywhere.

"What was that?" The strawberry smell permeates the air but in a soft, fresh way.

Mia brings her finger to her nose and wafts in air, or the smell, or something. "I really don't know. I—"

The door opens, revealing the little short girl who brought us to the room. "You can join us in the waiting lobby now."

My sister storms to her. "What the—"

Girl-guide holds up her hand, stopping my bull of a sister with just that motion. "You came in with a suspected Polio case. Your contagion had to be eradicated." Lowering her hand again, she adds, "Now, come with me," and waves us forward.

Mia glances back toward me, and with a quick shrug from me, we both follow the short girl.

Down another white hallway, through three sets of double doors, and into a room with a sign that actually says 'Waiting Lobby', we go. Better yet, the room is two sides of glass and two sides of a pale blue with dark, soft-looking furniture topped in colorful pillows. On the far wall, an entire bank of nutrition boxes is full of snacks and packaged drinks.

"You can wait here for your friend. His interviews will take a few hours. In the meantime, help yourselves to any nutrition. If you need assistance, press this button, and someone will come to you. Any questions?"

"Lavatory?" I ask.

"Across the hall." She points back through the open door.

Through the glass, I can actually see the sign. "Thank you." It's so much better to be able to see, than like in that other room.

As the girl turns, Mia says, "What was that spray, exactly, and why didn't you tell us it would be applied?"

Turning back, the guide smiles. "That would be privileged and proprietary information." The door closes with a soft click as she departs.

Mia spins to me and mouths the last thing the girl said. "I should have known better."

Sitting in the corner of the long divan, I pull my knees to my chest. "About the spray? Or going in here? Or what? I mean the plan did get us in here, and now we're free to ... you know ... do whatever we want. For a few hours. So, how do we find Zane? Is he even in this building? I mean, District One is huge."

Her pacing restarts. "I should have known to expect it and not get so worked up."

"What about Zane?"

"I can't believe I didn't see it coming."

"What about *Zane*, though?"

My sister doesn't stop moving. "I really can't—"

"Mia!" My exclamation comes out quick and loud.

She freezes. "What?" Her eyes are glassy.

I rise and walk to her. "Are you okay?"

Blinks happen. A few of them.

"Mia?" I take her by her arms and guide her to the divan. "Are you okay?"

She stares at me as if she has no idea who I am and blinks repeatedly.

"Sit down." I help lower my sister until she's seated and watch for a moment as she goes from eloquent leader to confused, lost and out of it. "Stay right there." Up again, I hit the button for help.

"Yes?" a voice asks through a speaker in the room.

"Uh ..." I lift my chin, facing the ceiling, searching for the source. "My sister's acting weird. Could that stuff from the other room ...? I mean, does it have any side effects?" *And if it does, will I be like her soon?*

"Only if you've been exposed to an active virus in the last forty-eight hours. Has she been?"

Glancing her way, I don't know how to answer. She's just sitting there, still as can be, slow-blinking every once in a while. "I-I don't know. Any other reason?"

"She'll be fine," the voice says.

She does not look fine to me. The Mia who made all the decisions thirty minutes ago is gone. "Shouldn't someone come look at her?"

"If she has any life-threatening symptoms, push the button." A light beep follows.

"Hello?" I ask.

No response.

"Great." June is separated from us, Mia's having some sort of episode, and Zane is who knows where. Sitting with my sister again, I take her hand in mine.

Her lids droop.

"Maybe you need some rest." As I nudge her onto her side, she curls up on the soft cushions and closes her eyes, her breathing shallow but regular. "Maybe you've just been going for so long that your body can't handle whatever that was, and I actually did rest, so I can." I pull a cover, one conveniently at the end of the divan, over her.

I start to pace like Mia did. Maybe if it helps her and Zane think, it will me, too. I'm alone. With no knowledge at all of the building, technology, or anyone communicating with me. No matter what, we came to the city center to find Zane. So, what do I do?

Think.

Think. Think. Think.

Why did Mia think Zane would be here? Or did she? She never said. Just said we had to get into the city center. There are thousands of buildings in the city center.

She knew we could get in with June's condition once he mentioned it. So, did she want us to go to *this* building?

Yes, because this is where Osso is.

Is Zane where Osso is, though?

This is a medical building.

Where they probably do medical stuff.

Back and forth I go, just like my sister, glancing up through the glass windows as I walk.

How is extracting information from Zane medical?

Because it requires a drug. And drugs generally require medical personnel.

So Zane has to be in this *building.*

Unless there's another building, and he's not.

My subconscious is notorious for casting doubts on all my ideas. My sister and Zane can just make decisions and go with it. I can't.

Where are you, Zane?

How do I find you?

The door opens, and two men push through. "... just need one more session with hi— oh, sorry. Didn't realize we had visitors." The man's smile is wide, and his chuckle is as fake as any I've ever heard. The scary part is that his voice is the same as from Zane's uncle's living quarters. "I'm Bradley Osso, but you probably already know that."

Uh ...

His head tilts a little. "You look familiar. Have we met?"

Uh ... I shake my head and stare at the floor, but glance up as he walks past toward the nutrition boxes. Walking backward, I slink toward the divan and my sleeping sister, folding into myself to keep from being more recognizable.

He types in a code at one of the boxes and retrieves a bottle of water. "If there's anything our staff can do for you, don't hesitate to ask. One for you, too, Bryan?"

"No, thanks." That voice is absolutely the same as Zane's uncle from the visit, but there's a sadness to his tone. "We should ... ah ... get going."

Osso pops off the top of the bottle. "Never waste a moment to meet the people," he says and tips the bottle up at his lips. I try hard not to make eye contact again. "Enjoy your stay."

I nod.

The swish of the door opening has me eyeing that area of the room as footsteps indicate they're walking past the windows in the direction of where Mia and I came.

Follow them.

If I follow, will they lead me to Zane?

What if I get caught?

What if they go somewhere else, and I get lost?

What would Mia do?

What would Zane do?

Why can't I just decide what *I'd* do?

Another glance toward my sister, and I know I'll get no answers from her. It's just me here. Me, all alone.

Go, before you lose your one and, maybe, only shot.

28

I've never been a spy. I'm not Zane, or Mia, or June. I don't know how to disappear like them. I have no idea how to do things undercover at all. If there are cameras, they'll record every one of my movements. If there are people, they will see me.

So, stop trying to think, or act, like them.

At least Osso didn't recognize me. I guess that means June's grandma wasn't quite right, and I have a shot at doing whatever it is I'm doing right now.

Shaking my head, I scurry down the hallway to the first intersection and peek around it to the right.

A set of double doors, with small windows near eye level, are to the left. Moving to it and peeking up through the windows, I find Osso Jr. and Zane's uncle walking side by side toward yet another double door. Zane's uncle motions with his hands as he moves, and not in that excited, happy way, but with rough movements as if he's angry.

I have no idea how to open the doors in front of me, so I tap in the middle and hope for the best. On silent hinges, they swish open.

Realizing I'm standing right in the middle, and the two men will likely hear the movement, I slink off to the side and wait until the doors are fully opened.

Peeking back in, I catch Osso and Zane's uncle as they turn

left before reaching the second set of doors, and I squeeze through as the ones I'm at begin to close.

The right one catches the back of my heel, sending a squealing echo down the hall. I freeze, wishing someone had, in fact, invented a person-sized invisibility cloak. When no one appears, I tiptoe forward, increasing my speed and staying as silent as possible as I come to the left turn and yet another set of doors.

Through the small windows, a whole hallway of doors greets me. Ten, at least, with all sorts of people bustling about, some in white coats, others in suits, standing in front of doors with their hands at their crotches, unmoving.

Security forces?

Slinking back and leaning against the wall, I have no idea how I'm going to get by, or through, them. Or if I should.

Think, Anna, think. I'd pace, but I don't want anyone to see me moving in this corridor.

Behind me, there's a swishing sound, and the doors I just came through open up.

Caught between set one and set two, I have absolutely no idea what to do and raise my hands in surrender.

A guy in a white lab coat, pushing a gurney, enters, with two other people carrying bags and poles. "What the hell are you doing here?" he asks.

"I—wha—"

"Didn't I tell you, if you come in this zone, you gotta be in scrubs, or a coat?"

"Uh—"

He shakes his head. "If I've told her once, I've told her a dozen times." As he reaches the second door, he stops. "Well?"

I have no idea what to say.

"Open the door already, and this time, since you're so behind, follow like a puppy dog and don't get lost." He eyes me with a serious glare. "Got that?"

I nod and press the 'Open' button. The doors swing inward, and I tag along, as directed, with the other two pushing at the back of a bed.

At a groan coming from beneath the sheets, I glance down. *Zane!*

"Quiet him. We don't want patients bothering other patients, and Osso really doesn't like *staff* bothering *staff*."

I'm sure that comment is directed to me.

The person to my right flicks a little button on the bag she's holding, and Zane goes silent, his arm falling off the side and out from under the sheet. Tubing feeds into the crook of his elbow. The attendant nudges it back under the sheet while we walk.

The men standing guard at each of the doors don't move, and though the lab-coated people do, they say nothing. Since the guy told me to get moving, no one has said a word. I'm even more glad I didn't barge in, given the circumstances.

Through the calm commotion, we go to a room at the far end of the hall. The four of us roll the bed right into the middle and back it up against a beautiful art-covered wall. Nothing in here is white. The wood on the floor has to be something old, with cracks and giant knots, all of which have been finished into a pristine, smooth surface. Floor-to-ceiling windows line the far side, looking out onto a green lawn, which shouldn't be possible, given it's the dead of winter.

"Don't just stand there, hook him up," the man says.

I return from my perusal and find Zane, uncovered to the waist, tubes in both arms, circular discs affixed to his temples, neck, chin, chest and who knows where else.

The other two people leave, and I stand alone in the room

with the main guy. "Now, since you're here … you get to stay. Got that?"

I nod.

"And since you never remember what I tell you to do, let me say it once more. Are you listening?"

I nod again.

"Your job is to stay here with him for twenty-four hours. No one comes in or goes out. He's not to be asked any questions, at all, if he wakes. Set your watch."

What's a watch? I glance away.

"You forgot that, too?"

Offering yet another nod seems appropriate, so I do.

"When are you going to learn?" The question comes out completely exasperated. Whoever he thinks I am must be a total and absolute horror to work with. "Why do I even try?" His grimace turns even farther south. "Just stay here, and don't leave. Can you do that one thing? Don't walk out of that door." He points with a sternly stretched finger. "Sit your butt down, and don't move until I get back."

"Yes, sir."

His head cocks a little.

Did I give myself away with my voice?

"You better be here when I get back." He presses a button on the device on his wrist, and it beeps once. "Twenty-four hours. Don't mess this up, or this time, I will go to your uncle, and I will tell him you have no idea how to work. You think he's going to like that?"

I shake my head but keep mute.

"You got that right. Twenty-four, Angelica."

Angelica?

The man turns and walks to the door, mumbling, and just before it closes, I hear, "Osso family, or not, that girl's trouble."

Oh, my Oz, he thinks I'm Angelica Osso.

Osso Junior's niece, and the only female in the administration poised to take on the role of CEO from Osso Junior, according to our government studies from Level three Educenter.

How did he mix us up, but her own uncle didn't? Or did he?

I drop to the seat next to Zane's bed, cheek resting against my knees, and stare out at the gorgeous green grass and the blue sky. It looks peaceful—except for the barricade on the far side and the buildings on the two other sides.

What am I going to do? I've found Zane, but he's unconscious. I can't just roll the bed out and back down the hall, lift Mia on to it and push them both out to the car. I can't carry him, either. I can't do anything. I can't go out by myself, because someone else is bound to recognize me.

Forehead to palms, I heave a giant sigh. Once again, I'm as stuck as a mouse in a trap. Walked right in with no exit.

What happens if the real Angelica shows up? What do I do then? Or if they figure out I'm not her.

Slipping my hand under Zane's unmoving one, I entwine my fingers with his and squeeze. "I need you to tell me what to do, Zane." Warmth flows through me, radiating into my palm, but he doesn't move. Doesn't share any Zane-esque insight. Laying my head down on the edge of the bed, I want to cry. To tell my dad he had it all right, that this is a mission far too complicated for me and Mia. Really just me. Mia would know what to do, if she were here.

The door swishes open, letting in outside sound.

I lift my chin, remembering what the guy said. "No one's supposed to come in here."

A girl, no older than me, stares at me. Her dark hair is longer than mine, hanging all around her face. Her attire is far more trendy with wide color bands on her shirt and what has to be the latest in fashionable jeans. Oddly, she's wearing flip-flops, when it can't be more than twenty degrees outside, even in the sun, and a long trench coat that extends all the way to the floor.

"Who are you?" she asks as she steps farther into the room.

"Wh-who are you?" The stutter makes me cringe, but I hold that inside and try not to let it show. At least, I think I don't.

"I asked you first." There's no mistaking who she is, though I'm not going to say her name in case I'm wrong.

"Well ... I ... was here first."

"Touché. But I could get you thrown out," she says.

"Or I could, since, apparently, they think I'm you, and *I* was here first." *Please let that be right.*

She slips a hand behind her. "Yeah, but I have a—" Both hands go behind. "Dammit." She stalks toward me. "Where is it?"

Standing no taller than her, I ask, "Where's what?"

"My security card, you dimwit." She's not a very nice part of my family tree which makes me doubly happy I'm a branch once or twice removed and normally far, far away.

"I don't have it. I don't have any ID." For that I'm oddly thankful.

Her eyes narrow. "Then, how'd you get in here?"

"We look alike, I think. Someone told me to follow them and stay put."

"Whatever." She angles a finger toward the still-sleeping Zane. "They tell you to stay with him?"

"Yeah."

She turns a device on her wrist toward herself as she scoots over toward Zane's bed. "Damn. He's hot. Probably why they haven't just gotten rid of him."

"What do you mean?"

Angelica gets close to Zane's cheek and breathes in. "Smells good, too."

"What do you mean *gotten rid of him*?"

She shrugs.

"No, seriously, what do you mean?" Even I can tell my tone is expectant, and I want to jump up and shake the answer out of her.

Her brow furrows. "Why the twenty questions? You got a thing for this one?"

"I—no. I just—"

"Whatever." The thing on her wrist dangles as if it's way too large, and each time she twists it, it slips back out as she lets go and taps her fingers together. "So, if they think you're me, and you're stuck in here ..." A devious grin alights her face. "Then, I can get back to my party." She moves straight to the windows, taps a button on the side, and two panels slide open, bringing in fresh, ice-cold air. "So, don't leave, or I will tell them who *you* are." Pushing the window closed from outside, she stops it with just a crack open and asks, "Who are you, anyway?"

"I'm no one." Like I'm going to give her my name.

"Whatever." That seems to be her favorite word. She slams the glass shut, bounds across the grass and to the building on the left, which she opens up and walks right into, disappearing from view.

Thanks to my clearly temperamental and selfishly, terminably late cousin-of-sorts, I now know how to get out of here.

I just have to wake up Mia, find June, and get an unconscious Zane out, too.

Piece of cake.

Right.

⚬━┿━⚬

Zane taught me one thing about sneaking around: doing

it at night is much easier than during the day. Not only does darkness help with cover, there are less people around.

In the last six hours, no one, not another soul, has entered Zane's room, and as the sun went behind the horizon, blanketing the room first in orange and pink and eventually losing luster, I, at least, now know we face west. The same way we need to go.

If my orientation is right, June's somewhere to the right, whether or not he's actually in this building. Mia's still back in the waiting lobby, and the car is on the opposite side of us all, in the holding lot.

Given Zane hasn't moved, and despite the orders from *the guy*, I grab the white lab coat hanging on the hook by the bathroom and slip it around my arms. On the lapel, AUWHM has been embroidered.

Turning back to Zane, I stare at him for a few seconds. "Don't do anything stupid," I whisper and open the door.

No one even walks the hall. Not a single guard stands at attention next to the doors. No other people in white lab coats move about. It's as if the entire area is deserted.

Empty.

Silent.

The hallway is no longer lit with a bright intensity, but has a dull, shadowy, spooky, haunted feel.

Here goes nothing.

My step into the hall produces no alarm, no security scramble to push me back in the room. Two feet into the hallway doesn't set off any alarms, either. The door closes without a sound behind me, and I start back toward where I left my sister.

No one greets me.

No one stops me.

No one is anywhere.

Retracing my steps is easy, and I go through both sets of double doors without hesitation.

Back down the hall.

Back to the waiting lobby.

An *empty* waiting lobby.

With no Mia.

I whirl, expecting her to sneak up on me, but she doesn't. No one does.

What if everyone is gone? What if I go back and Zane's not there anymore, and I'm here all by *myself*?

Racing down the empty hall, my feet slap against the tiles. I slide as I reach the doors, jam my palm against the entry lever, run through the gap, make it through the second, and getting back to Zane's door, I open that.

He's still there, resting just like before.

My heart pounds in my chest as I try to figure out what in the world has happened.

Are there any other people in this wing?

With Zane safe, I sneak back out and over to one of the other doors. There is no viewing window, no way for me to peek inside and double check that we're not the only ones in the entire building.

If I open it, will someone freak out? Call security? Get me, or get Angelica, rather, in trouble?

Not wanting that possibility to play out, I go back to Zane.

Other than the rise and fall of his chest, he hasn't moved at all. Not in more than six whole hours.

Without Mia, without June, without anyone, there's no way I can get out of here with him. Staring through windows, to the dark, open space beyond, only tiny pinpricks of light dot the area. No way can I push a bed through the lawn. I don't have that kind of strength, on top of the fact that it will create a path that, to anyone who looks, will show exactly where I've gone and what I've done.

How would I even get him beyond the gates? What about away from the building, at all? I can't even operate Zane's car.

Dropping to the seat next to him, I leave my elbows on my knees and cringe as my stomach grumbles.

"Delta Street ... compromised. Don't—"

Whirling to my right, Zane's eyes are closed, but his lips are parted just a tiny bit, and those words definitely came from him.

"Zane?" Could he have awoken, and I just didn't notice?

He doesn't respond.

I clasp his hand with mine. It's still warm, still alive, but unmoving, and when I let go, he doesn't try to hang on. "This is so weird. Everything about it is, Zane. You're here in the White House Medical Facility. They did something to you. Mia's gone. June's somewhere else. I don't know what to do."

No sound emerges from him.

Maybe I'm going crazy. Maybe that spray has hit me like it did Mia, and I'm hallucinating. Maybe I'm hallucinating this whole thing, and really, I'm at Zane's house, hidden under the bed, listening to his uncle and ... mine ... talking about going back to District One with Zane. Maybe I'm just still asleep.

That's it. That has to be it.

A sound on my left has me jolting upright. The windows slide open from outside and someone appears in the room, cloaked in darkness.

"Angelica?" a female voice asks.

"I—"

The figure rushes to me and grabs my arm, pulling me off the chair. "Let's go before they catch us."

My feet slide on the floor as she pulls me closer to the open window. "Stop—" I try to pull free, but she's seriously stronger than me and her grip doesn't even budge. "I'm not—"

"You are, too, going." She stops. "I've been looking all over hell and back for you. We had a commitment to Moe to be at his party, and you're going." She starts again, and as she's outside and I'm inside, I brace my feet against the window frame and yank as hard as I can.

My hand slips, and I fly back, landing with a butt-bumping thud on the floor, the back of my head smashing into the edge of Zane's bed. Luckily, the soft part.

The girl comes back in. "What's wrong with you? Why aren't you dying to get out of here? Why are you—" In the dark, it's impossible for me to see her eyes, but I'm guessing she's figured out I'm not the friend she came for.

If I'm not her, where is she? Why do I even care?

"I see now." The girl walks into the room, the dimly lit side light on the far right of Zane bringing her into more relief. "You like this one. Geez, Ang, why didn't you just say?"

"Um—"

"Get him a rolling chair, and we'll take him with. We can get you both back by oh-six-hundred. You know, before anyone even knows. And if anyone asks, you won't even have to lie about being with him all night." This is not the kind of girl I'd have expected Angelica Osso to hang out with. Then again, who am I to judge? "And, hell, this time, if you actually want to keep him, we just won't come back." She whirls toward me, her face in full relief, pudgy cheeked, unkempt hair, and a shirt torn at the shoulder. "If you're just going to sit there, I'll get the chair." She goes over to one of the panels by the shower room, opens it, and pulls out a contraption that unfolds into a wheeled chair.

I didn't even know stuff hid behind there.

Turning back, she pushes on a second area and reveals an entire cabinet of pre-packaged food. "Gonna need something. Not like they'll charge *him* for it." She chuckles and opens a package. "Want something?" she asks.

"Sure." Not wanting to give away my entire face and body, if she's truly a friend and knows the real Angelica, I stay low.

She tosses me a package as she stuffs three into the pockets of her black pants. "'Kay. Let's go." After wheeling the chair to Zane's side, she strips off the top sheet, lifts him as if he weighs nothing, and drops him into the chair.

His head flops to the side, and I jump up and right it so he doesn't break his neck. "Careful," I say. At least he's got a pair of shorts on under the sheet. Outside, though, he's going to be way too cold.

"Yorealdolifisone," she says, mouth full. I'm pretty sure she's commenting on how much I like Zane, but I'm not going to attempt a verbal interpretation and get it wrong. "Get those tubes."

Detangling the tubes and attaching them to the back of the chair, I settle Zane in and prop up his torso with pillows. Taking both covers from the bed, I drape them over him.

"Awful lot of effort for a guy, you know," my helper says.

"Yeah," is the only response I give her.

"'Kay. Let's go." She pushes Zane to the windows, presses the button, and moves out into the cold.

I take one look back and commit everything I can about the room to memory, in case I need to reset it if we get caught. Without the sun, it can't be more than zero degrees, and once again, I have no coat. I follow her, as she takes the chair straight across the lawn, through the dark, until we reach the fence. She heads right. I go with her. At the side of the building, she stops and moves to the front of Zane's chair.

"I lift. You push," she says, as she hauls him out of the chair and drapes him over her shoulder.

"Okay."

She crouches down and shimmies through a small opening between the fence and building, just enough for a body to go through sideways, but not for the open chair. Snapping the bottom latch, I fold the chair, slide it through, open it while still on the wrong side of the fence and Herculean-girl places Zane, far more gently than before, back in the seat. It takes nothing for me to slip through the same space, along with Zane's equipment, and reunite with him and this girl who must have some serious muscle.

I should ask her name, but I'm sure that'll out me before light does.

We head down the sidewalk, walking tightly against the side of the building. Rough edges turn to smooth, and back to rough, repeatedly as we walk.

A frantic banging sounds from inside one of the smooth spots.

"They should keep those sickos in there calmer," the girl says.

We continue, as does the banging, though it grows fainter by the second, I'd swear I heard someone yell 'Anna'. "Did … did you hear something?"

She keeps going, but I think she's shaking her head.

"Anna …" Once again my name hits me.

Stopping, I listen.

"Anna …" it's muffled but definitely my name.

June!

Racing back, I realize, like our building, each of the smooth areas is a window. At the third one we passed, I stop, and on the other side, June sits in his chair, in the dark, his forehead and palm against the window as if he has sapped all his energy trying to get my attention.

I knock, and his head pops up, lips curving. Pointing to the right, I mime pressing a button, hoping his room mirrors Zane's.

June moves across to the side but comes back to the window and shrugs, shaking his head.

"What are you doing?" The exasperated voice of the girl comes back to me. "You can't let out a sicko! You'll get us all dead."

I turn and lean into the one spot of light coming from across the barren road.

Girl shifts back. "You're not Angelica." She thumps a closed fist against her open palm. "I should—"

"What?" I ask. "Report me to the closest authority? I could do the same to you."

Her grimace fades, but the hardened eyes remain.

"Yeah, you screwed up, but I'll help you and tell you the last place I saw Angelica, if you help me get this *one* person out of this *one* room." I can't help but think about my sister and where she might be, too, but I'm going to have to wait on finding her.

"He'll kill us."

"No, he won't."

"Yes, he will. That's a quarantine room. You'd know that, if you were legit."

"Well, I'm not legit. So tell me how you got in my room, so I can get him out of here."

She shakes her head. "You can't. Only ID'd medical staff can get in, because they're in the system. Ang just always leaves the room door she's supposed to be in unhinged if we need to come get her."

"How do they get in if they are?" I ask.

"Thumb to the button. But you don't want to do that. Really." She backs up as if I'm about to release a plague. "Not that you can, anyway, since you're not Ang." More backpedaling takes her ten feet away at least.

"Button," June says, still muffled but clearer through the glass since we're so close. "Just try it."

I press my thumb to the button. It immediately releases a latch, and I jump back.

"Your funeral!" Amazonian-girl races off into the dark.

June and I grab the window and slide, pulling it until it opens fully. "Strange people you hang out with. Who was that?" he asks.

"Long, *long* story. I'll tell you in the car."

He maneuvers his chair over the lip of the window.

"Where's Zane?" he asks.

I point toward the other chair—the one that's not moving—twenty feet away.

"Let's go," June says and rolls after me. "I assume he's unconscious?"

"Hasn't said a word in hours. Well … at one point, he said 'Delta Street … compromised. Don't—', I think, or I was just hearing things, or my head was making stuff up. I don't know. He hasn't moved since."

"Let's get out of here."

29

Not a soul stopped us as we raced our way to the car—the only thing in the holding lot at all. Guards didn't question us when I opened the back and showed them not one, but two folded up medical chairs as we exited, or when I claimed Zane slept because of his illness, and they should step back unless they wanted to catch it. June, awake at the wheel, and fake-coughing, further propelled us out the final gates with an insane amount of speed.

No one in District One wants to catch what June, or Zane, supposedly have

It also seems no one in District One remains in their work environment longer than assigned, and that no one has a late-night shift.

I don't get it, but what do I know?

June didn't ever have a room monitor, because, according to him, no one wanted to risk their lives around him. No one shared in his supposed treatment plan, or study details. They locked him in the room, turned on a speaker, and talked to him through it whenever he called them, though they never had anything to say. They sent no one in. They tested nothing. They asked him even less—if that were possible.

As he shared the most boring day of his life, I recounted one that ranked pretty high up there on the eventful meter.

"Should I have waited for Mia?" I ask for the third time through a mix of worry, at having left her, and happiness that I managed to get Zane out.

June navigates us out of District One, the car once again offering the proper and necessary credentials to get through all districts and barriers. "Like I said, based on what Zane's told me about her ... she might already be out."

She wouldn't have left me, would she have?

Yes, she would've.

"*And* ... I think he said that she said never to worry about her, or something like that, too."

She has said that. Several times. Mia always manages to find her way around, or out, of whatever situation. I have to think that's happened again. Have to, or my guilt-o-meter will ratchet up too high.

A deep shiver makes my feet jerk and creeps its way up me, ending with a weird spasm of my hands. "Eww. Sorry. Weirdness."

"Tell me about it," June says. "Everything about today has been weird. So, Angelica is your Doppleganger, huh?"

I shrug as my eyelids droop, and I force them open again. "I wouldn't say that, necessarily. I mean, we did look alike, and we are technically family, by blood, I guess, but we aren't exactly the same, or anything."

"Yeah, but if you look *that* alike ... so alike it takes a really detailed look by someone who obviously knows her really well to pick you out, I have to wonder."

"Why is that weird? Don't they say everyone has a twin in the world?" Numbness creeps up my legs. Shaking them makes it stop. "And even twins don't always look alike-alike. Except for Marlena and Lucie, of course."

June laughs a little. "Resemblance is one thing. Cloning is

another."

"What?" Shock coats my exclamation. "I'm not a clone." Rubbing my calf helps stop the spreading unease.

"She could be."

"No way." My left lid won't stay open, and forcing it up with my fingers brings nothing but blurriness to my vision. I blink and rub it, hoping it'll help as tingling encompasses my arms.

What's happening?

"Or vice versa."

What were we talking about?

My right eye does the same thing as my left, and my head drops forward, but I yank it back as if I've fallen asleep for a moment and didn't plan to.

June glances my way. "You okay?"

I nod, my lids falling again. *This is not right. Tell June.* "Actually ... I might not—"

"Anna?" His voice is muffled. "Anna ..."

Buzzing fills my ears.

Chin falls to chest.

World closes in.

All.

Goes.

Black.

⊙══╪══⊙

A zing of fear jolts through me, and I blink open my eyes to nothing but darkness. Closing them, I breathe in, the scent of brewing coffee reaching my nose. Eyes open again, the dark still greets me, but blinking a few more times brings a little clarity to the space. A bedroom. I'm on a bed. *A bed.*

I rise, fast, and turn.

Zane's laying prone next to me.

Keeping my eyes open, and wishing they'd adjust faster than they are, I stare at his chest to make sure he's breathing.

With the slight rise of his ribcage, my entire body relaxes.

The tubes that were connected to him are gone, but he's still laying there as peaceful as the dead.

I poke his shoulder, wondering if maybe he's just asleep.

He doesn't move.

"Zane."

No response.

A light brightens a part of the floor, and I lay back down and close my eyes, hoping I haven't given away the fact that I'm awake—if it matters.

"Anna?" June's voice asks in a whisper.

I launch up. "June!" The exclamation is a hurried whisper. "Zane's not waking up."

The light grows as June opens the door and rolls in. "He's got a ways to go, I think, before he comes around."

"How long—how long have I been out?"

"Uh . . . it's about four-thirty in the morning, so seven hours. Ish."

I rub a hand over my temple. "What happened?"

June motions for me to follow him, and I slip from the bed, a weird Deja-vu sensation overwhelming me. Walking into the hallway, I realize exactly why I feel this way: I'm in my mom's living space.

"Oh, my god, it was all a dream." A happiness takes over me, knowing all this torment really happened in my head. When I turn to June, though, he doesn't share the same smiley-grinny-happy face I'm sure is plastered on mine. "It's not a dream, is it?"

He shakes his head.

"Well, at least I'm home." A deep breath steels my spine in

preparation for talking to my mom and dad.

June's head goes side to side again.

"Uh … what's that for?"

"You're not home."

"Not home?" How can I not be home? This looks just like my mom's space.

"Not exactly."

Slumping shoulders precedes my continuation through a hallway that is as much a duplicate of my house as anything. Worse, when I step toward the living-kitchen combo, my feet refuse to move, stuck in the frame of a space that absolutely, without a doubt, *is* my mom's space. "This is where I liv—*lived*, June." The divan is the same. The table clearly has a tilt, and while my mother isn't sitting there with a cup and her comms unit, it's in the exact same place.

I know what June's squished lips mean: 'I don't want to tell you'.

Marching my way to the kitchen area, I turn on the back burner. It doesn't work. Just like normal.

"This *is* my living space!"

"It's not." June's head goes back and forth.

"Where are we, then?"

"It's a long story, and I promise to tell you, but I can't right now."

"What? Why not?"

Something beeps, and June withdraws a tablet. "Because we have to go. Like, right now."

"Go where?"

He rolls to me and takes me hand. "Anna, do you trust me?"

There's that trust thing again. I do trust June. Zane, too, but Zane's not even awake to help.

An old lady appears at the back door, a door that looks and

acts just like the one in Mom's place. *My* space. "Glad to see you're awake, Erianna." She nods toward June. "Guess you were right, young man."

"Grandma?" The word is out of my mouth before I can stop it because my grandmother is dead, not here, where here is apparently not actually here.

"Come with me." She disappears just as quickly as she showed up—out through the same door.

I stare a June. "What the—" *My grandma?* Here, in a place that's eerily identical to my own. On top of that, I've met my clone, and Zane's still unconscious. This has to be some sort of dream. *Has* to be.

The old woman comes back in. "I said *now*." She leaves for a second time.

June rolls her way, tugging me along by my hand. "Come on, Anna. We have to go."

"But ... wha ..." I don't even know what to ask anymore. Or what to say. Or what to do. Digging in my heels, I stop our forward progress like some spoiled kid who wants her candy before dinner.

The Grandma-lady—no way she's actually my Grandma—returns yet again. "So, this is how it's going to be? We're in the middle of a war brokered on the strength of the human mind. Now, get a move on."

"Huh?"

"Don't even try. Just do," June says.

What is going on? Is this some other dimension? Have I traveled in time? Did I sleep for a millennia and my frozen body defrosted and now— "Just do ... *what*? Where are we going?" I am beyond confused.

Another beep sounds, and June tugs harder. "Come on, Anna. We *have* to go."

"Go *where? Where* are we going, June? *Where* are we? Why are we *here?* Where *is* here? What's happening?"

June stares straight at me. "We're at a safe house. A ... passage house, actually. I can't explain all of it now, because it took me hours to figure it out, get here, and all that, and we have, like, ten minutes, or everything is going to fall apart."

"*What* is?" My hands fly in the air and smack down on my thighs.

June reaches out, pleading with his palms together. "We're at the border, Anna. Twenty feet away. We're going to the U.S.."

I spin and point back at the room where I know Zane is sleeping. "But—"

"He'd want us to go."

"I'm not going to the U.S. without him!"

"Five minutes!" The Grandma-person's voice comes through from the back.

June rolls closer, my dangling hand still against his. "She'll take care of him."

I yank free. "I am *not* leaving Zane here with some woman I don't know, but who looks like my dead grandma, in a living space that looks like mine less my parents. I'm—"

"We have to."

"Why?"

June's shoulders slump. "Because they know."

A tremble shakes my entire body. "They ... know what?"

"Delta street *has* been compromised. A hundred percent. This is our last and only chance to get out of here before all hell breaks loose. To save ourselves before every person is individually accounted for, every generation line is tracked, every person is tagged, everything is searched, everything—"

"Hurry up, you two!"

"I'm *not* going without Zane!" I don't care what's happening in the A.U., I'm not saving myself if he can't be saved. I'm a fluke. I'll find a way to be safe. They'll want me because I'm easy to keep around.

June reaches down and places his tablet on the floor. When he grabs the handles the way he does, I know he's about to get out of his chair and sit on the floor. I've seen that move enough times.

"What are you doing?"

"Take Zane. He'll probably wake up ... maybe ... or you can get him help." June slips from his seat and lands with a thud on the floor.

"Where's the other chair? The one in the car."

"I had to get rid of it. The whole thing." He scoots back until he leans against the divan. "Put him in my chair and roll him out."

"I'm not going without you, June."

The back door slams shut. "What is it about you two that you can't tell time?" There is no way this is my grandma. She'd never talk like that to me.

"Look ..." I storm up to her. "I'm not going wherever it is you're taking us without the guy in the bed back there and the one on the floor there. Either all three of us go together, or we all stay here and face whatever's coming." A tremble rolls through my body, and I try to force myself still so it doesn't show.

Grandma-person's eyes narrow. "You're more like your mother than your mother even thinks." The old lady reaches toward me and pulls me into a hug that lasts way too long and is way too tight for a complete stranger. As she pulls back, her lips curve. "I knew one day you'd be a part of this. I just hoped it would be under better circumstances. Now ... I have an idea how to get someone who can't walk *and* someone who isn't moving through the wall behind his place, but it's all going to come down to what you're willing to do, Erianna?

30

Zane had, jokingly, once told me that going to the U.S. could be dangerous, that it could require us having to crawl through mud and dirt and grime. Never once did I think that part would be real, especially not squeezing through a two-foot hole, in the frigid night.

Yet, here we are. It's dark. It's long. It's cold. Dirty. Hard. Dusty. Claustrophobic. This is much worse than I could have ever imagined. I'm crawling, not walking, and Zane isn't leading.

I am.

I do believe this is the only way to get to the U.S., though. Why? Because June agreed with my Grandma, and without Zane, he's the only one I can trust.

Digging my elbows into the ground and pulling myself forward, I focus on the shaft of light I've illuminated in front of me with a little flashlight. The rope that's attached to me is what I'll need when I get to the other end. If I get to it.

My breath comes out in cold puffs, fogging up the air in front of me as I drag my legs along the ground behind me.

My muscles burn as I continue my crawling motion, one I figure June won't have a problem with, given how strong his upper body is. Mine? Not so much.

I can't see June or Zane anymore. No one guides me. No

one encourages me. All I have right now is me, to get us to the U.S., to give Zane what he wanted most.

His uncle, and mine, used him. As a tool. Not caring. Probably even watched and helped get the information they wanted from him. Maybe Zane's uncle let him live, I don't know. Maybe they wanted more from him, and getting Zane out is the only way to save him.

Grunting my way farther, I tug on the rope and note that it's tight. According to Grandma-lady, that means I only have about ten feet to go and need to release some of what's in my hand as I reach the end.

Unfurling some of the rope, I pull myself more, and a windy sound reaches my ears.

Tunnel's end?

A few more crawling motions bring a deeper cold to my bones. Even the borrowed coat isn't enough to shield me. My nose is running, but I can't wipe it; I've sniffed at least a hundred times, and I'm pretty sure ice is forming around my face.

Keep going.

I release more of the rope and use my arms to pull forward.

Keep going.

Another foot of rope. Another foot-ish to the end.

Keep going.

One more length of rope. A step closer to the end.

Again and again I go, until I escape my tunnel and find myself in the midst of open space.

In a field.

In the dark.

Under the waning moonlight.

Moving faster, knowing that my time is limited, I wiggle my way out through the hole, grab the rope and tug three times to show June that I'm through.

A pull back says he's ready.

Altering my position to sit facing the U.S. side of the wall, and pressing my feet against the surface, I pull, slowly, carefully. The weight on the other end is far heavier than anything I've ever had to haul in my life.

Like my own journey, one foot at a time, the rope grows longer on my side of the tunnel.

One foot at a time, I know Zane's coming through, and as heavy as he is, I will get him to the U.S..

It's the least I can do.

Despite the cold, sweat beads on my forehead and drips down my nose. My muscles burn, and the coat around me is making me too hot.

No time to take it off.

I pull more. Harder. Keeping my pace the same, hoping that while I'm pulling Zane's feet, June's able to both follow and push and deal with the claustrophobia himself.

Never did I imagine this is how we'd go to the U.S. How Zane would get here. That this is how we'd have to cross over.

That I'd go at all.

I don't even know what to do now that I'm here. We ran out of time for explanations; my timing has been terrible through this whole ordeal.

Another pull brings Zane's booted feet into view. I can see them because the sky is lightening—the sun coming up.

Scrambling and leaving the rope aside, I grab his feet and slide him halfway out of the tunnel. One more tug reveals the rest of him along with a visual of June's smiling face.

"Fancy meeting you here," he says, bringing a grin to my own.

"Never a dull moment." Maneuvering behind Zane and working my arms under him, I get him so he's leaning on the wall, still out cold.

June crawls the rest of the way out and props himself up next to Zane. Actually, both of us do, sandwiching Zane between us. At least he's dressed. Well dressed, thanks to Grandma. Not as dirty as me, due to the tarp we put him on. June, though, he's just as filthy as I am.

Heaving a sigh, I stare out at the rising sun, pink and yellow against the dark sky.

It doesn't look any different on this side of the wall than it did on mine.

It doesn't rise any slower.

It doesn't change how I feel inside, how much I don't get what's happening to my country, and how much I already miss normal.

It doesn't change how much I wish Zane would just wake up.

"What do we do now?" I ask, hoping June knows.

"We wait."

"Wait for what? Or should I say *who*?"

June chuckles. "According to your grandmother, someone will eventually sweep the wall."

"Eventually?" Could we be here for days? Weeks? We'd be dead by then, of course, since we couldn't pull June's chair through and don't have a second for the unconscious Zane.

"Probably sooner than later, given what's going on. Of course, they might not check it, at all, since they'll probably assume the people coming through can get wherever they're going on their own."

Oh goodie.

"And, of course, because comms were shut down to prevent additional breeches, Delta Street won't know that anyone is coming through. They'll probably even think the other side was officially sealed, like all the other spots have been already."

"Why wasn't this one?"

"Your grandma let me wait for you to wake up. Or until five a.m. whichever came first."

"What happened to me?"

June shakes his head. "I don't know. Haven't had enough time to investigate."

June and I stare out at the rising sun, the yellow ball above the horizon. "What do we do now, then?" I ask.

"You could go."

Me? "Go where? Where am I supposed to go?" I turn toward June, wishing he could hand me a map and a list of steps to take that would get us to wherever we need to be.

He holds a paper in his hand.

Now I ask for something useful and get it? Taking the paper, I open it, and on it are nothing more than the words: Independence Avenue. *So not helpful.* "What is this?"

June's lips squish to the side. "A street, I think. But then again, most people think Delta Street is a street, too." He shrugs.

Leaning back against the cold wall, I try to imagine how my so-called Grandma thought that two words on a piece of paper would help us once we got to the other side of the giant wall. Did she not know this landed us in the middle of a winter-deadened field? Didn't she know we'd have nowhere obvious to go? No shelter? No food? No contact? Nothing.

Balled fists are about the only outlet I have for my growing frustration.

June coughs as if clearing his throat. "I could start crawl-ing—"

"No," I say, shaking my head. "I'll go." If I've learned any-thing in the last eighteen years, it's how to walk from one place to the next. Cold, wet, hot, dark, light, I can walk, and I don't need a lot of food to make it through, either.

Being a fluke may finally pay off.

"Where will you go?" June asks.

I point out into the distant field. "That way. Toward the sun. East. Somewhere over there. If the sun starts to set before I get somewhere, I'll ... turn around, even if I've found nothing."

"If someone finds us, I'll make them follow your tracks. So leave breadcrumbs."

"I don't have any food to—"

June chuckles. "It's an expression. Leave me a trail of some sort, and we'll find you. Or come back, and we'll be right here waiting."

With the sun just high enough for me to see that I have a long, *long* way to go, I stand. My higher point of view doesn't help. Worse, wind whips up my jacket, freezing the sweat that accumulated on my skin and creating an air conditioner between me and my cover. Shivering doesn't help the cold, but it does get me jumping.

Pointing again, toward the sun, I say, "That way," and glancing at June, I fake a smile. "I'll be back."

"I know you will." He offers a small salute. "Welcome to the U.S."

It's not quite the welcome I expected, but Zane would probably say something like, "We're here, and that's all that counts."

I can only hope what he really wanted out of this is what's coming.

Acknowledgements

Gigantic thank yous to my daughters who, when they read Perry Road, told me I had to get moving on finishing this book. It's because of them, that I finished the major overhaul of some of the book's structure and pursued those last edits, and last read-through. Gotta love having fans in the same house.

Thank you also to my amazing, consistent beta readers, J.A. Belfield and Wendy Seagondollar, without whom this book would not be anywhere near written like it is.

Thank you, also, to the readers of Perry Road for your patience in waiting for me to get this one finished. Lots of life happened between the two books, but I do promise to work on the finale (Independence Avenue) as soon as this one is published. Promise. Remember, I have in-house pushers, now, too, so I won't have a chance to pause!

Gratiousness also goes out to my husband who deals with all my griping and troubleshooting tools on my computer when they don't work right, especially the ones I write and edit in!

As always, giant thank yous to YOU, the reader of Delta Street for choosing to spend time in my made-up world. I hope you enjoy the story!

EMI GAYLE

Emi Gayle just wants to be young again. She lives vicari-
ously through her youthful characters, while simultaneously
acting as chief-Mom to her teenaged son and searching for
a way to keep her two daughters from ever reaching the
dreaded teen years.

Ironically, those years were some of Emi's favorite times.
She met the man of her dreams at 14, was engaged to him
at 19, married him at 20 and she's still in love with him to
this day. She'll never forget what it was like to fall in love
at such a young age—emotions she wants everyone to feel.

Dawn *conceals*
what the dark
of night *reveals*

EMI GAYLE

AFTER DARK

Book One of the 19th Year

AVAILABLE NOW

EMI GAYLE

His life is no longer
the stuff of *fiction*

DAY AFTER

Book Two of the 19th Year

AVAILABLE NOW

EMI GAYLE

Choose him,
or let him *go.*

DARKEST DAY

Book Three of the 19th Year

AVAILABLE NOW